You
(VERY IRRESISTIBLE BACHELORS, Book 1)

LAYLA HAGEN

Dear Reader,

If you want to receive news about my upcoming books and sales, you can sign up for my newsletter HERE: http://laylahagen.com/mailing-list-sign-up/

Chapter One
Hunter

"Ready to get out of here?" I asked my best friend, Josie.

"Oh, yes."

We were in the Hamptons, attending a brunch one of my clients had thrown to celebrate the Fourth of July.

"What time is it, anyway?" Josie murmured. Her eyes widened when she checked her phone. "Hunter, it's already three o'clock. We won't make it in time to Amelia's. She'll roast our asses for being late."

"Not if we show up with her favorite dessert," I said. Amelia was my aunt. We had to be at her place in Brooklyn for dinner.

"Of course. Bribing people with food *is* your favorite strategy, after all." She flashed me a smile. Josie Gallagher knew me like no one else. After bidding our goodbyes, we left the building and hopped into my BMW, passing a plethora of New Yorkers just arriving into the Hamptons.

I was glad we were spending the rest of the

day with my family. Amelia loved celebrating holidays, and the Fourth of July was one of her favorites. It was an opportunity for everyone to gather—my four cousins, Josie, and me. Amelia was more than an aunt to me. She'd practically raised me. Come to think of it, she'd practically raised Josie too.

When we made it over Shinnecock Canal and hit a traffic jam, I wondered how smart it had been to drive into the Hamptons today knowing we had to make it to my aunt's annual party. But I couldn't turn the brunch down. I owned one of the largest real estate development companies in the country, and the client who'd invited me was about to sign another deal with me.

"Thanks for coming with me today," I said.

She pulled her dark brown hair into a ponytail, flashing me another one of her gorgeous smiles. I routinely asked Josie to join me at events. Everything was just ten times more entertaining when I had my best friend with me.

"Anytime. Oh… and if you want to buy my favorite dessert too when you stop to buy Amelia's, I won't mind."

"I'll do that. Any other requests?"

"Hey, don't tempt me."

I laughed, focusing on the road. Out of the corner of my eye, I noticed Josie looking at her phone. She'd done it a couple of times since we left the brunch.

"Why do you keep checking your phone?"

"Sent my parents something for the Fourth.

It's a surprise. Can't wait to hear from them."

"What did you send them?"

"Their favorite dessert."

"Who's bribing who now?"

She shrugged one shoulder, smiling from ear to ear. "Hey, we've been friends for fifteen years. It was about time I stole some of your tricks. Besides, I'm not bribing them. Just... hoping it'll motivate them to visit me soon." Her parents lived in Montana.

Josie and I had attended the same school. We'd been friends since she'd gotten into a fight with the school bully and I'd defended her. She'd been fifteen, and I'd been seventeen. Since then, she'd stuck next to me. I'd resented it in the beginning, like any teenager who didn't want a younger girl shadowing him.

But Josie had slipped under my skin, and soon I'd been the one shadowing *her*. Trouble seemed to follow her around. I had no idea when Josie and I had become best friends. I also had no idea when my friend had turned into a smoking-hot woman. She was tall and curvy, with legs that went for days. She tempted the hell out of me, but I knew better than to give in to those instincts.

"Why didn't you fly out to visit them?" I asked.

"I'm in the middle of a huge case. I just can't take time off."

I knew just how true that was. Once you jumped on the corporate hamster wheel, you were either all in or all out. Josie was a successful lawyer, but the hours she had to put in were even crazier than mine. One of these days, I was going to surprise Josie by flying in her family for a holiday. I just had to be smart about it. My best friend wasn't a fan of extravagant gifts.

"We should have planned to go straight to Amelia's after the event," Josie murmured. "But I want to change out of this dress."

Damn it. I did *not* want that visual in my brain. She was wearing a tight white dress and high heels that had already been messing with my thoughts the entire morning.

"I know. I need to get out of this suit too," I replied. There was no such thing as a casual brunch with a client.

We were lucky and made it into the city with some time to spare. I dropped off Josie first. She almost jumped out of the car, only pausing to look over her shoulder. "Don't forget about my dessert."

I grinned. "Wouldn't dare show my face without it."

***

Josie

My phone finally beeped with an incoming message when I had only two subway stations left. I'd changed as fast as possible into a cotton dress with spaghetti straps. I stretched my toes in my flip-flops. This outfit was perfect to face the July heat.

Mom: We just got the sweets. They're DELICIOUS!

My entire family had a sweet tooth. I could vividly imagine my mom's expression when she'd received the package. I clasped the phone tighter, smiling at the other passengers in the subway. The energy was very different than my daily ride to work, when everyone was in a hurry, either clasping coffee cups or already typing furiously on their laptops.

Now, everyone was relaxed, in a celebratory mood. I even spotted a few passengers holding tiny flags. New York transformed on the Fourth of July. Some of the passengers spoke about heading to Central Park for a picnic. Others were going to take the fireworks cruise. Spending the Fourth at Amelia's place was tradition. She was family to me, as were Hunter's cousins.

As for Hunter himself, the best description was "it's complicated." I'd had a crush on him when I'd first met him, but who wouldn't? Hunter had looked like a man even at seventeen. But I'd extinguished that crush long ago... at least, I thought I had. Most of the time. With light brown hair, intense blue eyes, and a body that made me drool, the man exuded so much masculinity that sometimes even being in the same room with him was difficult. But thirty-year-old women didn't have crushes. They dated and had relationships, and if they were lucky, they found someone who swept them off their feet. Someone to marry and have kids with. I wanted that. I hadn't been lucky yet, but I was persistent in the dating department.

Amelia lived in a low-rise apartment building in Brooklyn with her husband, Mick. When I arrived, all Hunter's cousins were already there: Tess, Skye, Ryker, and Cole.

"Hey, Josie. Where's Hunter? Thought you went together to the Hamptons," Tess said.

"He's on his way. We had to change first. He's bringing dessert too."

Tess lit up. "Oh, now we're talking."

Skye rubbed her stomach, grinning. Ryker and Cole each hugged me. I'd met all of them at a birthday party years ago. I came from a large family myself—I had two brothers and one sister—but the Winchester siblings were something else.

I'd nicknamed Ryker "the flirt" instantly. I'd mistakenly dubbed Cole "the gentleman" before amending that to "the charmer." Tess was "the hurricane"—she often set the tone, mobilizing everyone. Truthfully, I'd just met so many people that remembering names was more difficult than assigning nicknames. Skye had been the only shy one in the family, though that changed over the years. I loved the entire family to pieces.

No sooner did I greet everyone than Hunter arrived with flowers, the promised apple pie, and panna cotta—my favorite.

I noticed his frown before he headed to the kitchen to Amelia. He'd been in a great mood when he'd dropped me off. What had changed since then?

Time to find out.

Chapter Two
Hunter

I first stopped in the kitchen, where a wisp of a woman with gray hair pulled back in a severe bun was checking on the roast beef. Amelia smiled at me when I handed her a bouquet of flowers and dessert.

"Thank you." Just as I bent to kiss her cheek, Amelia's radar kicked in, and she asked, "What's wrong with you, my boy? You seem preoccupied."

She was right. I'd checked my mail for the first time in a week before leaving my apartment this afternoon and had discovered a very troubling letter. But I didn't intend to ruin her or anyone else's mood today.

"The usual pressure at work," I said vaguely, hoping that assuaged her interest for now.

"You'd better forget about it today. I'll have none of that at my table, Hunter Caldwell."

"Yes, ma'am."

I was determined to leave the issue at the doorstep. I'd fix this, just as I usually obliterated any inconvenience in my path. I'd built my company when the odds had been stacked against me. I'd find a solution for this too, but it wouldn't be tonight.

I just had to focus on my family, and with

some luck, no one would guess anything. I headed to the living room, where my cousins and Josie were gathered.

"Hunter, did you come to a consensus at the brunch?" Cole asked. He was my business partner, but we'd agreed that only I would attend the brunch today, otherwise we'd look too eager to close the deal.

Skye, who stood right between us, shook her head, pointing from Cole to me.

"Boys, a word of advice: don't get on Mom's bad side by discussing business right now. You know her rule: family celebrations are no place to talk shop."

"Skye's right. I'll update you later."

We chitchatted about the upcoming fireworks show. My mind wasn't on the brunch or the client, anyway. I had bigger worries on my mind. I thought I did a good job of hiding that—until Josie pulled me aside.

"Spill it. What's wrong?" she asked. My best friend never missed anything. I should have known there was no way I'd fool her. I could try to deflect, but experience had taught me it would lead me nowhere. So instead, I tilted my head in the direction of the library.

"That bad? Let's go," she said.

In the general mayhem, no one noticed us slip away.

"Want a drink?" I said once I'd closed the door behind us. Amelia kept a small bar in the library.

Josie scrutinized me but nodded. I handed her a glass of red wine, then opened up to her.

"Found a letter from immigration services in my mail. They're not renewing my E2 visa."

I'd lived in the United States for twenty-eight years, but I still had a British passport. After finishing my studies, I'd applied for a work visa and then an entrepreneurial visa. I'd always meant to apply for residency or citizenship, but I kept putting that on the back burner. I'd just never had time to deal with everything. It hadn't been a priority, because my visa had been renewed periodically. Until now. I'd lived here, in New York, since I was four years old. My father had been one of the most successful businessmen in the city until he went bankrupt. Shortly afterward, he passed away from a heart attack, when I was fourteen.

Mom moved back to their native London. I'd chosen to stay in the US because I'd gotten a scholarship at a local private school, which also offered a boarding option. It was a tumultuous time in the family. Mom and Amelia are sisters. Her then-husband had worked with Dad, managing the Boston office. After the bankruptcy, he left Amelia and my cousins for a younger woman. Amelia had been a homemaker until then. Getting a job and raising a family on her own was something she was not prepared for. Mom had been good friends with my school's principal, and she pulled some strings to secure a teaching position for her sister. Amelia moved her family to New York and became my legal guardian.

I visited Mom a few times a year in the UK, but my business was here. My *life* was here. New York was my home.

"Do you have a digital copy of your current visa?" Josie asked.

"No, it's all at home."

"Take a picture of it and send it to me as soon as you get home, okay? I'll start looking into it tonight."

"Thanks, Josie, but this isn't your area of expertise."

Josie was a brilliant lawyer, but she specialized in corporate law.

"I've dealt with the immigration services in a few cases. I know my way around those laws. I can't believe it has come to this. We'll fix it, don't you worry."

I was worrying, because there was a real risk I'd have to leave the United States. Even if only temporarily—I couldn't do that. I had zero connection to the UK except a British passport. I didn't even have an accent.

Josie closed her eyes briefly, taking a huge gulp of her wine.

"Easy there, tiger, or Amelia will have my ass for getting you drunk before we eat."

She flashed me a gorgeous smile. "All these years later, and she's still on *your* case for getting me into trouble?"

"You can set her straight anytime you feel like it. Anytime," I said.

"I quite like her thinking I was the innocent one all those times. Who knows what she'd do if I fess up? Maybe she'll stop inviting me over for the Fourth of July dinner."

"Doubt anything would make her stop inviting you. I don't want to tell them anything. They'll just worry for no reason."

"Ok."

I put my hand on her lower back, guiding her toward the door.

"Let's go back before they get suspicious," I said. I was close enough to notice a few freckles on her shoulders and the exposed part of her back. She only got them after being in the sun. Her skin looked so smooth that I barely stopped myself from touching her. Jesus, I had to stop that line of thinking.

Josie grinned. "I'm sure Tess already noticed we've disappeared. You just wait."

My cousin Tess had noticed everything even as a kid, and that hadn't changed. She pointed a finger at us the second we returned to the living room.

"So... what's with the secret escape?" she asked.

Josie laughed, giving me an I-told-you-so look. "Hunter and I can keep our secrets, can't we?"

***

Josie

I was on pins and needles for the rest of the dinner. The second I arrived at home, I kicked off my shoes, grabbed my laptop, and dove headfirst into my research.

Deported.

The word sent a cold shiver all over me. I wouldn't let that happen. I knew he had the best lawyers on hand, but I couldn't just do nothing. I was a lawyer too, and a very good one at that, and I was determined to help out my best friend.

Hunter was a powerful man. If he had a problem, he fixed it. If he set a goal, he reached it, no matter how many people told him it was far-fetched.

He'd been headstrong and emanating an unshakable sense of power since the day I met him. The two of us were scholarship students at the private school we attended. The other kids picked on me because of my clothes—my family didn't have the money for fancy ones. But where I'd been short and scrawny, Hunter had been tall and muscular and not one bit afraid to use his physique to intimidate others into leaving me alone.

I checked the immigration services requirements for green cards and visa extensions, then investigated some statutes. The knot in my stomach turned tighter as the hours went by, because these were murky waters, especially once they'd decided not to renew your existing visa.

It was three o'clock in the morning when my phone buzzed with an incoming message.

Hunter: Are you asleep?

Josie: No, still researching.

I'd made lists upon lists but had no definitive answer for him. I scrunched my nose when he called.

"I'm not done with the research," I said instead of greeting him.

"Josie, go to sleep. I'll have my team deal with this on Monday. Hell, I'll have a new team brought in."

"I want to look everything up too. The immigration services are pretty exact in their terms."

"All right, hit me up. What did you find?"

I was lying on the bed on my belly, dangling my feet, chewing the end of a pencil. I didn't like talking about my work until I had researched every possible angle of the law to exhaust all available options.

"Come on, Josie. I'm your best friend, not a judge. Just hit me up with whatever solution you have."

"Okay, okay.... Short of marrying an American, you're stuck with going through complex paperwork and keeping your fingers crossed. I mean, paperwork will be involved anyway, but this is a more straightforward route."

He gave a strained laugh. "You're joking."

"Unfortunately, not. Look, you have options of course, especially because you have a huge business, but they didn't renew your visa... so I'm not quite sure what they're looking for. Anyway, you *need* a green card. Your lawyers never mentioned that?"

"They did, I just didn't have time to deal with it."

"Okay. So, about the green card. Many people marry to obtain it. As a lawyer, I definitely don't recommend that course of action. It's a felony. If you're discovered, your American counterpart can get up to a few years in prison, and you'd be deported."

"But as a friend, you'd recommend it?"

I hesitated. "From my experience, it's the easiest route. It's not *easy* by any means, but easier than other options."

Hunter said nothing for a few seconds. He sounded dejected when he spoke next. "I haven't found anyone to marry in thirty-two years. I don't think I can just whip someone up on demand…."

Interesting. I hadn't known Hunter *wanted* to find anyone. He'd made it clear on more than one occasion that he didn't intend to settle down anytime soon. I supposed when you looked the way Hunter did and had so much wealth… why settle?

"It doesn't have to be real, Hunter. Just an arrangement with someone you trust until you're done with this. But, again… that's against the law, so you're better off exploring your other options. Do you want me to email you after I'm done with my *legal* suggestions?"

"Yes, please."

"Okay."

"You're amazing, Josie."

The timbre of his voice was deliciously sensual. Most times I managed to ignore that, but not now, in my sleepy haze. Heat coursed through me with an intensity that made the muscles in my belly contract. My own voice was a little uneven as I bid him goodnight.

Some days, being Hunter Caldwell's best friend was a dangerous endeavor.

I finalized my research at four o'clock in the morning and sent it to Hunter. Thank God tomorrow was Saturday. As a lawyer, I often worked long hours, but I hadn't pulled an all-nighter in a few years.

I'd assumed I'd sleep the second my head touched the pillow, but ugly thoughts pummeled my mind.

What if Hunter didn't get this sorted out? I'd gotten so used to him getting his way that it had never occurred to me that he'd ever encounter an obstacle he couldn't overcome. What if he had to relocate?

For a few seconds, I reverted to that teenage girl who'd had no one but him, and an icy shiver slid down my spine.

I almost reached for my phone to check if he'd replied to my email. I was ridiculous. What was I expecting? That he'd emailed me back in the last five minutes, informing me that he'd found a miraculous solution, as always?

By the time I fell asleep, it was early morning.

I woke up four hours later, feeling as if my head weighed a ton. I was truly too old for all-nighters. I intended to head straight into the shower, but the phone caught my attention. I had an unread message from Hunter.

Hunter: You're probably going to sleep in, but shoot me a text when you wake up.

Josie: I'm up.

He answered right away.

Hunter: Do you have plans today?

Josie: Just in the evening.

Hunter: Can I drop by in an hour or so?

Josie: Sure.

I was certain he wanted to go through the list I'd sent him this morning. I hurried with my shower, wanting to have some time to read through it again. I was still too sleepy to form any real coherent thoughts, so after showering, I settled on my couch, sipping a large coffee. I lived in a comfortable one-bedroom apartment in Kips Bay. It was a good compromise between not having a killer commute to work and not wasting half my salary on rent. Most days, the lack of décor in my home didn't bother me, since I wasn't here much, but on my days off, it did become obvious how simple it all was. White walls; furniture in various shades of cream and gray. I had one single painting from IKEA, depicting a rainforest, hanging next to the TV.

Interior design had never been my forte. Neither was fashion, but that was easier to wing. I owned suits—practically my lawyer uniform—and a few cocktail dresses. I was still a plain girl at heart.

I'd just reread the email for the second time when the doorbell rang.

When I opened the door, Hunter was grinning down at me, holding a take-out bag from my favorite breakfast joint. Why, oh why did that smile have to be so damn sexy and alluring?

"I come bringing gifts."

I smelled grilled cheese and pancakes. My mouth watered. I narrowed my eyes.

"Are you trying to bribe me into going to one of those fancy-pants galleries with you?

Because I've got to tell you, once was enough for me." I was grinning, but I kind of meant it. He usually started buttering me up by bringing me breakfast on the weekend.

His smile widened. "I'm trying to bribe you to marry me."

Chapter Three
Josie

"Wait, what?" I blurted out.

"Let's have breakfast. I'll explain everything."

I opened the door wider, letting him in. My mind was racing, and so was my pulse. He couldn't be serious.

Hunter went straight to my living room, kneeling at the oval coffee table. As soon as I handed him plates, he unloaded the goodies.

"All my favorites. You've gone all out."

"You know me. I don't do anything half-assed."

I sat on the floor next to him, waiting for him to talk but almost afraid to ask him anything more. Maybe it had been a spur of the moment impulse and now he'd thought better of it. I hoped. He couldn't be serious.

My hopes plummeted when he cleared his throat. "I went through your email. I also talked to Robert this morning."

Robert was a lawyer and a mutual friend. He specialized in immigration law, which made him an excellent choice.

"He said that the options you laid out are

pretty much everything."

Crap. I'd hoped that in my sleepy haze I'd overlooked something major that could help Hunter out of his pinch.

"His only other suggestion was marriage."

I stopped in the act of cutting my sandwich and opened my mouth to protest. Hunter placed his hand on my right thigh. The contact singed me, warmth spreading from the point of contact, electrifying me. I sucked in a breath.

"Hear me out first, Josie. You're the only person I trust. It's a huge risk, and if I had a viable alternative, I wouldn't ever ask you this."

"Hunter, this is madness."

"I would take care of you no matter what. You know that, right?"

Crap. I knew, and therein lay the problem. Hunter had looked after me when no one else had. My family was great, and there was nothing they wouldn't do for me, but they all lived in Montana. Leaving home at fifteen had been one of the hardest things I had to do, but I couldn't turn down the scholarship—it had been my one shot at attending a great private school. When I'd come to New York, we'd spoken on the phone as often as we could afford, which wasn't often at all.

Hunter had never asked me for one thing. Not one damned thing. And now he needed my help. I couldn't possibly say no.

"You're not seeing anyone, right?" he went on.

"Not seriously. No."

I'd had a second date with a guy I'd met at the theater a few days ago, but that was all.

"So, this wouldn't inconvenience you in that regard. It's just a piece of paper."

"Such a romantic proposal."

"You know what I mean."

"Hunter, we'd have to keep up the sham for two or three years, minimum. It can take up to a year for the immigration services to approve your green card, and it's usually best to stay married for two years after you receive it to avoid suspicions. I researched that yesterday. It's good that your current visa is still valid for one year."

He pulled back his hand and nodded. "You're right. Forget I asked. I'll tell my lawyers to start the legalities for one of the other options first thing on Monday."

"I didn't say no," I said quickly. I didn't want to leave him in the lurch. "I'd do anything for you. This is just so.... I need some time to process everything."

"It's too risky. I didn't think this through. I just jumped at the opportunity because it seems to be the one most likely to guarantee a positive outcome."

"How involved would this have to be?" I was thinking out loud more than directing the question at him. "We'd have to live together... pretend for everyone. My family and your mom don't live here, so that would be easier... but Amelia and the rest of the Winchester clan? Not so easy. Unless you want to tell them the truth?"

"I don't like the idea of lying, but I don't want to tell anyone the truth because that's more of a risk overall. Plus, then I'd be asking them to lie for me too. Everyone would get in trouble if the immigration services got wind of it."

"No one would believe us, you know. That we'd marry."

"That we're suddenly in love? Why not? Would it be so unbelievable that I've fallen for you after so many years of friendship? That you're the one?"

He shifted closer, smiling down at me. God, why did his smile have to be so dazzling?

I cleared my throat, shifting a little, seeking a bit of distance.

"You're good, I'll give you that. I suppose given our long friendship, a spur-of-the-moment marriage with me is more believable than with anyone else."

With a pang of disappointment, I realized this was probably why he'd asked me in the first place. Not because deep down somewhere, he was attracted to me.

I mentally slapped myself. I didn't want him to be attracted to me. The reason our friendship had survived all these years was because it had been strictly platonic. Hunter wasn't the type to settle, and I wasn't the type to be friends with benefits with anyone. I'd resisted all that sex appeal he had going on until now.

If I lived with him for three years? I wasn't sure I was strong enough to pretend he wasn't drop-dead sexy. I mean… just looking at all this deliciousness that was Hunter Caldwell, I realized my chances of ignoring it were zero. And what if that torch lit up again? This would be a heartbreak for me waiting to happen.

"Josie," he said softly, cupping my cheek. My skin heated up. Was he touching me more than usual today, or was I just more sensitive?

"Forget about it. You're already stressed out. I don't—"

"No, no. I'll think about it, okay? I'll think about it and let you know."

"You're sure?" The anxious look on his face slayed me. I wanted to say yes right then and there, but I didn't.

I just nodded.

"If you say no, I will completely understand. Okay?"

I nodded again.

He drew his thumb in small circles over my cheek, resting it dangerously close to one corner of my mouth. A shiver skittered along my spine. Every nerve ending was on edge. Holy shit.

I *was* more sensitive, no doubt about that. I averted my gaze quickly, afraid I'd give myself away. Besides, those blue eyes were my kryptonite.

I only took a deep, relaxing breath after he left.

I wandered around the apartment, unsure

what to do with myself. At last, I pulled out my iPad to make one of my trusty pro/con lists. I could assess a situation better once I saw all aspects in writing.

Half an hour later, I gave up. I still hadn't typed one word down in any column. There was just one big pro: Hunter would get his green card. The list of cons was a mile long.

Aside from the legal risks, I had to lie to my family. I was also essentially putting my personal life on hold for three years, and after that, I'd be Hunter Caldwell's ex-wife. He was famous in New York. He came from old English money, but his father went bankrupt when Hunter was in high school.

People had sneered at the name Caldwell back then. Some still did, especially because Hunter had gone into the real estate business, just like his father. I respected him, because it hadn't been an easy path. Investors had been reluctant to back him, associating his name with his dad's financial fiasco.

Hunter was my best friend, but in many ways, he was still a mystery to me. He rarely spoke about his dad. When I'd met him at school, he'd been a loner, despite having his aunt and cousins nearby.

A lot of people knew him: he was rich and had succeeded despite his dad's legacy. He also ran charity events with his cousins. To be honest, I think many in the city knew him more because of those events than his business. They were called the Ballroom Galas, because they took place in an actual ballroom, and the dress code was very fancy. There were no two ways about it, he was famous in New York. What would it be like to be his wife?

Usually, my go-to people when I needed advice were my family or the Winchester clan. Ryker and Cole were younger than their sisters, and I was smack dab in the middle. I was as close to Tess and Skye as I was to my sister.

My fingers were itching to grab the phone and call my sister or one of my brothers. But Hunter was right. I couldn't involve them or the Winchesters, though I could imagine their reactions. My family would have a lot to say on the topic.

Amelia would probably tell us both to not even think about going through with this. Despite being in her seventies, she didn't want to retire. She'd worked her way up from teacher to principal and still ran the school with an iron fist. Tess would hand us our asses for taking this risk. Skye would insist Hunter check out every other option.

Ryker and Cole would laugh and give us thumbs up. Cole would probably tease Hunter relentlessly about giving up his bachelor status—even if it was temporarily. Ryker would too, but since Cole worked with Hunter, it wasn't easy to escape his teasing. Not that Ryker was easy to escape either. His office wasn't far away from Hunter's. He was a successful Wall Street analyst.

I blew out a breath, pouting. I couldn't involve anyone in this.

Clearly, this decision wouldn't be rational, but emotional. The lawyer in me struggled with that. But it all boiled down to whether I'd leave Hunter in the lurch or not. If the one time he truly needed me, I'd turn my back on him and tell him to take his chances with the immigration services.

By dinnertime, I still hadn't decided anything. I felt like I needed more details, and yet I couldn't come up with them on my own.

What would our life together look like? How often would we have to be seen in public?

As husband and wife, we'd be expected to show some PDA. My skin tingled at the prospect. And therein lay my problem. Could I live with Hunter for three years, pretend I was head over heels in love when we were in public, and not actually fall for him?

At five o'clock, I still wasn't sure about my course of action but canceled my evening plans. I wasn't in the mood to go out.

I wondered what Hunter was doing tonight. Was he on a date? My stomach churned unpleasantly at the thought. I circled back to my sheet of paper, crossing over the words "pros" and "cons." The new title was Demands and Conditions.

I had no problem coming up with a lengthy list. I was a lawyer, after all. Setting up a framework and boundaries was second nature to me.

After I wrote down everything I could think of, I surveyed the list, biting the end of my pen. Hunter would think I was out of my mind.

I jumped when my phone started buzzing. Hunter was calling. No time like the present to bring this to his attention, but I couldn't work up the courage to answer. I could barely bring myself to write down some of the conditions. How was I supposed to say them out loud?

I fretted so long that the phone stopped buzzing. But I couldn't put this off. If I was going to go through with this, I needed all the facts. Drawing in a deep breath, I called him back. He answered right away.

"Hey. Are you still out?" he asked.

"What? Oh... I stayed in. Wasn't in the mood for anything. I've been thinking about what you said...."

"I'm listening."

"So... I made a list of things we should discuss."

He laughed. "You have a list?"

"Hey. Don't mock me. I think better when I see things in writing."

"Hit me up."

"First things first. We'd sleep in separate rooms."

"It wouldn't be real, Josie. Of course, I wouldn't expect you to share my bed."

"I'm glad we clarified it."

"What's the next point?"

"I just want paperwork. No wedding."

"Amelia will flip her shit. Mom too. Your family too. Why no wedding?"

"Because when I do wear a white dress and walk to the altar, I want it to be real."

"That's fair," he said after a few seconds. "Do you want anyone to be at the courthouse, or just the two of us?"

"Amelia would disown us both if we didn't invite her, so I don't think we'll get away with that. It would make my family happy too. And your mom."

The more I thought about it, the more I realized it wouldn't work. "Crap. I don't think we'll get away just with a courthouse wedding."

"I don't think so either. We'll need a party. This is pretty much the only wedding anyone'll get for me." I wasn't sure why he didn't want to marry, but this wasn't the first time he'd made his thoughts on the subject clear.

"Party's fine," I muttered, even though I'd secretly hoped we could just spring it on everyone that we got married in secret.

"What's the next point?"

I cleared my throat, tapping my pen against the sheet. There was no point beating around the bush.

"Neither of us can see other people during the duration of our engagement and marriage. You're well known in business circles. If anyone gossiped that you're sleeping with someone else behind my back, I'd be everyone's laughingstock. The reverse is true for you. And it would give the immigration services serious reasons to suspect we're just putting on a charade."

There was a long pause, and I was convinced this was a deal breaker for him.

"You're right. I hadn't thought of that," he said finally. "Why don't I take you out to dinner and we'll go through the rest of the points on your list?"

"No need."

"You canceled your plans because of me, future fiancée. The least I can do is make it up to you."

I grinned, flipping on my back, deciding on the spot to go through with this. "When you put it like that, it sounds like a great idea. I've already eaten, but I won't say no to dessert and cocktails. Take me somewhere fancy."

"Demanding fiancée."

"I'm still your girlfriend for now, right?"

"You're right. Demanding girlfriend."

Hot damn, I liked the sound of that.

"Any other demands?"

"I'm in the mood for crème brûlée, and I want a great view. Oh, and a comfy sitting area where we can plot after we eat."

"You're enjoying this already," he teased. I actually was. And more than that, I was happy that I could help Hunter.

"Big time, almost fiancé. Big time."

Chapter Four
Josie

I *almost* regretted asking Hunter to take me somewhere fancy, mostly because our idea of fancy differed. As a lawyer, I was a high earner, but I was nowhere in his league. Hunter's paychecks had at least two more zeros than mine, and he wasn't shy about spending it. He'd brought me to a Michelin-starred restaurant in Manhattan.

That was the beauty of New York; you could find anything you wanted. We had a spectacular view of the Empire State building, and I was captivated by all the lights.

That building had been the height of sophistication for me when I first moved here as a doe-eyed teenager. Honestly, it still was. Sometimes I still felt as if I was in a movie when I walked around New York.

"This place is gorgeous," I said, glancing around.

"My bossy girlfriend requested a fancy outing. I complied." He winked.

"Good thing I put on this dress. Oh... I just realized you attend about a million fundraisers and functions. I'll have to come with you, right? My wardrobe will need a makeover. I have a few cocktail dresses, but I'll need gowns for those events, especially the Ballroom Galas. How much do you think I'll have to spend on new clothes?"

Even though I made good money, I remembered only too well what it was like to not have any to spend it on frivolities.

Hunter set down his menu. "Josie, I'll pay for any extra costs you'll have because of this… issue."

I rolled back my shoulders. "What? Why?"

"Because it's fair. I can't expect you to empty your account to keep up with my lifestyle. You're the one doing me a favor. Don't forget that. You can use the money only to buy whatever it is that you need for these outings. You can sell or donate all the clothes once it's all over if it makes you feel better."

Damn. He actually was making sense. I would be needing fancier clothes to mingle with his crowd, and I certainly wouldn't want to blow my paycheck for that. Until now, we'd mostly spent our time together doing things we could both afford. But if I were his wife, I would have to join him everywhere.

"This sounds a lot like I'd be… kept."

"That's not what it is. You know I'm making sense."

He held my gaze stubbornly, as if daring me to contradict him. I felt my cheeks flush.

"I forgot how persuasive you are," I said finally.

"I sense you're going to give me many opportunities to prove that skill."

"Are you saying I'm stubborn?"

"Very stubborn." His gaze dropped to my mouth for a split second before snapping back up to meet my eyes.

I swallowed, then sipped my cocktail to give myself something to do. Why was I suddenly out of sorts?

"We should plan our next steps," I said. "Your current visa is still valid for a year,

but I think it's best to move things along as soon as possible. You'll get your green card quicker."

"You want us to announce it to the family Saturday at Amelia's birthday?"

My stomach rolled. This was it, right? Once we told the family, there would be no going back.

"Okay. I'll talk to my family too. And the wedding?"

"As you said, the sooner the better. Three weeks?"

"That's not very believable."

Hunter leaned in, dropping his voice to a conspiratorial whisper. "Josie, no one would question that I'd convince you to marry me in three weeks. We've known each other for most of our lives. We know everything there is to know about one another. Why wait when we're so in love?"

Well, damn. He sounded so persuasive that I wasn't questioning it either. And I couldn't argue. The faster the better.

"Fine, Mr. Fiancé. I'm accepting your very romantic proposal."

Hunter grinned. "And I didn't even have to get down on one knee."

I flashed my left hand. "I'm still expecting a ring. Don't think you're off the hook about that."

"Yes, ma'am. Your wish is my command."

Our dessert was delicious, and the cocktails complemented it perfectly.

"I know you want another round of the crème brûlée," Hunter said after we'd cleaned our plates.

"Who wouldn't? But it's best if I stop while I'm ahead. I have a wedding to get ready for."

"You are fucking sexy, Josie."

My breath caught at the raw edge in his voice. He'd never called me sexy. He'd complimented me often, but this felt different. Carefully, I glanced up. The look in his eyes was feral. I didn't want to read anything into it, but my body hadn't gotten the memo. My pulse sped up.

"Don't argue with me." He leaned in slightly, dominating the space—and me.

"I'm not."

His eyes flashed, and I felt all that power he emanated like a physical force.

We ended up ordering ice cream and panna cotta and shared them. It was a good thing Hunter asked for the check right afterward, because I was eying the strawberry pancakes as well, and I really couldn't indulge in that too.

When I rose from the table, I accidentally caught my heel in the leg of the chair.

"Easy there, tiger." Hunter hurried to my side, and before I knew it, he had an arm around my shoulders, his fingers pressing slightly into my arm. He held me so close that I couldn't help registering that he smelled like both the ocean and the forest.

"Hunter, Josie, what a surprise running into you two here."

Bernard Wagner stopped in front of us, watching with a curious smile. He was a mutual acquaintance from our school days.

"Hi, Bernard," I said smoothly.

"You're not leaving, are you? It's been ages since I've seen you. Anything new?" he asked.

Hunter wasn't loosening his grip on me. If I hadn't been so lost in him, perhaps I would have foreseen his next move. He pulled me even closer, so that my right breast was pressed against his steel chest.

With a wolfish smile, he told Bernard, "As a matter of fact, yes. Josie and I are engaged."

Even as Hunter tipped his head down to mine, I didn't realize he intended to kiss me—until his mouth touched mine. I parted my lips without hesitation. I nearly moaned at the unexpected shot of pleasure. Every cell in my body seemed lit by a fuse, reacting to the kiss.

I was completely overwhelmed by him—the possessive grip on my arm, the delicious feeling of his lips on mine. When the kiss stopped, I nearly pulled him back by the collar of his shirt. I didn't have time to gauge his reaction, because he focused on Bernard, who congratulated us.

I was in a daze as we exchanged some more pleasantries, and none of the words registered. I was still acutely aware of Hunter's grip on me as we walked to the elevator. Once inside, we were alone.

"We did well out there, didn't we?" he asked, and I instantly deflated. What was up with that?

"Yes, I think we did."

Hunter watched me carefully. "Josie, did I do something wrong?"

"No, no. Just... took me by surprise."

I'd assumed our first kiss would be when we announced it to the family, that we'd talk about it before. But that didn't explain why I was so out of it, and I felt uncomfortable with Hunter still studying me.

"You're a hell of a kisser. Threw me off my game," I said, to lighten up the mood.

Hunter grinned. "I see. Now I know what to do next time we have an argument."

I narrowed my eyes. "I think we need to set some rules."

"I'm all ears."

I cocked a brow. "Why are you so agreeable? You're not a fan of rules."

He leaned into me as the elevator doors opened. "I didn't say I'll follow them."

He resumed his hold on me as we walked out. There was no need for it, and he knew that. My heel was fine. Did he just want to make a public statement? I stopped short of asking him, because of course he was making a public statement. The show had started when he'd kissed me, and now I had to roll along with it. The valet already had a cab ready for us. We'd arrived together, and by the looks of it, Hunter wanted to take me home, but I couldn't be this close to him right now. Not after he'd kissed me like that.

"I can take a cab by myself." I needed to whip my thoughts back on track and possibly fan myself.

He looked at me funny, and I immediately knew I'd given myself away. Now he knew for sure that something was off.

"I'm taking you home, Josie. That way, we can talk some more, and you'll tell me exactly what's wrong."

I was silent in the cab because I honestly wasn't sure what to tell him or how to act right now. He didn't push.

He walked me to my door in silence. After stepping inside, I stood in the doorway, unsure what to say.

"Josie, talk to me. What's wrong?"

"I'm not sure, honestly. I... just don't know."

"I don't want to leave things like this."

I turned around, biting my lip.

"You mentioned something about rules," he said.

"Yes." I could do this. I was an excellent lawyer. Rules were my specialty. "Let's keep kissing only for the public, okay?"

He stared at me. What was he thinking? As if

in slow motion, his mouth curled into a smile. "How about touching?"

"Hunter…."

"Looking?"

"You're not taking me seriously."

"Sorry, I'm not. Of course I'll only kiss you in public, Josie. I know the drill. But now I'm curious as to why you think it was necessary to remind me. Was that kiss so good that you're afraid you'll ask for more?"

He was close enough that the tips of his shoes nudged the tips of mine. The tip of his *nose* was almost touching mine.

"You're insufferable," I murmured.

"So you've been telling me since I was seventeen, but you've stuck around."

"You're lucky I like you. There's nothing wrong, Hunter. I guess I'm just a bit overwhelmed with everything going on."

"Josie, we can do this."

"Always so confident."

A sly grin spread on his handsome face. "You like that about me."

"Oh my God. You keep being cocky, and I'll throw you out."

He came, if possible, even closer.

"Why, are you afraid I'll kiss you again?" he murmured. His hot breath tickled my lips. I licked them, almost involuntarily. His eyes turned feral.

"Goodnight, Hunter."

He smiled as I closed the door. I was smiling

too, but my heart was beating at a hundred miles an hour, because the truth was... yes, I *was* afraid.

Chapter Five
Josie

I felt a bit jumpy the next day, already feeling guilty about essentially breaking the law. On the way to work, I was so lost in my thoughts that I kept bumping into commuters. That earned me several glares. New Yorkers were extra moody in the morning.

Usually, in the hustle and bustle of the crowded streets, I couldn't hear my own thoughts. But today, not even the symphony of cars honking, and strangers yelling was enough to quiet my mind.

It hadn't helped that I looked up information on the US Citizenship and Immigration Services as well as Immigration and Customs Enforcement websites whenever I got a chance. They were on the lookout for sham marriages between US residents and foreigners. If they suspected anything, they could interrogate us. I was half expecting that, honestly, considering the timing of it all. But I hoped we'd only be going through a normal procedure, and not the Stokes interview. Apparently, the questions were so detailed that even real couples had problems answering them.

During my lunch break, I walked the few

blocks from my office to Central Park, sitting on a bench that was hidden from the sun by the thick foliage of a tree. I had to take off my suit jacket; the July heat was suffocating.

As usual, the view calmed me. Something about the lush green lawn and people sitting on it, relaxing, was soothing. I came here from time to time during lunch break. My other lunch distraction was the Met, especially when they brought in new collections.

On Tuesday, I was miffed to find an email from Hunter with an attachment. It was a ticket to a rock-climbing hall that had recently opened in town. I called him immediately.

"What's with the ticket?"

"You like rock climbing, and this is the best place for it in town. You need to blow off some steam."

"Hunter, I'm fine."

"You're not. You've been my friend for fifteen years. Trust me to read you."

My fingers were a little shaky around the phone. My heart was racing. Could he also tell why I was so nervous? That I wasn't just afraid we'd be found out, but that the prospect of living with him, kissing him scared me?

"Thank you. I'm going to give it a try, but only if you come with me."

"Climbing? Hell, no. This is a gift for my fiancée."

My stomach flipped at the word. Silly stomach.

"No one knows yet, so no need for the ticket."

"Yes, there is. And this is something you need to get used to."

"What?"

"Being showered with gifts."

"Why?"

"You're doing me a favor. I intend to make everything go as smoothly as possible for you. And I won't accept a no."

"You won't accept it?" I teased.

"No. Just have some fun, Josie. You deserve it."

I was seeing a whole new side of Hunter. He was right, of course. I did need to blow off some steam. I was working my butt off at the law firm because I was hoping to be promoted to partner by the end of next year. And now with this additional stress, I was not myself.

I went climbing later that afternoon, and it was glorious. When I arrived home, I picked up my phone, intending to scroll through Instagram, and discovered a message from Hunter. He was inescapable. He'd always been this way, only now, after the kiss, it all felt different. My stomach flipped each time he called or texted.

Hunter: Are you free tomorrow in the evening?

Josie: Yes. Why?

Hunter: I was thinking we should pick a ring.

Josie: Already?

Hunter: Amelia's birthday party is on Saturday, remember? It would be good to have it by then.

Oh... he was right, of course.

Josie: Sure.

Hunter: I'll be at your place at six o'clock.

I had one night to process it all. One night. Oh heavens. I was a little nervous... but why was I smiling from ear to ear?

***

Hunter

When I told Josie I'd be at her place, she assumed I was picking her up and we were going to Tiffany. I wanted to make things go as smoothly as possible for her, which was why I had someone from Tiffany come to her place.

On the way, I called Mom. I checked in with her once a week to make sure everything was alright.

"Hi, Mom," I greeted.

"Hey!"

"Do you have time? I have some news I want to share."

"Of course."

"You remember Josie, right?"

"She's your best friend, Hunter. Of course, I remember her."

"We're getting married."

A short pause followed, and then my eardrums exploded.

"Oh my God! What? When? You didn't tell me anything. Is she pregnant? Since when have you two been dating? You've been lying every time I asked you when you're planning to settle?"

I chuckled. "Mom, slow down. Breathe."

"Okay. I'll breathe. You talk."

"We've known each other forever…"

I went on, telling her a version of what Josie and I had agreed on. Mom would have to travel all the way from London for the wedding.

"Three weeks? This is a shotgun wedding, isn't it? You don't have to pretend. I want grandkids anyway."

Guilt twisted my insides. I was getting her hopes up, and three years down the road, I'd disappoint her.

"It's not a shotgun wedding, Mom. I promise."

"Have you told Amelia already?"

"No, you're the first person I've told. We'll tell everyone on Saturday."

"Can't wait to gossip with Amelia about it. Sometimes I think she forgets you're not her son."

I laughed, because Mom was spot-on. And Amelia's second husband, Mick, was the closest I had to a father.

"I'm so happy for you, Hunter. So happy."

"Thanks, Mom. Are you okay? Need

anything?"

"I'm good. I'm about to get into a subway station though, don't think I'll have reception anymore. Talk to you later?"

"Sure."

I'd been taking care of Mom for years. While in college, I worked odd jobs on the side, and fresh out of college, made big bucks working in management consultancy. After a few years, I'd had enough capital to start my own business, and attract further investors.

I sometimes wondered what would have happened if I'd moved back to England. But I hadn't wanted to leave the States. I'd been at a good school and had managed to secure a scholarship, because I had good grades. My fellow classmates hadn't let me forget about my new status. They'd also claimed I'd gotten it because Mom and the principal were friends. They'd nicknamed me "the stray."

I'd learned to ignore them. I just wanted to graduate, get a scholarship to Columbia University, then buckle down to work. By the time Amelia started teaching at the school, the raucous comments were just background noise.

When Josie arrived three years later, they directed the comments at her, and I hadn't wanted her to go through the same. I'd only meant to protect her at first, but somehow, she ended up being my friend.

Then again, Josie could be friends with anyone. She'd quickly become close with my cousins.

Before I knew it, she was a regular at Amelia's place.

The realization of it all was hitting me hard; I had some big problems. That I was about to break the law, for one. That I had to lie to everyone I cared about, for the other.

But right now, my biggest problem was that I couldn't stop wanting Josie. I'd always noticed she was gorgeous, always been attracted to her. But I'd compartmentalized that easily enough. I'd made a clear distinction between Hunter the man and Hunter the friend.

Those walls had completely shattered when I'd kissed her. The way she'd responded... fuck. I almost got hard just thinking about it. She'd opened up without a second's hesitation. But I knew the moment I'd tasted the cocktail on her lips that the only reason for that had been the alcohol.

I repeated that mantra, but it was no use. The second Josie opened the door, I could practically taste her on my lips. I drank in the curve of her waist, the way her dark hair bounced just above her breasts. It was as if that one kiss had opened the floodgates.

"Hey!"

She smiled brilliantly at me, then looked over her shoulder toward her living room.

"Kendra's already here. That's a nice surprise."

I was very pleased with myself when Kendra greeted me. I'd personally called before and talked to her. I had a little surprise in store for Josie.

The vendor winked at me when Josie wasn't

looking and said, "Shall I begin taking out the selection?"

"Yes," I said.

"Right away. Congratulations, by the way."

I laced an arm around Josie's shoulders, pulling her closer. She smiled shyly. My heartbeat intensified. I couldn't wait to see her reaction when she saw the selection.

Kendra turned to the metal case next to her, opened it, and pulled out a tray with forty rings.

I studied Josie's face closely as she perused the rows, and knew the exact moment she found the sapphire, because she didn't look away from it.

"Shall I take that one out for you?" Kendra asked excitedly. Then, as if deciding there wasn't any reason to continue keeping the secret, added, "Your fiancé called before and asked if I had it in the store and to include it in the selection. I thought that was so romantic."

Josie looked up in surprise.

"Kendra, can you excuse us for a moment?" I asked.

"Of course."

Josie and I went into her small bedroom. Once Kendra was out of earshot, Josie asked, "How did you know about the ring?"

"I asked Tess."

"That's sweet," she murmured.

"What's wrong?"

"It's just that... I want that ring when I get engaged for real."

I hadn't thought about that. And what was it with the knot in my stomach? I nodded tightly.

"Do you think Tess will catch on if we show up with another ring?" she whispered.

"No, I'll just tell her I messed up and had the wrong ring brought up or something."

"I'll just say I changed my mind. Which one do you want to buy?"

I shrugged. "Whichever you want. Doesn't matter to me. Something you see yourself wearing for some time." I forced myself to sound detached, like it was all the same to me. When we returned to the living room, Josie glanced at the rings again, and ended up picking one with a round, modest diamond.

Kendra didn't seem all too surprised that Josie had chosen another ring.

"Don't sweat it. We women sometimes change our minds," she said.

I just nodded curtly. What could I say? Josie hadn't changed her mind. She still wanted the sapphire ring and a future. She just didn't want that future with *me*.

I'd known all that, I had no idea why I was feeling so off-kilter. Because I'd wanted to do something nice for her, and it had completely backfired. That was the reason. The only reason.

As Kendra packed up the tray and Josie put the ring on her finger, I wondered if we shouldn't act more like a couple.

No, this was just fine. We didn't have to put on a show twenty-four seven. That would get tiring fast. Even real couples weren't all over each other all the time. Buying the ring was probably one of those moments that *did* involve emotions though, judging by the disconcerted look Kendra gave us.

But I sensed that Josie needed some space, and I wanted to give it to her.

For the first time, it occurred to me just how much I was asking of her. I'd never given marriage any thought, mostly because I didn't think anything could last. My own parents' marriage crumbled when the financial problems started.

But Josie was more optimistic than I was. This was harder for her, going through the motions while possibly comparing it to what she'd imagined.

She was silent after Kendra left. I wanted to leave her with her thoughts but gave up after exactly twelve minutes.

"Let's call this off. It's not too late," I said.

Josie blinked up at me. "What? Why?"

"Because this is obviously going to be much harder than I anticipated. For you, I mean."

She shook her head. "No, it's fine. I'll be fine. Just… I imagined the day I was getting my engagement ring to be different."

"That's exactly what I mean."

"Hunter. You've done so much for me. This is the least I can do."

I stepped closer, tilting her head up.

"Josie. Look at me. I don't want you to go through with this out of some skewed sense of obligation."

"Right."

"I don't want you to feel like you owe me, because you don't."

"That's a lot of don'ts."

"There's a lot more where that came from."

"Is that so?"

"Yes."

"I'm discovering a new side to you. Not sure how much I like it."

"Judging by your shit-eating grin, you love it."

She tried to rein in her grin—and failed.

Chapter Six
Josie

On Saturday, I was a basket case as I paced my apartment, waiting for Hunter to pick me up. We'd decided this was the best tactic. It would be natural for us to arrive together. Hunter had suggested we wait until after dinner to break the news, so we wouldn't spend the entire meal answering questions. I countered by saying that I couldn't hide the ring until dessert. He'd agreed with me in the end.

I startled when the doorbell rang and hurried to open the door. I twirled once, showing off the light green dress.

"What do you think? Worthy of an engagement announcement? Does it say 'I've secretly been in love with Hunter my entire life'?"

I'd spun with so much enthusiasm that I got a little dizzy, swaying when I stopped. Hunter's arm was on my waist the next second. Strong. Warm. Steady.

I laughed at myself as I looked up. "So? What do you think?"

"You're sexy."

My eyes widened. "It's inappropriate?"

"No. It's just perfect."

I became aware of just how possessive that arm was on my waist. That his other hand was on my shoulder. The skin-on-skin contact singed me. I wiggled out, smoothing my dress.

"Let's go. Can't wait to show off my ring. I did some research. Apparently, scorned wives can turn engagement rings into something else. A pendant, or earrings. I'll turn this into something beautiful after you're going to break my heart."

"Maybe you'll break mine."

I rolled my eyes. "You're the heartbreaker. I'm just me."

"You're fucking beautiful."

"I already said yes. You don't have to butter me up."

He touched my chin, his thumb resting almost at the corner of my mouth.

"You are beautiful, Josie. If I haven't said it before, it was only because I was afraid you'd think I was coming onto you."

"And now you're not afraid anymore?"

He smiled. "No, I'm not, fiancée. So you'd better get used to it."

I felt slightly off-balance. Was he flirting? Was he joking? My heart was beating insanely fast as I looked straight at him, trying to gauge his true intentions. I ended up averting my gaze, afraid he'd be able to tell what I was thinking. It was difficult not to get wrapped up in his charm when he was so focused on me.

We took a cab to Amelia's but got out a few blocks away, deciding to walk for a few minutes and make our game plan.

"I told Mom," he said. "She was… psyched. I'm guessing Amelia will be too."

"Hunter, sorry to rain on your parade, but all the girls will be psyched."

He sighed. "True."

"I think our best bet is to divide and conquer."

"Elaborate."

"We try to talk to everyone separately, or at least in small groups. If everyone bombards us with questions at the same time, we're more likely to slip up and make a mistake."

He ran a hand through his hair. "You're right."

"The guys are probably just going to roll their eyes and leave you alone."

"If they don't, I'll hand them their asses."

"Yeah, but that means you have to save me from the girls, okay?"

"I'll do my best. Oh, and take two weeks off after the wedding."

"Why?"

"We'll have plenty of stuff to deal with," he said.

"Okay…" I wasn't really sure what he meant, but I trusted his gut feeling.

Hunter took my hand as we walked toward Amelia's door. Sweat dotted my palms. He must have sensed my distress, because he squeezed it reassuringly. Neither of us said it out loud, but after tonight, there was no going back.

Amelia opened the door, kissing both our cheeks. Then she noticed our interlinked hands.

"Oh my God," she said with a smile.

"Josie and I have news. Let's join the others." Hunter brought his hand around my shoulders as we headed to the living room.

Five minutes later, everyone present was pouncing on us.

Amelia pulled me into a heartfelt hug.

"I've always known you two would eventually see what was right in front of you. You'll make my boy so happy."

I felt so guilty that I nearly confessed everything on the spot. I looked around for Hunter, wondering if there was a way to talk to him alone. Surely, we could tell Amelia? She wouldn't tell anyone. It wasn't fair to lie to her. I couldn't bear imagining the look of disappointment on her face when we'd "divorce" a few years down the road. She'd be crushed, especially since she went through a divorce herself. I couldn't even imagine being a mom of four and my husband just announcing he was leaving me for another woman.

When I'd met the Winchester family, they were still dealing in their own way with their father leaving, but they'd had one thing in common: they were all very protective of Amelia. She always joked that she'd had a household full of rebels before the divorce, and afterward, they always took turns being up to no good, as if they'd known she was too overwhelmed by life to deal with all of them at the same time.

Amelia was one of the people I loved and respected most. I couldn't lie to her. But I was almost certain the immigration services would question Amelia about Hunter if they even had the slightest suspicion. No, I had to soldier on with this. I wouldn't put Amelia in danger just because I couldn't deal with a guilty conscience.

"When is the wedding?" Ryker asked, sipping his whiskey.

"In three weeks," I answered.

Ryker nearly choked on his drink.

"What?" Tess exclaimed. "Are you pregnant?"

"No," Hunter and I answered at the same time. He kissed my hand, adding, "I've loved Josie for most of my life. She's the one. She's always been the one. Why wait?"

Had we agreed to this? It wasn't exactly what we'd rehearsed, was it? It sounded so real, and my heart felt about to explode. For the second time, I was too wrapped up in Hunter to realize his next move. My knees weakened the moment our lips touched. This kiss was even hotter than the first one, and the entire family was watching. What was he thinking?

"Ohoho. We get it, lovebirds," Cole said.

Ryker whistled when we broke apart.

Ryker and Cole had a similar build—both were over six foot two. Both had deep blue eyes, but Ryker had dark blond hair while Cole's was jet-black. Somehow that gave him a (completely unearned) gentlemanly air, while Ryker often looked as if he belonged on a concert stage rather than on Wall Street. He *did* play the guitar in local bars after work sometimes, when he unleashed all that bad boy charm.

All of our plans to tackle the family one member at a time went down fast. Skye and Tess were cornering me. To my astonishment, the guys were cornering Hunter. At least, that's what I thought they were doing. They were at the opposite end of the room, but Hunter looked pretty surrounded to me. I'd have felt sorry for him if I wasn't so desperate myself.

Amelia and Mick were chatting, occasionally glancing at me or Hunter.

"We need to throw you an epic bachelorette party," Tess said. She and Skye exchanged conspiratorial glances.

Skye clapped her hands. "Yup. Alcohol will flow. We need to lure out every single detail. When did you first start having the hots for Hunter? Why didn't you tell us? How long has this been going on?"

Shit, shit, shit. I was certain I could survive an interview with the immigration services and lie through my teeth. But I wasn't sure I could survive Tess and Skye, especially if there was alcohol involved. I'd never been able to lie to them. And they looked at me as if they were expecting answers *right now*. I didn't have any.

I glanced in Hunter's direction and blew out a relieved breath when I caught his eye. I hoped my expression conveyed just how desperate I was.

It must have, because Hunter stalked toward us. I got up from the couch where I was sitting with the girls, and he walked right into my personal space, placing an arm around my shoulders.

"Hey! Stop accosting my future wife."

I shuddered. It was the first time he'd said wife.

"But she won't tell us anything." Tess pouted.

"Maybe it's a sign you should stop asking."

Tess grinned. "Or a sign that I have to dig deeper."

Skye elbowed her. "Let them keep their secrets for now. We have all the time in the world to question her during the bachelorette party."

"When are we going dress shopping?" Tess asked.

"I don't want a white dress."

I realized this was a mistake the second the words were out of my mouth. Because guess who knew that I'd dreamed about a white dress forever? Tess.

She might have bought my change of heart about the ring, but she'd never believe I didn't want a white dress.

"You're kidding, right?" Tess asked

incredulously. "You've always wanted a white dress. Remember that time we went shopping for bridesmaid dresses for Mom's wedding and you tried one on for fun?"

I blushed. Of course, I remembered.

"There's not enough time to find the right one," I said lamely. "Better just to have an evening dress."

"Nonsense. With a body like yours, you'll find something off the rack that fits you."

Hunter came to my defense. "Girls, don't pester her. Let her have whatever she wants."

"Promise me at least that you'll try any dresses off the rack that catch your eye," Tess said.

And maybe it was the fact that Tess was giving us a funny look, or that I couldn't resist the idea of trying on wedding gowns, but I found myself nodding. Oh boy, it was easy to get swept up in all of this.

"I don't understand the rush," Tess said.

"When you know, you know," Hunter declared confidently, and everyone within earshot melted…including me.

Chapter Seven
Hunter

Next week was a shitshow. Somehow, everyone in my circle had gotten wind of the engagement. I had to field calls left and right. I had no time to answer questions like *When's the wedding? Where? When can we meet the bride?*

The biggest problem was that everyone I spoke to was expecting an invitation. I'd promised Josie a small party, and I wanted to respect that promise.

That proved to be wishful thinking when Tess showed up at my apartment one morning with breakfast.

"To what do I owe this surprise?" I asked as we sat at the bar counter just in front of my kitchen.

"I need to talk to you about the wedding."

"Okay."

Amelia and Tess had declared they wanted to be the official organizers. Josie and I had been relieved. Neither of us was in a state to deal with that.

"You said you want a small party, but I don't think it's possible. The sheer number of people who expect to be invited is astronomic."

"How is that even possible?"

Tess grinned. "Hunter, you're famous in this city. Not only because of your business. Our charity parties are notorious. Everyone knows and loves the Ballroom Galas. We've done well with that."

She was right. Years ago, my company renovated an older building on the Upper East Side. I ended up keeping it. Now it houses two different ballrooms where we organize charity events we call the Ballroom Galas. All my cousins were involved. It was our joint project.

Cole and I brought in high-profile donors. Ryker, Tess, and Skye were masters at organizing events. We'd come up with the concept together, betting on the fact that fancy events would make donors part with their money easily, and we'd been right.

The ball season ran from September to June. We had several events spread throughout that period. Whenever we didn't have galas, we rented the rooms out to event companies.

"And I had an idea. Given the size, we should have the wedding in one of the ballrooms."

"Do we really have to invite everyone?"

"It would be rude not to invite your business partners and the biggest donors at the galas."

"I'll run this by Josie and get back to you." I didn't want to make this even harder for her.

Tess watched me carefully.

"What?" I asked.

"My spidey-senses tell me something's not right... but I can't quite tell what. Why don't you fess up?"

"What do you mean?"

"You tell me."

I stubbornly held her gaze, hoping she'd change the subject. She narrowed her eyes but shook her head.

"By the way, Ryker's throwing your bachelor party."

A real bachelor party to go with a fake wedding? I needed to stop it.

"Can you get me out of it?" I asked.

"No. And even if I could, I wouldn't. It's a milestone. You can't miss it."

"So why did you tell me? To torment me?"

She grinned. "No, to give you time to prepare."

"How generous."

"I'm throwing Josie's party. Man, I've dreamed about finally throwing one of the girls a bachelorette party forever. I'm bringing out the big guns."

"No strippers."

Tess laughed. *Laughed.* "I don't remember asking you."

The thought of Josie putting her hands on another man... goddammit. No. I was getting increasingly possessive, and she was not mine.

"So why are you telling me this? Also to get me prepared?"

"No, *this* was just to torment you." Damn. She was throwing my own words at me.

I tried another angle. "Have you asked Josie if she wants a party?"

"She does, believe me."

"Okay." *Okay*. If Josie did want it, I'd be a jerk to say anything against it. Did she also want a stripper? Shit, I needed to focus on something else. The thought made me want to punch the table or crush my cup.

"Any chance whatsoever I can skip this... milestone?" I asked.

She smiled sweetly. "You've said that about every milestone I've coerced you into having. And in retrospect, you've always been happy I did."

Prom, graduation, graduation trip. I'd wanted to skip all of those. Tess was one year older than me and had moved out of the Winchester house by the time I was a senior, but guess who'd come home to visit the weekend of my prom? Tess.

She'd practically shoved me out the door. I hadn't asked anyone to go with me, and I still didn't have many friends aside from Josie, but I ended up having fun. Same with graduation.

"I've always hoped you and Josie would get together," she went on. "I'm happy for you two." Guilt kicked in again.

Tess glanced at the screen of her phone and sighed. "I need to go or I'll be late for my morning meeting."

"Tess, I'm grateful you want to organize the wedding, but I can hire a wedding planner. You have a lot on your plate."

She and Skye were setting up their own lingerie business, and it took a lot of work. They both still worked full-time in the fashion industry, so they did everything in their spare time. So far, they had a small online shop, but their aim was to open a brick-and-mortar store soon.

"I'm never too busy for family."

"Thanks."

I had no clue why that still got to me after so many years. Maybe because I *had* felt like a stray dog in the few months after Mom moved to England and before Amelia and my cousins moved to New York. They'd given me so much, and I was trying to give back every chance I got.

Which was why I wanted to talk to Tess about something that was still a touchy subject.

"How is the financing going?" I asked her. She and Skye were pitching to investors for their business. They were as bold as they were hardworking. New York was a playground for the fashion industry, but also fiercely competitive.

"We have offers and are now assessing."

"You've already decided which of the investors you want to take on?"

"Not yet. I'll—wait a second. You have that look."

"What look?"

"The corner of your mouth is a little lifted. Like… you're not curious, just want a confirmation. Which means you've already got your way."

"I might have set up precautions."

"Like what?"

"Might have done thorough background research on all investors."

In my defense, it wasn't unwarranted. One of the business partners they worked with early on had scammed them. I was still pissed that he'd gotten away with it, but one of these days, it'd catch up to him. He'd get what he deserved.

She kissed my cheek. "Thank you for looking out for us. I just can't believe we messed up so badly."

"Tess, it happens."

"Really? How many people nearly lost their business because they trusted the wrong people?"

"Many. I can make you a list. It'll be at least ten pages long."

"You're just trying to make me feel better. Is that so I don't grill you anymore?"

"I thought you were late for a meeting."

"Ha! You're deflecting. I knew it. My spidey-senses are spot on. Something's not right here. I'll get it out of you at the next family council."

I was a dead man. Family council was a fancy term for lunch in one of my meeting rooms, where the five of us gathered to talk about the charity, but more often than not talked about personal matters. I had a feeling I'd be the focus for the foreseeable future.

I arrived at work later than usual. Our building was on the Upper West side. We were surrounded by tall structures and narrow streets, but I hadn't bought this building for the view, more for the practicality. My company took up six floors, and I'd rented out the rest.

Cole was already there, looking over the plans for our next project. Usually, I was all business at the office, but time was of essence now. I waited until I was alone with him and mentioned, "I heard Ryker's on bachelor party duty."

He snapped his head up from the iPad. "He told you that?"

His bewilderment told me he was in on it.

"Tess did."

He chuckled. "Then you probably already know more than you should."

"Get me out of it."

"You're joking, right? That's your night, buddy. And by extension, our night. Not skipping it."

"Cole—"

"Trust me on this. Come on, we make a good team."

"I don't feel like you're on my team right now. More like you're banding against me."

Cole flashed me a shit-eating grin. "Sometimes we have to. For your own good." He clapped my shoulder. "Don't worry, we've got your back."

That was *exactly* what worried me.

That afternoon, I held one of our bimonthly meetings, where we reviewed our progress and goals.

"To sum up, we're on the right track to meet this month's goals, but we can be more aggressive. I'm sure that if we put our mind to it, we can achieve 110 percent."

"Always pushing for more," one of the managers said, shaking his head.

I leveled a stare at him, and he held up his hands in defense. None of the other twenty attendees said anything. I commanded the respect of my team because I was demanding, but not unfair. I wanted us to be the best. I was proud of the business and liked what I did.

Our projects were mostly commercial buildings, though we'd done a few residential buildings just outside the city. It was a dynamic industry. Some things hadn't changed since my father had done business, but a lot had. At the core of it was building things that improved people's quality of life one way or another, no matter if they spent their free time there, went to work or lived there.

We were one of the biggest real estate developers in the country, and New York was our main playground. Headquarters was here, but we were working on setting up another office in Miami. I dismissed the meeting after outlining the operative steps to achieve the extra goals.

My head wasn't in the game afterward. I needed to talk to Josie about the wedding. I didn't want to do it over the phone, and I'd intended to give her room to breathe for a few days. I had a hunch she was already overwhelmed by everything. I didn't want her to feel pressured.

I'd been there for her through highs and lows over the years, but this time I couldn't really be there, because *I* was the cause of everything. This was already putting a strain on our friendship.

I told myself that this strain would only last for a few weeks while we got used to this, and then everything would go back to normal, but deep down, I didn't think it was possible.

In the afternoon, I heard back from the real estate agent I'd instructed on the search for a new apartment. My company hadn't built a residential project in a while, which meant I had to try my luck on the market. I could no longer postpone talking to Josie.

Pulling up my favorite numbers, I called her on the way to the gym. She answered right away.

"Hunter, hi!"

"Hey. Remember I talked about buying a new apartment?"

"Yes."

"I've got an appointment with the real estate agent tomorrow. Do you want to come? I'd like your opinion, and—"

I stopped myself just as I was about to say it would make our engagement more credible—couples went house-hunting together.

Maybe I was being paranoid about the immigration services recording phone conversations, but I didn't want to take any chances. Then I remembered we'd already talked about our relationship on the phone… damn. I was going to do better from now on.

"Sure," Josie said in a tone that indicated she knew what I really meant.

"Perfect. I'll text you the details."

The next day, we met at the address that the real estate agent, Darla, had indicated, in Chelsea. She and Josie were already there when I arrived. I assessed Josie. She was relaxed, chatting with Darla. That changed when she noticed me. She squared her shoulders, holding her chin high. Her gaze darted to the engagement ring, and then she gave me a nervous smile.

"Darla, I see you've met my fiancée."

"Yes. Ready? I can give you a rundown of what I've prepared."

Nodding, I placed an arm around Josie's shoulders. She stiffened for a fraction of a second and then she leaned into my touch, as if she'd been expecting it. Was she just playing her part, or did she want this? Me?

Her breathing was labored, her chest moving up and down rapidly. She turned her head slightly in my direction. Her blue eyes widened when she realized I was watching her. She bit her lip before looking away. It was all I could do not to cup her face in my hands and kiss her. Everything about her tempted me: her slender neck, the way her dark hair fell over her shoulders.

There was no going back to the way things

were before. The faster I accepted that, the better. But could she accept it?

"We're seeing five apartments in the condo building. It's luxury real estate with a gym and sauna. On the other edge of the property, I have a renovated townhouse, if you'd like to see it? You'd still have access to all the facilities in the building."

I'd opened my mouth to tell her I wasn't looking for a house when I noticed Josie nodding enthusiastically. She looked like a kid on Christmas morning.

"Sure. Let's see the house," I said. Why not make Josie happy? I always bought real estate as an investment, not just a place to live. I was the condo type all the way. Less hassle, and easier to resell.

The house had five bedrooms on three floors and a generous terrace on top. There was plenty of space for both Josie and me to have home offices. Hell, I could even bring in a treadmill in one of the rooms. That would still leave us with a guest bedroom.

"Perfect for two kids, even three," Darla was saying. I stiffened, pretending to inspect the windows.

Josie was over the moon. She touched every wall, every door, smiling every time she looked out a window.

"What do you think?" Darla asked when we were back in the living room.

Josie was positively glowing. "Oh my God. I can already see us roasting marshmallows at the fire...."

"Kids love fireplaces," Darla said. There she went again, bringing up children.

Josie's smile faded. She cast her gaze to the floor. What was she thinking about? The life she could have if she had the right man beside her, not just a stand-in groom?

"And the kitchen has a built-in pizza oven."

Josie was glowing again. She could see herself living in this house, I could feel it in my bones.

"We're buying the house," I said.

Darla gave me a thumbs-up. When she excused herself to make a call, Josie tugged at my sleeve.

"I got carried away. You don't want a house. We can go see condos," she whispered.

I shook my head, lacing our fingers, kissing the back of her hand. My heart was beating wildly. Every fiber inside me wanted to please Josie.

"We're buying it, Josie."

Josie looked adorably conflicted. I was betting she wanted to convince me this wasn't necessary, while already falling in love with the house.

Darla assured us she'd have all paperwork ready within a week, and then it was just Josie and me, walking around the neighborhood.

"Hunter, are you sure about the house? I know you're not a fan."

"It's a great house. And you like it."

"I *love* it. And that fireplace. And the pizza oven. But it's so huge. Darla couldn't stop talking about kids. I think she suspects this is a shotgun wedding."

"That makes sense."

"By the way, you looked as if someone slapped you every time she brought up kids."

"That obvious?"

"To me it was. You don't want any, do you?"

We'd never spoken about this. It just hadn't come up.

"I've never given that much thought, honestly. Family, kids. Just... not something I focused on when thinking about the future."

It wasn't that I didn't want them—it was just that life was easier if I kept expectations low, didn't look forward to a future that might not happen. It was easier if I wasn't actively thinking about what was missing from my life.

Would I even make a good husband?

I avoided asking myself those questions, because I couldn't help thinking about my own parents. After Dad passed away and Mom moved to London, I'd missed them terribly. I'd longed for everything family stood for: warmth, security. I'd been forced to get used to being on my own. The only way I managed that was to focus on what I had and on my goals, not what was missing. By the time Amelia and my cousins moved to New York, I'd gotten used to being on my own.

I'd spent many years just focusing on being the best: at school, in college, at work. Building something I could be proud of. Superficial relationships were all I knew. I didn't know if I could be a good husband, much less a good father.

"Not sure I have what it takes, Josie."

She gave me a look I couldn't decipher.

"But *you* do want kids?" I asked.

She grinned. "Two of them, hopefully girls."

"Why girls?"

"'Cause I'd have no idea what to do with boys. And man, this house would honestly be perfect to raise kids."

"The house will be yours after I get my green card. I'll sign it over to you."

Josie stopped walking.

"What are you talking about?"

Shit. She'd narrowed her eyes at me. Still, I persisted.

"I want you to have the house."

"I can't afford to buy it from you."

"I wouldn't be selling it to you. Just signing it over."

"Why would you do that?"

"Because you're doing me a huge favor, Josie. And you like the house—"

"Hunter!"

"What's so bad about what I'm saying? You like the house; I can afford to buy something else and move out once I receive the papers. You just said it would be perfect to raise a family."

How would this even work out? What sane man would like an ex-husband hanging around, being his wife's best friend? Perhaps if we told him the truth?

The thought of a nameless man being able to give her what she needed made me want to punch something.

She pointed a finger at me, then poked my chest.

"I just want to make you happy."

She sighed, letting her hand drop. "Why do you say these things? I can't fight you when you do that."

"Does that mean you'll accept?"

"No."

"Josie—"

"Hunter. I am not just going to accept a house." She held her chin high, crossing her arms over her chest. I nearly kissed her, right then and there. Then she flashed a wicked smile. "What's your stance on foot rubs?"

"What?"

"You said you want to make me happy. Foot rubs make me happy. You'll have plenty of opportunities to learn the skill. At the end of the day, when I'm tired, sitting on the couch and reading or watching TV."

My heart started beating faster again at the image she was painting, at this version of our life together. Maybe I wasn't the only one who was actually looking forward to this, crazy as it was.

"Want me to put you in contact with Leonie so you can take care of decorating the house?"

Josie blinked, shaking her head. "My taste

isn't that great. Just have Leonie deal with everything, as usual."

Leonie was my assistant and overall lifesaver. She held the keys to my life. She'd taken care of decorating every place I'd lived in over the last seven years.

I couldn't keep the disappointment at bay. I'd wanted Josie to decorate it. I wanted her to feel at home… make a home for us? For a split second, it had seemed she'd wanted that, but maybe I'd just been imagining… projecting.

"Okay. I'll have her coordinate everything."

We were already looking around for cabs when I remembered I wanted to run something else by her.

"Josie, I don't think we can keep the wedding small."

"Why not?"

"Everyone's getting wind of it."

"And let me guess, they're all checking their mail already to see if they've got an invitation."

"Something like that."

She bit her lip, running a hand through her hair. "So… how many guests are we talking?"

"Two hundred, give or take."

"Wow. Okay. Okay. I guess everything's going to be at a grander scale than I imagined. The wedding, the bachelorette party…."

"How's that coming along?" I tried to sound casual, not like I was already a jealous, possessive bastard.

I wasn't fooling her. She looked at me suspiciously, smiling slyly.

"I'm not telling you anything."

"Josie…"

"What? Are you going to *make* me tell you, fiancé?"

"You know I can do just that."

I leaned in closer, touching my fingers to her cheek, resting my thumb right under her lower lip. She gasped, widening her eyes. There was no one with us. No one to pretend for. But I couldn't be next to her and not touch her. Hell, I was barely refraining from kissing her. She exhaled sharply, licking her lower lip. I very nearly took what I wanted but stopped just in time.

There would be plenty of occasions to kiss her, and I was going to take advantage of them. A lot.

Chapter Eight
Josie

On Wednesday, Hunter surprised me yet again. An employee from my bank called me at 8:00 a.m.

"Ms. Gallagher, someone by the name of Hunter Caldwell has transferred one hundred thousand dollars to your account. We just wanted to check a few things. Our internal compliance requires us to ask a few things when sums this large are transferred."

I nearly fell off my chair. "That's my fiancé... I think our wires got crossed somehow. But don't approve it."

What was he thinking? He'd said that he'd take care of all extra costs that arose because I was married to him, but I hadn't explicitly agreed to this. And we weren't even married yet. After ending the current call, I pulled up Hunter's number on my phone but disconnected before it rang.

No, I wanted to talk to him about this in person. The money weighed on me the entire day, as I shifted through statutes for my clients, billing hours like crazy.

I was on track to become partner—my bosses

had heavily hinted that I was in the running to be promoted by the end of this year. I couldn't wait for that to happen. It came with a hefty salary increase. I'd already budgeted the extra dollars for the first year—I was going to reimburse my parents for helping me with law school.

I left work at seven o'clock and headed to Hunter's office. I wasn't even sure he would still be there, so I called him.

"Hey, fiancé," I greeted when he picked up. "Where are you?"

"Not sure you want to know."

"Oh?"

"On second thought… wait a second. Ryker's been killing me with planning my bachelor party for the past hour. Care to rescue me?"

I chuckled. "You can't rescue yourself?"

"Not after I just asked him to be my best man."

"Right… that *does* require outside intervention. Where are you?"

"At the Greek restaurant near my condo."

"I need about twenty minutes to get there. Think you can handle Ryker on your own?"

Hunter groaned. "I'll try."

"Won't he be suspicious that I'll just show up there?"

"No, he'll just think we're madly in love."

"Of course he will. Can you order a moussaka for me? I'm starving."

I took a cab to the restaurant, pressing the

side of my head against the cool window. When we'd visited that house, I could practically see myself living there, raising kids, growing old… with Hunter. My heart was getting involved in this already, and that was dangerous.

When he'd suggested I decorate the house, I'd been dying to say yes but couldn't. That house already felt like a home. I didn't want to get even more invested in it. It would just make it harder to say goodbye. Or… maybe we'd become a real family. Could that happen? Could he fall for me? Jesus, thinking like that was going to lead me to heartbreak… and yet, I couldn't stop.

When I climbed out of the cab in front of the restaurant, I drew in a deep breath and nearly choked. New York was stifling hot in July, even in the evening. And the humidity was inescapable. My hair had already curled at the temples.

The restaurant boasted Corinthian-style columns and alabaster statues at the corners. Hunter and Ryker were sitting at a table for four on the left side of the room.

"Hello, boys."

Ryker tilted his head, smiling. "I see I'm on my way to becoming the third wheel."

"Don't want to hurt your feelings, but I can't contradict you," I teased.

"Well, I've got what I came for anyway."

"Giving me white hair," Hunter said in a grouchy tone. Ryker laughed. Even I laughed.

"I haven't seen him in such a good mood in a

long time. Someone's in love."

Ah... if only.

Ryker rose, kissing my cheek, then trapping my right hand between his palms. "Josie, you're my only hope. I need you on my side on this."

"You charmer, you."

"Hey, I'm The Flirt, and proud of it. Don't you get me mixed up with Cole."

I laughed, shaking my head.

"Wouldn't dream of it."

"I can flirt just to prove I'm worthy of my nickname."

"Go ahead."

Hunter's eyes snapped fire.

"Or maybe not. Someone's jealous." I batted my eyelashes at Hunter. "What? I'm not marrying Ryker, am I?"

I winked at him before focusing on Ryker.

"Hunter wants to have the bachelor party the night before the wedding. I have big plans, and I don't think that would be wise," Ryker said.

"We're just going to have some drinks," Hunter grumbled. Ryker smirked. They were definitely not just going to have some drinks.

"Are you going to return him to me in one piece?" I asked Ryker.

"I cannot promise that."

"Without a hangover?"

"Also can't promise that."

I turned to Hunter. "So, since you'll probably be hungover and in bad shape, I can't have that on our wedding day. You should have your bachelor party the weekend before."

Hunter narrowed his eyes. "You were supposed to come here to rescue me."

"Yes, but Ryker's case is so much more convincing than yours."

"Thank you, Josie," Ryker said jovially.

Hunter still looked grouchy as Ryker bid us goodbye. I slid into the chair he'd just vacated.

Hunter asked one of the waiters to bring the moussaka he'd ordered for me. I was so hungry that I'd completely forgotten why I'd wanted to see him in the first place, but I remembered after a few mouthfuls, once the couple next to us asked to pay.

"I got a call from my bank," I said.

A grin appeared on his face.

"Of course. As we agreed."

"I don't remember the agreeing part."

His grin broadened. "I suggested it, you gave me shit. I persisted. You said I was very convincing."

Damn it, this was where I was supposed to have a smart comeback. Instead, I was lost in those blue eyes. I couldn't look away from his lips. They were so full. They always had been, but after knowing how they felt against mine, I couldn't unthink it anymore.

"Tess called today to inform me she wanted you all to herself one afternoon this week to go dress shopping for the wedding. You *will* need that money."

"Has it ever occurred to you that Tess will

never believe I'd let you pay for my wedding dress? Or let you give me money, for that matter? She knows me too well."

"She also knows me well, and I have no doubt that she's sure that if you were really mine, I would make sure you're taken care of and want for nothing."

God, that was sweet. A bit tyrannical, but sweet.

"You'd have a hard time convincing me."

"I remember you saying my kiss threw you off your game. Want to test that theory some more?" Hunter moved from the chair opposite me to the one next to me.

He was slightly towering over me, and by the delicious glint in his eyes, I could tell that if I pushed, he'd kiss me just to prove his point.

I shook my head. "This is insane."

"I know."

I crossed my arms over my chest, glaring at him, but he seemed unfazed.

"I didn't authorize the transfer. Aside from my personal reasons, it would be a huge red flag for the immigration office, Hunter."

His smile fell. "I didn't think about that."

"It would look as if you're paying me to marry you."

"You're right."

"So... this arrangement will have to work differently. I will deal with my wedding dress. As to all the other dresses I'll need for functions and so on... you and I can go shopping before every event. It would make me feel better than having a joint account or credit card."

He stared at me. "That's my punishment, right? I hate shopping."

"Right. Of course, you do."

"You can bribe me into coming."

"How?"

"Promise me a peek while you're changing."

His eyes smoldered. I was so overwhelmed that I didn't have a comeback. Was he joking? But that heat in his eyes... Oh, God, he wasn't joking.

There were two sides to Hunter. One I knew: my friend, my rock. The other: the man. Pure masculinity. Pure testosterone. I was more aware of that now than ever. My body reacted to it on a primal level.

"Cat got your tongue?" he whispered playfully.

"I don't know what to say."

"Just tell me what you want."

He placed his hand over mine. Holy shit. My skin sizzled everywhere he touched me... and everywhere he didn't, as if my entire body was anticipating his touch—craving it.

"Shopping. Tomorrow" was all I managed to say.

Hunter's grin turned triumphant. Damn, I loved making him smile. "We have a deal."

***

Hunter

The next afternoon, we headed to a shop Tess recommended on Fifth Avenue. The street was packed, but there were only a few other patrons in the shop. The salesperson led me and Josie to a changing room all the way at the back.

There was a leather armchair directly in front of the changing rooms, and on the small coffee table next to it there was a bottle of water and a glass. Maybe this wouldn't be so bad.

Josie turned to me. "The Ballroom Galas only start in September, but we'll be attending other functions in the meantime, right?"

"Yes."

"Are they as elegant as the galas?"

She'd come to a few over the years.

"I don't know how to answer that. I always wear a tux."

She laughed, patting my shoulder. "Okay, I can handle this."

She went directly to a salesperson and they spoke about lengths and styles and God knows what else before the woman disappeared. Josie closed the curtains.

I poured water in my glass and nearly toppled it over when I heard a zipper. She was undressing. I drew in a sharp breath, focusing on my glass.

The woman—Honor was the name on her

badge—brought a handful of dresses, handing them over to Josie. When Honor left, she didn't draw the curtains to the changing room all the way together.

I played with the rim of the glass, determined not to look.

Five seconds later, I lost the battle with myself and glanced up. I was getting more than an eyeful. Was she doing this on purpose? To torment me? No, that wasn't her style.

The right thing to do would have been to tell her that I had a direct view, but as of late, when it came to Josie, I couldn't seem to be able to do the right thing.

She was gorgeous. I got an eyeful of her legs and—

Fuck me.

The panties she was wearing… were those even panties? They covered nothing of her ass. The front was semitransparent.

I glanced at the glass in my hand again, attempting to calm down. It was useless. I had a raging hard-on.

I fought to get it under control, and by the time she came out, I'd succeeded somewhat, but I was hanging by a very thin thread.

She was wearing a red dress that was just… perfection.

"What do you think?"

"You're beautiful."

"Does it fit the bill?"

"Definitely."

"Okay. We're done, then."

"Buy more. More than the ones she brought you. About ten. You'll be situated then for a few months."

"Okay."

Forty minutes later, Josie came out wearing the last dress. White with silver streaks, showcasing every curve. She was so goddamn sexy in it that I nearly swallowed my tongue. Her breasts were peeking out of the top of the gown, her neck and shoulders on full display.

"I love this dress. But I want something to cover my shoulders."

"I can call Honor to find something."

"No, just give me that scarf, I think it will work with all the dresses. I can throw it over my shoulders and just knot it in the front."

She pointed to a mannequin with a silver scarf around its neck. I brought it, but instead of handing it to Josie, I wrapped it around her shoulders myself.

I rested my thumbs on her clavicle, desperate to steal a touch under the pretense of playing the fiancé.

"This took longer than we thought," she said.

"I'm not complaining."

"How so?"

"You didn't close the curtains completely."

She gasped. "Naughty fiancé."

"That's not naughty, Josie." I dragged my thumbs up the sides of her neck, stopping at the nape, coming closer. "If I'd been naughty, I would've come after you in that changing room and kissed you until you moaned."

"Hunter, you can't say these things," she whispered. Her cheeks turned pink. Her pulse accelerated. I felt its thrum under my thumbs.

"Of course, I can. I'm your fiancé."

"You're impossible."

"Just wait until I'm your husband."

The skin on her arms broke out in goose bumps. Her breath caught. Her reaction to me was intoxicating. A touch wasn't enough anymore. I *needed* a kiss.

The salesperson was coming our way. I could pass this off as a kiss for the public, right?

I sealed my mouth over Josie's the next second, and every doubt I had subsided, because she was kissing me back with a fervor that nearly brought me to my knees. When she sucked on my tongue, instinct overpowered every rational thought.

I wanted to kiss, claim, fuck.

I had no idea how I managed to pull back, but I did.

Josie averted her gaze, turning to Honor, who was looking between us with a wide smile.

"We're taking everything," I informed her.

"I'll just change, and you can pack this up too," Josie said.

She busied herself for longer than necessary inside. I didn't feel too guilty, because Josie had enjoyed the kiss. It had been there in her body language, the way she'd kissed me back. The way she'd pressed her thighs together.

I poured myself another glass of water while Josie changed, even though she'd pulled the curtains all the way together this time.

Dammit, I was a jerk. What was I thinking, convincing myself it was okay to kiss her just because she liked it? Why wouldn't she enjoy kissing? That didn't mean it was okay for me to do it.

But ever since we'd decided to go through with this, it was as if a switch had gone off in my brain. Every time I looked at her, all I could think of was that she was mine. Which, of course, she was not. But I was beginning to realize I'd have to constantly make an effort to remind myself of that. She was my best friend, and I knew better than to push that line.

Chapter Nine
Josie

The next day, I met Tess and Skye early in the afternoon. We headed to Soho, in Lower Manhattan.

Many people swore by Fifth Avenue, but I loved Soho more. It used to be full of galleries, but a lot have been replaced by shops. The city kept reinventing itself constantly, as if it was determined to keep the sense of wonder alive among its residents.

Soho boasted an old-world charm, with its narrow cobblestone streets—even though I had to be careful not to misstep with my heels. The buildings with wrought iron facades housed artsy cafes and shops ranging from mainstream brands to unique boutiques.

I'd be lying if I said I wasn't looking forward to this. Was it nerve-wracking? Sure. But I also felt an excitement I couldn't even begin to describe.

Skye and Tess were waiting for me in front of the store. I'd never seen them more excited. I was so happy they were shopping with me, because they had excellent taste in clothing. They could get away with wearing anything.

Skye was curvy and tall. She'd been like that as

a teenager too and often said that was why she wanted to go into the lingerie business. She wanted to create sexy things for curvy girls. She waved at me so enthusiastically that a few chocolate brown strands bounced around from her high ponytail.

Tess was tall too, but willowy. Her light brown hair was interspersed with blonde strands. She didn't follow trends. She knew what she liked and made no apologies for it. I loved Tess and Skye to the moon and back. I'd do anything for them. If they hurt, I hurt. If they were happy, I was happy. Right now, I was feeling extra guilty for deceiving them.

The store had bridal gowns on the ground floor and evening wear on the top floor. Despite intending to head straight upstairs, I couldn't tear my eyes off the white dresses. I loved bridal gowns in any shape.

My heart gave a mighty sigh as I glanced at a rack. Belatedly, I realized Tess was watching me. Shit. The cat was out of the bag.

"Andrea, what do you have on the rack in my friend's size? She and my cousin have recently realized they're the loves of each other's lives and are getting married in two weeks."

"That's so romantic," Andrea said. "And you're so in love that you can't wait to get married and are willing to let any silly childhood dreams slide by just to tie the knot. What's your size?"

"Six."

"You go upstairs and pick what you like. I'm going to check what I have ready-to-buy in your size in the bridal selection."

Twenty minutes later, I entered the changing room with seven evening dresses. They were all to die for. How was I supposed to decide?

A few minutes later, my problem escalated, because Andrea told me she'd found ten wedding dresses in my size. She'd hung them on a rack in front of the changing room.

They were all absolutely stunning, and I knew before I'd even tried them that I was a goner.

One by one, I paraded the dresses in front of Tess and Skye. A mermaid-style one with a sweetheart neckline stole my heart. I looked like royalty wearing it.

"This is the one, isn't it?" Tess asked.

Skye clapped her hands. "Look at her dopey smile. Of course, it is."

Between their laughter and the beauty of the dress, for one moment I forgot altogether that this wasn't real.

I was being silly.

"I still want to try the rest of the evening gowns," I told them before taking refuge in the changing room.

I could easily tell Tess and Skye this wasn't what I was looking for, that I'd had an image of my perfect dress in mind for years, and instead of settling on something that wasn't what I'd envisioned, I preferred no bridal dress at all. They'd understand.

But we were getting married in one of the ballrooms. We had two hundred guests. I couldn't show up in a cocktail dress. It would raise eyebrows.

I twirled in front of the mirror, grinning like a fool. I wouldn't let this dress pass me by. I opened the curtains to the changing room again and announced, "You're right. This is the one."

They cheered and came to hug me. I felt overwhelmed with emotion and a little guilt but hugged them back just as hard.

"You just need shoes," Andrea said. "I'll be right back."

"And keep Saturday before the wedding free," Tess said.

"Why?"

"For the bachelorette party."

I swallowed. "We need a whole day? I'd planned to move into the new house on Saturday."

"Change your plans, girl. We're kidnapping you and treating you to the whole bridal program."

"Should I be afraid?"

Skye placed one hand on her hip. "Is the Arctic freezing? Yes."

"Okay, then."

"We'll help you pack your stuff. I can't believe you've agreed to marry Hunter before you've lived with him. What if he's one of those guys who leaves his stuff everywhere?"

I gave a nervous laugh. This is the type of thing I should know.

"I'm pretty laid-back about everything."

Tess raised an eyebrow. "Have you met yourself? You're crazy exact about everything."

"No, I'm not."

"The shelves in your bookcase have labels with the first letter of the authors' names."

"Isn't that normal?"

"It is if you're a bookstore. You get my drift?"

"Well, it's all about compromise," I muttered, but I couldn't quite meet Tess's eyes.

Chapter Ten
Josie

Leonie was a lifesaver, as usual. She'd informed me that she'd take care of packing up my stuff while I was at work, as well as moving everything over to the house. All I had to do was separate everything in three piles: take with me, put in storage, throw away/donate.

Tess and Skye had offered to help.

Two evenings into the packing process, I realized *packing* was code for *interrogation*.

"Did he already make space for you in his closet?" Tess asked.

"Umm…." Shit. Every time I thought we were on safe ground, something new came up. I didn't even know what Hunter's closet looked like.

"I'm going to help him do it," I said vaguely. "He just moved in the house, so nothing's set yet." Now that I came to think about it, what would our arrangement look like? I slept in a different bedroom, but all my clothes would be in his closet? My toiletries in his bathroom? There was more than one bathroom in the house, but we had to make it look as if we were sharing a bedroom and a bathroom.

The thought of showering in *his* shower,

entering his room on a daily basis felt far too intimate. What if he slept naked? Nope... I would not think about that. Yet now that I'd let that thought in, it was all I could think about. A bout of heat coursed through me.

We somehow had to manage this, because there was no way I could keep my clothes in my bedroom. I'd have to move everything back and forth every time a Winchester came to visit, and they liked to drop by unannounced.

On Saturday, I was all jittery on the subway ride to the house. Leonie had already sent all my stuff there yesterday. I only had time for a quick tour before Tess and Skye picked me up for my bachelorette party. I couldn't wait. Sure, I was liable to get drunk and say something I wasn't supposed to, but I needed to blow off some steam.

Besides, Hunter and I had fabricated some more details about our relationship at the beginning of the week. We'd had dinner together and plotted. It had started out fun. We each came up with potential questions Tess and Skye would throw at me.

By the end of it, I was breathless and needy and thoughts I should never have about my best friend were now permanently branded in my brain. It had started benignly enough, but then I'd somehow dug my own grave.

"What if they ask me intimate details?" I'd asked.

Hunter had winked. "Just tell them I'm the

best you've ever had."

"Always so humble." My cheeks had heated up. Even now, I blushed as I remembered the conversation.

My face still felt hot as I knocked at the door. Hunter welcomed me with a lazy smile, gesturing for me to step inside. He was wearing a very thin shirt— it was practically transparent. I had to make a concerted effort not to trace all those muscles with my gaze. Damn it. The man looked like sex on a stick.

"Wow, this looks incredible," I said the second I stepped inside the house. It had been completely empty when the real estate agent had shown it to us, and was unrecognizable with all the furniture. The living room was split in two areas: the kitchen, complete with an island and barstools and a glass table, and the living area, defined by a celestial blue couch with three seats.

"Leonie outdid herself. She already unpacked everything."

I still wasn't sure how we were going to handle having separate bedrooms but keeping all our clothes in one place. It seemed like a lot of hassle and a lot of bumping into each other.

We didn't have time to talk logistics, because both of our bachelor parties were starting in a few minutes.

Skye and Tess arrived first.

"Ready?" Tess asked, rubbing her palms together in excitement.

"Depends, are you going to tell me what we're doing?"

They both vehemently shook their heads. I turned to Hunter, who was watching us with an amused expression.

"Fiancé, don't you have anything to tell them? A warning? A lecture?"

"Afraid you can't handle your own bachelorette party?" he asked lazily.

Tess snickered. "You talk as if you'll be able to handle yours."

Hunter's eyes flashed.

"Okay. Here are some ground rules. Don't get my girl too drunk. Don't let anyone come on to her. And whatever you do, don't torture her with questions."

Skye smiled indulgently. "Awww, that's so sweet. Completely useless, but points for trying."

***

Hunter

My cousin Ryker was a master at organizing events. He'd scheduled a full day. We'd started with a rafting trip on a river just outside the city and were finishing the night by going to a bar. It was just the three of us: Ryker, Cole, and me.

"Didn't think I'd see the day you married," Ryker exclaimed when we downed the second round of tequila.

"Ryker, don't start," Cole said.

"Why not? Need to understand what changed his mind."

"Why?" I asked.

"So I don't run the same risk."

I laughed, twirling the empty glass.

"When you know, you know, and there's nothing you can do about it."

Ryker looked glum at my explanation but didn't pry any further. I couldn't help wondering what Tess, Skye, and Josie were up to. I'd been wondering for the better part of the day, but every time I took out my phone, I shoved it right back in my pocket.

I lost the fight after the third round of tequila and excused myself from the group.

The music was loud enough that I had to step outside to make the call. My vision was blurry when I looked at the screen, but I somehow managed to pull up Josie's number.

Only it wasn't Josie who answered. It was Skye.

"You're one lovesick fiancé," she remarked.

"Can I talk to Josie?"

"Nope. It's a no-man zone tonight. If you speak to her, you'll convince her to bail on us."

"What makes you think that?"

"Because you sound like you've had just enough tequila to want to bolt on Ryker and convince Josie to bolt with you, and we can't have that. We still have *plans*. You'll have your fiancée all to yourself tomorrow, but tonight, she's ours."

"What exactly do those plans entail?"

"You know. Just fun."

That wasn't reassuring at all, but Skye refused to tell me anything more. My thoughts were running amok as I headed inside, back to the guys. Ryker had suggested a strip club, but I'd firmly put my foot down. Not my style.

But what about Josie? Had my cousins gotten her a stripper? The thought drove me insane. I didn't want any man to put his hands on her, let alone other body parts.

Fucking hell. Why was I feeling possessive? She was my friend. She was helping me out. That was all.

I was lying to myself, and I knew it. This past week, it had become clear just how close to each other we'd be over the next few years, and this morning... fuck. We were going to live in the same house.

"There you are. Tell me you haven't called Josie," Ryker said.

"I haven't called Josie."

"You're a shit liar." He dragged a hand over his face dramatically. "Skye will hand me my ass."

"Why?"

"Because we were supposed to keep you entertained enough not to call Josie."

The corners of my mouth twitched. "Skye was the one who answered the phone, so you'd better be thorough in preparing your defense."

***

I arrived at the house at three o'clock in the morning. Josie wasn't there yet. Despite the long day, I felt full of energy. The light buzz from the alcohol had evaporated, and I was too restless to sleep.

I heard noise at the front door about an hour later. It sounded as if someone was scratching the lock. I didn't see anyone through the peephole but opened anyway. Josie was bent, holding the key in her hand. She straightened up, batting her eyelashes.

"Umm... had a little trouble finding the lock."

"They got you drunk."

Josie pouted, lacing her arms around my neck as I scooped her up in my arms. "They invited all my closest friends. We were twelve. It was crazy. And Tess and Skye were merciless, Hunter. Merciless. I thought I was safe once we'd gotten to the club, but then after we had a few shots, they were at it again. I made a fool of myself."

"What did they ask?"

I laid her on the bed in the guest room, sitting at the edge. "Why I fell for you, what I like best about you, how I knew you were the one."

"What did you tell them?"

She wrinkled her nose, turning on one side with her face to me, hugging the pillow. "That you're probably the person who knows me best and you've charmed me since you were a teenager, and that I've dreamed about having mini Hunters forever."

"Fuck, you're sweet."

"My head's swimming."

"Close your eyes. Go to sleep."

"I should probably change…."

"I'll help."

She narrowed her eyes. "I'm not drunk enough to get seminaked in front of you."

She was out in a few seconds, but I didn't move from her side. Had she meant any part of what she'd told my cousins? Or did she just tell them that to appease them? It was probably the latter, but her words tugged at me for reasons I didn't understand.

The warmth of a home and the love of a woman were things I hadn't even let myself think I might have one day, because they'd always felt so far out of reach.

I honestly couldn't see myself in that position. A father. The head of a family. Did Josie see me in a different light?

When Josie turned on the other side, her dress rode up higher—and then even higher when she rolled onto her stomach. Holy fuck. She was wearing a thong that basically covered nothing. I didn't want to look, but I couldn't not *look*.

I had to get out of there. Now.

I darted out the door, taking refuge in my own bedroom. Jesus Christ. This was my life from now on. This gorgeous woman would be living with me for three years. I'd be tempted every single day, and I'd have to fight that temptation.

No matter how close she was, Josie was out of reach.

***

I slept like a rock. Next morning, I was surprised to find Josie was already awake… mostly. She was lying on the couch, knees pulled up to her chest, staring into space. She looked cute, in long pajama pants and a top. I couldn't erase the image of that perfect ass of hers from my brain.

"Morning, drunk girl."

"My head feels like it weighs a ton. Took a shower, but it didn't help."

"Alcohol will do that to you."

"Why are you so chirpy? You had your bachelor party."

"But I came home earlier."

"Boo, that sounds like a boring party."

"Want to take a grand tour of the place?"

She groaned. "I should, right? But I just want to stay like this forever."

"You need water."

I brought her a large glass from the kitchen. She reluctantly pushed herself to a sitting position, crossing her legs on the couch.

"I know the house anyway," she mumbled. "The agent gave us a tour."

"Yes, but it didn't have any furniture back then."

"You're right. Okay, let me finish this up and you can give me a tour of the kingdom."

I chuckled, helping her up after she emptied the glass. We covered the rooms where Leonie had set up home offices for us, then the guest room she was sleeping in and the one where I'd put the treadmill once it was delivered before coming to the master bedroom where I'd taken up residence.

"Wow, this room is even bigger than I remember," Josie said in wonder.

"I sleep on the left side of the bed... not sure if you'll ever need that detail, but there it is. So the right side would be yours."

She met my gaze, then quickly looked away. Damn, she was blushing, and she looked gorgeous. This was intimate information, and as a friend, she wouldn't know.

"You only sleep on one side? That's a waste of a big bed." Tilting her head, she gave me a sly smile. "Besides, I sleep on the left side too, even though I kind of roll around everywhere. So you'd have to switch to the right."

"Or... I could convince you to switch sides."

She waved her hand. "No chance."

"I can be very convincing."

"So you keep saying."

"You want proof?"

I knew I shouldn't go any nearer, and still I did. I stepped so close that I could smell the faint strawberry scent of her shower gel. Her breath caught. She licked her lower lip, then laughed nervously, turning to peek inside the bathroom.

I couldn't wait to see her reaction. She'd showered in the guest bathroom today.

"Wow. Wow. You have a Jacuzzi. This wasn't

here before."

"Leonie had it installed."

"I think I'm in love with her. I call dibs on it on Friday evening."

I laughed. "Whaaaat?"

"You heard me."

"We'll negotiate."

She spun around, zeroing in on me. "Negotiate what? I want one evening, you have six others to choose from."

I tilted my head, feeling the overwhelming urge to make her blush again.

"Maybe I only want to be in it when you are."

For a few seconds, she didn't say anything. She was so close that I had to clasp my hands behind my back to resist the urge to touch her.

Clearing her throat, she said, "Friday's mine. I don't want you cramping my style, Hunter."

"I'm not making any promises."

She let out a shaky breath, averting her gaze.

Did I know what I was doing? Not a fucking clue, but I didn't seem to know how to stop either.

"Leonie put all your clothes in my dressing room. Let's just take everything to the guest room," I suggested.

She looked at me in surprise. "Hunter, it would look suspicious if my stuff was there."

"You think anyone's going to check the bedrooms?"

"You never know when Tess or Skye will say they want to borrow something. Or what about the cleaning lady? What if someone from the immigration services questions her? We can't ask her to lie. It wouldn't be fair, and we're not even sure she'd do it. It's too risky."

"Wait, so what are you suggesting?"

"I think I have to keep all my stuff in your bedroom and bathroom. I'll just sleep in the guest room but do everything else in yours. I can't use the guest bathroom, like I did today. It would be a dead giveaway if all my cosmetics were there."

I wasn't used to sharing my personal space. As stupid as it sounded, this hadn't occurred to me. And I couldn't process the implications beyond the fact that Josie would be in my bedroom every day. In my bathroom. She'd shower there.

Fuck. Me.

"Okay," I said calmly. "Okay. So, then… let's start with the bathroom. Leonie just put everything in a corner, but I want to rearrange a few things."

"What's your morning routine?" she asked while we were making space for her stuff in the bathroom. It was easy. Besides cologne, aftershave, shaving cream, shower gel, and shampoo, I didn't have anything else.

Josie filled the space with a dozen bottles and jars.

"I get up, take a shower, shave, put on a suit, drink coffee, and eat whatever's in my fridge. You?"

She laughed. "Wow. Mine's a bit more elaborate. I get up at five, do thirty minutes of yoga, then eat yogurt with granola before hopping into the shower. I need about an hour in the bathroom, all in all."

I blinked. "An hour? What can you possibly do that takes one hour?"

She tilted her head playfully. "Have you ever lived with a woman before? Oh wait, I already know you haven't. Shaving takes some time, and then smearing on the body cream, massaging my skin until it sinks in."

Fuck, no. I didn't want those images about my best friend in my head.

"And my hair needs a wet conditioner, a hair mask, and a mousse once I've towel dried it. Then I blow dry it."

"You do this every morning?"

That was just not possible.

She grinned. "You thought I rolled out of bed looking the way I usually do?"

"I've known you since you were fifteen. I always thought you were beautiful."

She gave me a shy smile. "Looking all lawyer-y takes a considerable amount of effort. It's exhausting, to tell you the truth."

I leaned in, grinning. "I can help you apply that cream. If it helps ease the load."

Even I knew I'd pushed things too far. She frowned, as if she was wondering if the flirty comments were a joke. I could also tell the exact moment she realized they weren't, because her breath caught. When she glanced down at my lips, I nearly leaned in to kiss her.

She swallowed, shook her head.

"Aren't you a charmer? Keep all that testosterone bottled up for the next three years. You'll need it afterward to get back in the game."

Afterward? That seemed so far away, so unimportant right now.

"Let's set some ground rules for our morning routine," Josie continued. "I should probably start showering first, since I need longer, but that means I'll wake you up."

"I sleep like the dead in the morning. Trust me, I sometimes miss all three alarms."

"Good. One advantage of having me as a roommate: I'll make sure you wake up."

"Okay. That's settled. Just take care when you come into the bedroom."

"Why?"

"I sleep naked."

"Are you serious?"

"No. But it was worth it just to see you blush."

"I'm not blushing."

"I think you are. And you know what else I think?" I was so close to kissing her. So damn close. "I think you were just hoping to see me naked every morning."

Chapter Eleven
Josie

The following week was a doozy. Since Amelia and Tess had taken it upon themselves to organize the wedding, Hunter and I only had to decide between the various options they laid out for us. I loved every moment of it: choosing the flowers, the theme, the band, making seating arrangements, you name it.

Living with Hunter was... hard. I tried to pretend we were simply roommates, but there was no getting past the intimacy of it all.

I felt self-conscious about hopping in his shower every morning. I kept my ears perked to pick up any sound—what if in a sleepy haze he came inside without knocking?

Some things could not be undone or unseen. But he'd been right—he did sleep like a rock in the morning. Even so, I'd taken to tiptoeing with the blow dryer to the living room and closing all doors.

On Wednesday, he caught up with me in the kitchen while I ate my yogurt. He was already dressed to the nines. I typically only dressed after finishing breakfast, to avoid the risk of dropping yogurt on my suits.

"I have a proposition for you," Hunter said, grabbing coffee.

"Shoot."

"You take the master bedroom. I'll sleep in the guest room."

"Why?"

"It makes more sense. I only need fifteen minutes in the morning. I can just come in after you're done."

Well, hell. I'd have that enormous room all to myself?

"What's that?" he asked.

I caught myself smiling from ear to ear. "I might be imagining myself in that king-sized bed of yours."

"So, we have a deal?"

"Yes. Can I buy a vanity table? So I don't have to do my makeup in the bathroom? There's no natural light."

"Sure." He blinked. "I know you wanted Leonie to take care of everything, but... obviously if you want to redecorate any part of the house, you're welcome to do it. I want you to feel at home."

The dangerous part? I was already feeling as if I was at home. And yet, I couldn't help hanging on to that feeling of wanting more.

"I don't want to redecorate per se, but I was thinking that I can make a reading nook under the window next to the fireplace. There is enough space for a window seat and a shelf."

"You gave this a lot of thought already."

I blushed. "I've just looked around on Pinterest. I'm not very design savvy."

"I'll ask an interior designer to come help us."

"Really?"

"Yes. Oh, and those two weeks I told you to take off? We're going on a honeymoon."

"Wow. Why didn't you tell me before?"

"You would have said two weeks is too long."

"It is."

"It's just enough to relax."

"You've already arranged it? What if I I'm changing my mind about taking time off?"

He tilted his head playfully, placing one hand on the counter, right next to my hip. "I'd change your mind right back."

I exhaled sharply. "Where are we going?"

He dug a hand in the inside breast pocket of his jacket, taking out a folded sheet of paper and handing it to me. I set my bowl on the counter and carefully unfolded the paper.

He'd printed out the flight itinerary. We were flying via Dubai to... I scanned the rest of the page, zeroing in on the destination. We were flying to the Maldives.

I blinked repeatedly. My eyes were burning as I looked back up at him.

"Shit, you're crying. Did I do something wrong? You've been wanting to go there since high school."

I chuckled through the tears. By way of answering, I wrapped my arms around his neck, rising on my tiptoes and burying my face in the crook of his neck. I warmed all over when he brought his arms around my waist.

"When have you gotten so good at surprises? Thank you."

"You're welcome."

I *had* always wanted to go, but one thing or the other had always gotten in the way. Law school, then getting a job, then working long hours to make senior, now working toward becoming a partner, always worrying that it would count against me if I took so much time off, always wondering if I wasn't better off saving more instead of spending money on extravagant vacations.

"Why didn't you tell me until now, though?" I asked, pulling back.

"You would've tried to convince me to go somewhere nearer, cheaper."

I grinned. I definitely would have.

"How much—" I began, but Hunter shook his head.

"Everything's already taken care of, and you're not allowed to give me shit about it."

"Not allowed? We'll see about that."

On Friday, I went to work with one thought in mind: that Jacuzzi was going to be all mine this afternoon. All mine.

My family was arriving tomorrow morning. They were supposed to arrive yesterday, but their flight got canceled because of a technical problem.

They'd been rebooked for tomorrow.

I'd planned to take Mom, my sister, and my brother's girlfriend to a spa this afternoon, but that had fallen through.

I wanted to do something nice for them, and tomorrow we'd all go, but it wasn't the same thing. I'd wanted to spend some quality time with them today—my last full day as a single woman.

I got strange looks from my coworkers, but I didn't put two and two together until someone straight up asked, "We weren't expecting you here the day before your wedding. Brides usually take the day off."

"Oh." Shit. Shit. Shit. That hadn't even occurred to me. I tried to sound casual. "Everything is already taken care of. I just wanted to finalize a few things. Besides, my fiancé is taking me to the Maldives for two weeks. Need to sort out a few things."

There, that sounded like a solid reason. Katherine didn't look like she was buying it. Cold sweat broke out on my neck as I wondered if the immigration services would question my work colleagues. I hoped not, because this would be a red flag. Besides, if my boss found out I was being investigated by the USCIS, I could kiss that promotion goodbye.

"And I'm only here for a few hours anyway," I added.

Katherine smiled at last. "Excited about the honeymoon?"

"Oh, yeah."

Ironically, I didn't get much done, because I was too busy obsessing over whether my colleagues were suspicious or not. I ended up leaving right before lunch.

I began unbuttoning my shirt as I stepped into the house. That Jacuzzi would be so welcome right now. I had two hours before I went to get my pedicure. I didn't have time for it tomorrow, when I also had a manicure, hair, and makeup scheduled.

When the tub was full, I slid in the hot water with a sigh. I propped my head on the edge of the bathtub, plugging in wireless earphones. My phone was safely on the cabinet next to the towel rack.

I hummed the lyrics, closing my eyes as the Jacuzzi's jets of water massaged my tense body. *This* was the best relaxation money could buy. When I moved back into a place of my own, I'd definitely get my own Jacuzzi.

I shuddered thinking how much it would cost to have one installed, but honestly, I could invest in myself.

I couldn't wait to see my family tomorrow. I saw them so rarely. We were all spread out, and seeing everyone at the same time was a perk.

As a little girl, I'd dreamed Dad would walk me to the altar, that Mom would fuss over my dress and makeup… I wondered what they would think if they knew tomorrow was just a sham.

I was helping out my best friend. Surely they wouldn't be disappointed. Yet I was lying to them.

There was no other way to phrase it. Could I tell them the truth? At least tell Mom and Dad? The chances of any immigration officer interrogating them was slim. Still, they'd have to keep it a secret too, and that increased the risk. What if they slipped and told someone?

No, I couldn't tell them, as much as I wanted to.

I focused on the music and my breathing, clearing my mind, as I did during my daily yoga sessions. Yoga had been one of the things that had kept me from going crazy since starting law school. Before that, I'd laughed it off, thinking it was just a fad.

I was so relaxed, I almost dozed off. I had no idea how much time had passed before I heard a faint groan over the music in my headphones. I blinked my eyes open and froze.

Hunter was standing in the doorway, a towel wrapped around his lower body. My breath caught as I willed myself not to look below his face, but that wasn't helping much.

His eyes were wide and full of lust. His hands were clenching either side of the doorframe so hard, I was surprised the wood didn't splinter. I took my earbuds out, dropping them on the floor, then rose to my feet before realizing that made matters worse, because now Hunter had a full-frontal view.

And then I couldn't help myself, I looked down, and even through the towel, it was obvious he was hard. I'd never gotten aroused so fast in my life.

It was all I could do not to clench my thighs. I didn't hear what he grumbled under his breath as he grabbed a towel, handing it to me. Our fingers touched briefly, and energy zapped through me. And when his gaze perused me unabashedly, resting on my breasts before moving downward, I felt on fire, as if he was trailing his mouth across my skin.

He snapped his gaze away as I wrapped the towel around me, then turned his back completely, as if he didn't trust himself *not* to look if he was facing me. I shared his conundrum.

"I didn't hear you come in," I hurried to explain. "I was listening to music."

"I didn't know you were home," he said.

"Left the office early. Everyone was wondering why I didn't take the day off."

"Shit. I didn't think about that."

"Neither did I, but I told them I just wanted to wrap up a few things before the honeymoon. You can turn around now. Towel's on. All safe."

Hunter stayed put for a few seconds, and when he turned, my knees nearly buckled from the sheer intensity in his eyes.

I knew right then and there that we'd crossed yet another boundary. I lifted one foot, intending to swing my leg over the edge of the tub, but lost my balance.

Hunter caught my wrist. Shit, could he tell my pulse was out of control? I avoided looking at him as I stepped out. I wasn't sure what to say, how to manage this tension.

As gracefully as possible, I grabbed my phone and skidded past him, going straight inside my room. Except, it wasn't my space, was it? He'd have to walk through it when he came out.

Glancing at the clock, I realized it was already time to leave for the spa. I dressed quickly, then simply shouted, "I'm leaving for my pedicure appointment" while he was still in the bathroom.

Chapter Twelve
Josie

While at the spa, I tried to occupy my brain with an upcoming case. It didn't really work. My thoughts kept drifting to Hunter. We'd been living together barely a week, and everything was already awkward. I could feel our friendship changing, metamorphosing into something I couldn't define. I could only see this tension escalating.

We were adults, we both had needs, and a three-year dry spell wasn't exactly plausible, was it? And still, I didn't want to go back on that. We could be careful, of course. We wouldn't have to be seen in public at all with other people and the immigration services would be none the wiser. But the truth was, I couldn't bear the thought of smelling another woman's perfume on Hunter. Of hearing him come home in the morning and knowing he'd been with someone else. This already felt more real than it was supposed to.

I felt more confused when I arrived home than when I'd left. I lingered a little outside, not quite ready to go in. This place was just beautiful, with the mix of colors and explosion of smells: a gardening company had brought pots with anemones and freesias, laying them on the steps in front of the house. In the hot summer night, the smell felt more intense, somehow, perhaps because of the humidity.

Tearing my gaze away from the flowers, I headed toward the front door, finally gathering the courage to push it open.

When I stepped inside, I sighed. It smelled absolutely mouthwatering.

Hunter was in the kitchen, cooking steaks.

"Hey!" I greeted.

He winked. "Dinner's almost ready."

"Want me to set the table?"

"Already done."

I squinted. "Are you trying to bribe me again?"

He chuckled. "Just wanted to cook you dinner, future Mrs. Caldwell."

"What?"

"What what?"

"There will be no future Mrs. Caldwell. I'm keeping my name."

Hunter set down the steak fork, frowning. "No, you're not."

"I can't believe we're arguing about this the day before the wedding. A real couple would have discussed this ahead of time. How the hell are we going to pull this off?"

"You're gonna take my name, and that's that." His voice was dominant, but he didn't think I'd just relent, did he? I liked making Hunter happy, but I did have some solid reasons for sticking to my guns.

"No, I'm not."

"No one would believe I couldn't convince my wife to take my name."

"I'm not going to the hassle of changing my name only to change it back in three years."

"Josie...."

"Don't Josie me. It's not negotiable."

He tilted his head, a twinkle appearing in his eyes. "Everything is negotiable."

"You're so full of yourself. There is no guarantee a real fiancée would want to take your name."

"I would convince her."

"How?"

"Are you sure you want to know?"

He was looking at me with the same fire as this afternoon. Clearly, the hours apart had not only *not* extinguished it, but stoked it.

And when he looked at my lips, I felt that same fire coursing through me. His semi-naked body was imprinted on my brain, and I knew he was not faring better than me.

"I'm keeping my name, Hunter. I'm building a reputation for myself at the firm and among clients, and I don't want to confuse anyone by changing my name," I said eventually, stepping away from him. He didn't reply, which I considered a victory.

During dinner, the tension between us escalated. He touched me constantly. Brushed his arm against mine when he served the steak, rested his ankles against mine under the table. I just couldn't cool down.

After dinner, I helped clean up, trying to stay out of his way as much as possible.

"Josie, you want to talk about earlier?"

Damn. I'd been too obvious. I was at the sink, rinsing our glasses.

"What do you mean?" I schooled my voice to sound neutral.

I felt him right behind me when he spoke next. "You're avoiding looking at me. Is it because I saw you naked or because I sported a raging hard-on for you?"

Holy shit. Energy vibrated through me. My hands trembled lightly. His breath on the shell of my ear was messing with my senses. He wasn't touching any part of me, but I felt the heat of his body. There couldn't have been more than an inch distance between us.

I stopped the water, drawing in a deep breath. "I don't... I don't know. I don't know what to think or how to explain anything."

"Let me put you at ease and explain myself. You're fucking beautiful, and—"

I whirled around, thinking it was the easiest way to interrupt him. Unfortunately, that put me face-to-face with him. I hadn't miscalculated. He *was* close. And now he'd moved one hand on my waist. I felt every finger press against my rib cage as if they were touching my bare skin.

"Stop with the flirty lines."

"Why? They're true."

I swallowed. "Hunter... just, don't."

He watched me as if he was about to hoist me up on the counter, but after a few seconds, he reluctantly let go.

We slept in different bedrooms, but I didn't think even that could cut through the sexual tension. The lease to my apartment was still running until the end of the month. Maybe I should spend the night there? I was just about to broach the subject when he abruptly said, "I'm going for a run."

"Oh. But the treadmill wasn't delivered yet. And isn't the gym in the condo building closed for quality check tonight?" We'd gotten a memo about this.

"Yes, it is. I'll just run around the neighborhood."

"You hate running on pavement."

"I need to release all this tension somehow."

"What tension? Ohhh...."

My face felt on fire as I realized what he meant. Scratch that. There was so much heat in his gaze that my entire *body* was on fire.

He smiled, not taking his eyes off me as he pulled away. "I have a hunch I'll have to get used to it."

Chapter Thirteen
Josie

The next morning, I was giddy. The wedding might be fake, but my excitement wasn't.

I was determined to block out any negative thoughts and fears. The list of things that could go wrong was endless, but I wasn't going to dwell on that today.

I was far too excited to even be able to go through my yoga routine. Clearing my mind was impossible.

First things first, I called an Uber and headed to the hotel where my family was staying. It was right next to Hunter's ballroom, where the reception and ceremony were taking place.

Hunter had arranged for a driver to pick them up from the airport. The schedule was so tight that I only had time to say hi to everyone, and then my sister, Dylan's girlfriend, and I were meeting Tess and Skye at the spa. Mom had texted that she was too tired to join us.

I arrived at the hotel before they did, and when the gang came in, I took stock of everyone. Momma had cut her jet-black hair into a bob and had lost a bit of weight. Dad looked the same as ever. I swear the man didn't age. His dirty-blond hair was cropped short, and he towered over everyone.

My brothers, Dylan and Ian, hugged me first. They both took after Dad. God, I missed them.

"Where's Hunter? We want to talk to him," Dylan said at once.

"No, you don't. I don't need you to scare off the groom before he says yes."

Ian rubbed his palms. "We'll find him without your help, don't worry."

I rolled my eyes, exchanging a glance with my sister, Isabelle. She was younger than me, and since I'd left home so early, I'd left her alone to deal with our brothers for all these years.

She hugged me tight, and I didn't want to let go. After greeting everyone, I helped them check in.

When we arrived in the rooms, a surprise awaited us.

"The rooms are huge," Mom exclaimed.

Wow. Hunter had booked them suites. When I'd brought up my parents, he said he'd take care of it. I imagined he'd just book a few rooms, not suites.

He was spoiling my family. I had the overwhelming urge to see him and hug the living daylights out of him.

I settled on messaging him.

Josie: Thank you for the rooms. They're great. You've made everyone very happy.

Hunter: Glad to hear it.

Josie: Are you on schedule so far?

Hunter: My schedule only begins in three

hours.

Josie: Lucky you.

Mom patted my cheek as I helped her steam her dress. "My sweet girl. I can't believe you're finally getting married. You'll be so happy with Hunter."

I didn't know what to say, so I just smiled. With a bout of panic, I realized the whole day would be like this, and I'd have to look everyone in the eye and lie to them.

I could do this.

No negative thoughts. No negative thoughts. I repeated the mantra as the girls and I left for the spa.

I wasn't close to my brother Dylan's girlfriend, Lina, but I'd heard a lot about her.

"This is so fancy," she said once we entered the spa.

It really was. There was a small koi pond in front of the entrance, and the inside looked like something out of a fairy tale.

Tess and Skye met us at the manicure stations, where I sat next to Isabelle. We were a little further away from the others.

"How did it happen? When?" she asked. "You need to tell me everything."

"I already told the story at my bachelorette party."

"Which I did not attend."

"And whose fault is that?"

She wrinkled her nose. "Sometimes I wish I were more like you."

"What do you mean?"

"You came to the big city when you were a teenager, took the leap. I was always too afraid to get out of my comfort zone."

"But you're happy with your life, aren't you?"

My siblings had all left Montana for college and were now spread throughout the country. Unfortunately, none moved to New York. I was still hoping to convince them to join me one day.

"Most of the time, yes. But don't let me spoil your big day with my soul searching."

I wanted to ask her for more information, but she changed the subject, focusing on Hunter.

The next few hours were simply crazy. Never in my life had I undergone so many beautification processes in so little time.

Nothing was *just* something when you were a bride.

Makeup included a thirty-minute face massage as a first step. Hairstyling was preceded by a three-step care process.

Since the bridal package lasted two hours longer than a regular one, the rest of the party left before I did.

I would change into my dress at the hotel, as that made the most sense. Hunter and I couldn't very well both get dressed at the house. What if he saw me?

It seemed silly to care about all these superstitions, and yet I couldn't help it. I wanted to do things the right way, even though…

No negative thoughts.

No imagining what my actual wedding would be like. Truthfully, it couldn't measure up to this one.

My Dad was in the lobby when I entered the hotel, pacing around.

"Dad, what are you doing here all alone?" I asked.

"Wanted to look at this place. Stay with me for a few minutes? I've got a feeling this is the only time I'll get you to myself today."

"Sure."

We sat in a corner of the lobby, drinking coffee.

"My girl is a grown woman," Dad murmured.

"Still a Daddy's girl, don't you worry."

"You were always such a happy kid. We did well, didn't we? Your mom and I?"

My heart squeezed. "I had the best childhood."

Why would he have doubts? The wedding was bringing out emotions in all of us.

"You left when you were so young, and we didn't have much to give you."

"Daddy, I'm happy. I've always been happy."

He watched me carefully, sipping his coffee.

"So, your future husband spoke with me today."

"Hunter's here already?" I looked around instinctively. Dad grinned. "What?"

"You're head over heels in love with this

man."

"I'm not—"

Holy shit. I'd almost told him I wasn't in love. My breath caught. I gripped my cup tighter. Luckily, Dad didn't seem to notice.

"What did he talk to you about?"

"So, he suggested something. I wanted to run it by you."

"Of course."

"He suggested we all come down here at Christmas for two weeks. Business is closed during that time anyway. He said he'd cover all costs."

Something funny happened to my throat. It felt raspy all of a sudden.

"Sure. That sounds fantastic. Two whole weeks? Wow. We haven't had that in years."

"You've got yourself a great man, Josie."

I knew. Oh, how I knew.

The urge I had earlier to hug him returned in full force, but I honestly had no idea where he was.

Josie: Can I talk to you? I'm going to room 2118.

I had to start getting dressed. Securing the veil in my hair wouldn't be easy. The hairstylist had berated me for not bringing the veil with me—he could've sorted it out, but I'd honestly completely forgotten about it.

My dress was in Mom's room. The group was already there, drinking champagne. Amelia too, as well as her sister—Hunter's mother. I'd only met her twice, at high-school graduation and then college graduation.

"Darling, you look absolutely beautiful," she said.

I twirled once for effect, and as I turned to face her, realized that she was watching my belly intently. I pressed my lips together to keep from laughing. Throwing me a conspiratorial wink, Tess handed me a glass of champagne.

We all toasted to the wedding, and when I took my first sip, I heard both my Mom and Hunter's sigh. Their disappointment crushed me, but at least this cleared any doubts that this was a shotgun wedding.

I'd make sure to take a sip in front of all the guests to avoid being questioned.

"Okay, so, before you change into your dress... we've got a present for you," Tess exclaimed, handing me the sexiest set of lingerie I'd ever owned. Pearly white silk, with a pattern of lace at the hem. Two sets of panties, a bra, and a short robe.

"Wow."

"A little something for your wedding night," Tess said.

Which I'd be spending alone. Right... they didn't know that.

"And you can wear it under your wedding dress. We specifically picked something that would fit," Skye added.

"And that will completely blow Hunter's mind. He'll maul you before he manages to undress you," Tess said.

"I'll pretend I haven't heard that," Amelia said.

Tess grinned. "Whoops. Forgot to rephrase that in a mom-proof way."

Skye's cheeks turned a little red. I pulled her into a half hug.

"Mom, we need some wedding traditions. How come we don't have them? We have traditions for *everything*," Isabelle said.

That was true. We had traditions by the bucketload, especially for big holidays.

Mom smiled. "That's because Josie's the first to get married. We can start working on those now."

"Does Ian and Dylan wanting to give Hunter *the talk* count as tradition?" I asked.

Amelia laughed. "Let the boys feel like they're doing their job. Cole and Ryker didn't make things easy for poor Mick when he first asked me out."

I knew that only too well. They both made Mick jump through hoops.

I changed in the ensuite bathroom. I could have just packed the lingerie, and Tess and Skye would be none the wiser. But I wanted to be sexy. If the wedding were real, this was exactly what I'd be wearing, and since I was having my fantasy wedding anyway, why not wear the lingerie too?

While I was fastening my bra, someone knocked at the door.

"Hunter is here to talk to you," Tess said.

"Oh. Okay."

"Hunter, you're not allowed to see her. Talk

through the door."

"Tess, don't be ridiculous," he boomed.

"I mean it. I'll stay here and keep guard if necessary."

"No need," I replied, chuckling.

"Okay. I'll leave you two."

I waited until I couldn't hear Tess's footsteps anymore before asking, "What's wrong?"

"Nothing. You said you wanted to talk to me."

"Right."

"You're really going to talk to me through the closed door?"

"Tess is right. It's bad luck to see the bride on the wedding day."

"You do know this isn't real, right?"

"All the more. Want something to go wrong and you to be shipped across the ocean?"

"Josie…."

"So, I've talked to Dad."

"Good. I talked to him earlier too."

He sounded pleased with himself—which was when I realized that he'd gone to Dad on purpose.

"You can't pay to fly in my entire family for Christmas. It's very generous, but I can't say yes."

"Yes, you can. Things are different now."

"Why?" I almost pressed my ear against the door, not wanting to miss a word.

"Because you'll be my wife. And I want you to be happy. And I know that you're always feeling guilty about not spending more time with your gang."

My eyes burned at the corners, turning misty. This man! It was a good thing we were talking through a door and he couldn't see my face.

I cleared my throat, fiddling with the hem of my robe. I was beginning to realize that the problem wasn't that a real wedding wouldn't measure up to this one.

It was that I didn't think another man could measure up to Hunter. I doubted that anyone I'd ever marry would get me better than Hunter would, that he'd understand me on such a deep level—that he'd know exactly when to push because I was standing in my own way.

"I won't accept a no. So there you have it." That bossy tone was going to be my undoing.

"Thank you. It's a lovely surprise."

"My pleasure, Josie. I'll go now. Tess is giving me the evil eye from across the room."

I laughed, waiting until I was sure Hunter had left before coming out. I discovered that my brothers had joined our group in the meantime.

"The number of eligible bachelors at this wedding is astounding," Tess said.

"My girlfriends are already rubbing their hands in excitement," Skye added. "Awww, look at Ian. He's practically shivering with fear."

Dylan held his hands up, laughing. "Lucky I'm taken."

Ian turned to me. "As my sister and the bride, I beg you... save me."

"But this is so much fun."

Isabelle did a little shimmy, grinning. "These two always say you're their girl. So happy to finally see you throw them under the bus."

Chapter Fourteen
Hunter

I looked around the venue, chuckling. This had gotten completely out of control. It wasn't just a low-key party, it was an over-the-top wedding, but I supposed it was my own fault for handing the reins to Amelia and Tess.

"I can't believe Mom and Tess pulled this off in a few weeks," Ryker commented.

"Makes me wonder what they would've come up with if they had more time. But I'm sure I'll find out as soon as one of you gets marr—"

"Don't say it out loud," Ryker said with a grin. "Might jinx me. Can't believe you're the first in the family to marry."

I grinned back, silently agreeing with him. I hadn't thought I'd be the first one either. I hadn't envisioned marrying at all, period.

I looked around again. What did Josie think about everything? She'd been so adamant about not wanting this to feel like an actual wedding, yet looking around, I couldn't imagine anything looking *more* like a wedding.

I was waiting in front of the officiant. When the music started, I looked up to the end of the red carpet, and nearly swallowed my tongue. She was wearing a wedding dress. Why hadn't she told me that? Why hadn't anyone? Had Josie felt she had to do this in order to keep up appearances?

I couldn't say why this impacted me so much. Even through the short veil covering her face, I noticed that her eyes were a little glassy. I wanted to soothe her, to reassure her. With shock, I realized that there was some part of me longing for this to not be just for pretend. I mentally shook myself. I couldn't get caught up in moments like this and mess everything up. Josie was here today to do me a favor, to help me out. I'd better not muddle things.

I wasn't her forever guy. She was my best friend, and that was all she was ever going to be. She wasn't going to fall for me. She hadn't until now, so why would things change?

Her dad walked with her, beaming at the rest of the family on the way. Josie's parents and siblings looked beyond happy, which brought along yet another wave of guilt.

I had to do something about all the guilt. And if I was feeling this way, I couldn't even imagine how Josie felt.

She smiled at the crowd, a warm and genuine smile. Or maybe I just wished it so badly that I saw what I wanted.

"Take good care of her," her dad said when they reached me.

"I will, sir. I promise."

I planned to make good on my promise. The

Christmas trip was a good start. Josie wasn't one to easily accept things, but I wouldn't back down. When I took her hand, kissing it, I was overwhelmed by emotion in a way I couldn't explain or even comprehend.

Josie's hand was shaking. I squeezed it lightly as we both turned to face the officiant.

He began the ceremony, greeting and welcoming everyone. I was too caught up in Josie to hear him, and yet, when he spoke about being together for better or for worse, I couldn't block out his words.

I wanted to believe what he said, but more often than not, I met people who gave up when the going got rough. I glanced at Josie again, looking for any signs that she was as affected by this moment as I was.

When the officiant said, "You may kiss the bride," blood rushed in my ears, pounding with ferocity. I lifted her veil slowly.

She was stunning. Her eyes were bright, her lips full and beckoning me. When I leaned in to kiss her, I could barely hold myself back. I felt a deep, desperate need to claim this woman as mine.

***

Josie

Up until now, I'd felt as if I was watching everything, myself included, as a movie. But when Hunter kissed me, I felt like a princess in a fairy tale, awoken from slumber by the prince's kiss. Everything came into focus. Correction. Everything about *him* came into focus. His soft yet determined lips. The deep, lazy strokes of his tongue. His hand on my arm, touching my bare skin.

Someone cleared their throat.

"Easy there, we can all see you can't wait to be alone," Ryker said. Hunter smiled against my lips before pulling back, glaring at Ryker.

I blushed, but when Hunter took my hand, and we walked out arm in arm, I couldn't help but grin from ear to ear.

"You look stunning, Josie," he whispered as we lined up for pictures. In an even lower voice, he added, "You didn't tell me you'd be wearing a white dress."

"Thought I'd surprise you."

"Did my cousins force your hand?"

I nudged him playfully. "Show a bit more faith in me, will ya? I liked this one, so I thought what the heck? Why waste the opportunity?"

We smiled and posed for the pics, and I tried not to allow my emotions to overwhelm me *again*.

It was a testament to Amelia's and Tess's organizational talent that the wedding looked as if they'd worked on it for months, rather than a few weeks.

I had attended plenty of weddings lately, what with half my friends tying the knot, and this one was right up there with the most elaborate ones I'd seen. I was happy I'd chosen a bridal gown. A cocktail dress wouldn't have done all of this justice, and I didn't need yet another reason to feel guilt toward Hunter's family.

The ballroom was connected to the ceremony area by an archway with flowers. Hunter and I led the way, with the wedding party just behind us and the rest of the guests following suit.

The ballroom was simply beautiful. Understated elegance and more than a dash of romanticism. High ceiling supported by columns on the outskirts and a crystal chandelier hanging in the center. The room had two levels: the ground floor, and half a level higher, balconies with wrought iron railings. Twinkling lights were interspersed here and there, casting a warm glow throughout the room, highlighting the white freesias that served as centerpieces. The tables were arranged on the balconies. The ground floor was entirely used for dancing.

The next hour was a whirlwind as everyone congratulated us. By the time we finally sat at the bridal table, I couldn't feel my toes. But my reprieve didn't last long, because the DJ announced it was time for the first dance.

"Ready, Mrs. Josie Gallagher?" Hunter asked.

I laughed, taking his hand. There was a pep in my step as we headed toward the dance floor.

"You're not going to get over the fact that I didn't take your name anytime soon, are you?" I asked once he placed an arm around my waist. I was trying to distract myself, to focus on anything other than how close he was. It was to no avail; his presence was inescapable.

"I plan to make you feel guilty about it for a long time."

"No chance. I have zero guilt about not further inflating your ego. You *think* you have too much swagger anyway."

"Let me prove my swagger then, *wife*."

I shuddered at the word. I'd never imagined Hunter would say that word to anyone, much less to me. I'd been looking forward to the dance this morning, but now my hormones were still in overdrive from the kiss earlier. Even the barest of touches set me on the edge, and I wasn't sure I could dance with him and not give myself away.

When Hunter held me even tighter, I knew I didn't stand a chance. He'd take one look at me and just *know*.

"Thank God you made me practice," he muttered in my hair after twirling me once.

"See, listen to me. You'll get far."

He threw his head back, laughing. "Spoken like a true wife."

"And your best friend," I reminded him. He smiled wickedly.

"I'd say you've become more daring since you put on that first ring."

I could hardly dispute that. "Yes, but you seemed to need it, honestly. Besides, I had to get in character."

He watched me with warm eyes. "You're the

best person I know, Josie. Thank you for doing this. I promise I'll make the next three years as amazing as possible."

I wanted to tell him that he better not or I might not want the arrangement to come to an end at all. Instead, I braced myself for the final twirl. Hunter executed the move with perfect precision, just as we'd rehearsed it, but when he pulled me back, he didn't just catch me...

He kissed me.

I hummed low against his mouth, because I just couldn't help it. He stroked my tongue lazily, and I couldn't help but wonder... how was he in bed?

I'd been trying not to think about this, but now I couldn't keep the thoughts at bay. The way he kissed me... fuck, it was as if he was close to throwing me over his shoulder and leaving the party with me. I had no doubt that Hunter would know how to take care of me, no matter if he loved me slowly or fucked me hard. When he pulled back, there was no mistaking the lust in his eyes.

I danced the whole night. I had so much energy I didn't think I could sit anyway. I danced with anyone who asked me to. Unfortunately though, our guests were throwing questions at me left and right.

"When did this happen?"

"Have you always been in love with him?"

"How did he propose?"

"Are you pregnant?"

I kept the number of champagne glasses I

drank to a minimum, because I wanted my head clear.

For the most part, I had fun. So much fun, in fact, that I had to constantly remind myself this wasn't really my wedding.

I wasn't going to go to bed and wake up next to this gorgeous man. One day, another woman would have his ring on her finger, and if we managed to play our eventual divorce as "we were better off as friends," I'd even be at that wedding, celebrating the happy couple. Instead of cheering me up, the thought made my heart squeeze. *Oh, Josie, Josie, Josie, your hormones are wreaking havoc, that's all.* I just had to tell Hunter to stop with the panty-melting kisses. They'd mess with any girl's head.

I'd tell him just that, starting tomorrow. Tonight, I wanted to enjoy them for a while longer. Once the number of guests dwindled, I indulged a little more in champagne… and in Hunter. I didn't know if he was buzzed too or if I was feeling everything in a magnified way, but his kisses were becoming a little more frequent. A lot hotter.

By the time we climbed into the car that would take us home, my entire body felt like a livewire. My nipples were too sensitive, pushing against my dress. The pressure between my thighs was unbearable.

I'd never been more pleased by the sheer size of the house, and by the fact that the bedrooms were far apart, because I had to take care of myself tonight. The past weeks had been like foreplay, and today had just been too much.

I was so lost in my thoughts that I didn't realize what Hunter was about to do until he lifted me in his arms. I shrieked, grabbing onto his neck, holding on for dear life.

"What are you doing?"

"Crossing the threshold with my new bride."

I smiled. "You think the immigration services have spy cameras around here?"

"No, I just think that you're an incurable romantic and you secretly like that I'm carrying you."

I giggled, resting my head in the crook of his neck. I was too tired and too wired up at the same time to pretend with him.

"I do like it, Hunter."

We were quiet as he walked through the house with me. A five o'clock shadow already covered his cheeks. I stroked them absentmindedly. His skin smelled amazing. The aftershave and cologne had evaporated, revealing the scent of him.

He only put me down when he brought me to the master bedroom. For a brief second, I forgot we'd switched rooms and thought he was laying me on *his* bed. My nerves lit up in anticipation before I remembered the switch.

I wasn't ready for the evening to end, and yet, when he left, I didn't stop him.

Half an hour later, I paced the room, cursing. This damn dress just wouldn't come off. I'd tried to undo the laces at the back myself, and somehow I'd managed to make a knot of it. Even though I planned to keep the dress, preserve it like the prize it was, I was tempted to head to the kitchen, grab a knife, and just cut the string. I would have done it too, if I hadn't been afraid I might accidentally stab myself. How could this be so hard?

Brides aren't supposed to undo their own wedding gowns, a small voice said at the back of my mind. I sighed. I knew that, of course. But Hunter was probably asleep by now. I didn't want to wake him up. If only I'd started this process sooner. But I'd wasted twenty minutes removing my makeup, and the three hundred or so bobby pins from my hair.

After fifteen more minutes, I gave up. My only choices were to either sleep in it or wake up Hunter. I opted for the latter.

To my astonishment, he wasn't asleep. His bed was empty, but I could hear the shower in the bathroom.

I sat on the mattress, right up until the water stopped running and the door opened. I leaped to my feet.

"I'm in your bedroom," I yelled, then lowered my eyes to my lap just in case he was naked.

When I heard him step into the room, I asked, "Are you decent?"

"Yes."

His voice was a little hoarse.

"Umm... sorry to crash in on you, but I can't undo the ribbons by myself."

It sounded ridiculous, like a cheap pickup line. When Hunter didn't say anything, I added quickly, "I pulled at the laces, but on the wrong one, and ended up with a knot I can't undo myself."

"I'll take care of you."

I looked up to him as he walked to me. Holy shit. The man only had a towel wrapped around him. His chest was bare. I had a flashback to the moment he'd walked in on me in the bathroom.

I turned my back to him, glad that the room was semidark, or there would be no hiding my blush.

I sucked in my breath when Hunter tangled his fingers in the laces, pulling them open. The corset loosened, and I knew he'd succeeded. This felt so intimate. Even more intimate than his carrying me over the threshold. Each eyelet made a tiny pop when the lace was pulled out of it, and I knew Hunter had opened all of them when I had to press the corset against my chest with both hands to keep the dress from sliding down.

"Thanks," I said after he was done.

"You're welcome. It was too tight, I think. You've got marks here."

He touched his fingers to my bare skin in a slow, delicate move, and my knees weakened a little.

"They'll fade by tomorrow."

Please, stop touching me, or I might just turn around and kiss you.

"Josie, fuck... what are you wearing?"

It took me a second to realize he'd probably just noticed my lingerie. He only saw the back of it, but still...

"Umm... just... lace, and..."

I felt his fingers curl against my skin before he removed his hand, as if he had to fight his every instinct in order not to touch me.

"You're so sexy."

His voice was even lower, gruffer.

"Hunter—"

He silenced me by bringing a hand to the side of my waist. The pressure he applied was light, but it set me on fire.

I'd barely managed to calm down over the past half hour, and now I was on edge again.

"Fuck, Josie. Keep me in check, okay?"

"What?"

His mouth was dangerously close to my ear. His hot breath tickled the sensitive spot behind it.

"Since you've moved in—and after today—I can't keep the lines from blurring. I don't know how. You have to be the reasonable one between the two of us."

I didn't know what to say, how to react.

"You're the most important person in my life, and I don't want to screw this up," he said.

He whirled me around, bringing his hand to my face, caressing my cheek before kissing my forehead.

The first night in one thousand ninety-five. How were we supposed to make it through?

Chapter Fifteen
Josie

Next morning, I woke up with a headache, as if I was hungover. No surprise, since I'd only gotten a few hours of sleep.

I'd expected Hunter to already be up and about, but a quick peek in his room showed that he was still fast asleep. Then again, he'd already finished packing before the wedding. As usual, I'd left some details until the very last minute.

I still had to sort out my cosmetics. As I stuffed all my creams and scrubs in the toiletries bag, I caught a glimpse of my wedding ring, and it dawned on me that I was a married woman. Holy shit. I was legally bound to the six feet of sexiness currently sleeping in the guest room. I was married to Hunter Caldwell, my best friend, and teenage crush. A mix of panic and euphoria overwhelmed me, and I had to lean against the wall of the bathroom and press the heel of my palm on my collarbone to calm down. Then I headed to the foyer, where Hunter had already brought our bags. I wondered if he had a reservation confirmation from the hotel somewhere. He hadn't wanted to tell me the name of the hotel, insisting he wanted an element of surprise.

I had a sneaking suspicion he actually hadn't wanted me to research the price, but eh... he was asleep now. How would he know I snooped around?

I hunched over to find the zipper to his bag.

"What do you think you're doing?"

I startled so badly that I nearly plowed headfirst into the door. My heart was beating so fast, I felt I was going to be sick as I straightened up and whirled around to Hunter. He was wearing pajama pants and nothing else. The pants hung low enough on his hips that I had a prime view of the V-lines pointing downward. *Don't stare. Don't stare.*

I forced my gaze up. Right, at the first opportunity I got, I was buying him some decent pajamas.

"I just wanted to put my toiletries in the bag," I said with as much innocence as I could muster. Hunter narrowed his eyes, stepping closer.

"My bag?"

"I don't have enough space in mine." It was true, but I was sure my cheeks were pink.

"There's something else too. You wanted to look at what hotel we're going to."

"Not at all."

His eyes crinkled at the corners. In a fraction of a second, he wrapped one arm around me, pinning me against the entrance door. His hips were pressing against mine, keeping me immobile.

"Tell me what you were up to."

"Or what?"

"I can think about a few torture methods to

lure the truth out of you."

His bare chest was almost touching my torso, and then there would be nothing separating us except my very thin cotton dress. My senses were completely assaulted by this man and it wasn't even nine o'clock in the morning. Two full weeks in a romantic resort in the Maldives, where I'd be seeing enough of him shirtless to tempt me on an hourly basis? Things were *not* looking good for me.

"Fine, I admit it. I admit it. I wanted to know the name of the hotel."

"See? That wasn't so hard."

Was I imagining it, or was he looking at my lips? His skin felt so impossibly hot against me.

"You'll find out soon enough."

"How soon?" I grinned. I couldn't help it.

"Patience." He motioned to my toiletries bag. "That's all you need me to stuff in my luggage?"

"Yes."

"Good. Go get ready, and I'll pack it up."

"You don't trust me, do you?" I rolled my eyes. "I wouldn't peek."

"Think I'm going to believe you after catching you red-handed?"

He had a point, so I turned on my heels, heading to my room to change into my travel attire—jeans and a polo shirt.

Half an hour later, we were in the back of a cab, heading to the airport. Hunter was silent, looking out the window. From time to time he touched his wedding band—we wore identical platinum rings. I wondered if he felt the same panic and euphoria I did. The same *attraction*. I couldn't think like that. It was silly.

At the airport, the driver wheeled the carriage with our bags right inside the building.

"I wish you all the best on your honeymoon," he said.

Hunter took over, pushing the baggage cart toward the business class check-in area.

"Good morning, sir," the check-in lady said, taking the passports Hunter handed her.

She scanned them while a man took care of our luggage.

"Would you like me to print out the tickets, or do you have them on your phone?"

"Print them, please," Hunter said. After we received them, we headed to the TSA checkpoint.

"Still not going to tell me the name of the hotel? I want to do my research about the activities they offer."

"You'll have plenty of time once we arrive."

The line advanced, and I moved with it, startling a little when Hunter wrapped an arm around me from behind, bringing his lips to my ear.

"Told you I'd make these years the best, Josie. Just trust me on that."

I did trust him. The problem was, I didn't know how I'd manage to go back to how things were once we divorced.

"If you want me to trust you, that means you actually have to tell me things," I teased.

"We'll get to that. Baby steps."

After security, we headed straight to the business lounge. "So, this is how you travel all the time?" I asked him, sitting cross-legged on a leather armchair big enough for two of me. "I could get used to it."

We were served champagne and canapes right before boarding began. I already had a happy buzz going on and was a bit mad at myself for that, because I wanted to experience *everything*.

When we were shown to our seats, I immediately began poking every button and trying every single position for the seat.

I only stopped when I caught Hunter staring at me with a strange expression.

"What?"

"I forgot how much you enjoy new things."

Unfazed, I checked every item on the menu, accepting yet another glass of champagne. Then I glanced at my ring, touched it. "Does it feel weird?"

He gave me a small smile. "I honestly never thought I'd wear one. How about you?"

"I freaked a little this morning," I admitted in a small voice.

"So did I. But I think it's normal. It's not a small thing, and the implications are... well... we both know them." He frowned, then half turned, leaning in closer. For a fraction of a second, I thought he was going to kiss me, leave no doubt for everyone that we were in love, but instead he said, "If you regret it..."

"Too late, I already signed on the dotted line."

"We can get an annulment."

The mere word made me sad. What was up with that?

I tried to sound playful as I said, "And miss out on the Maldives?"

"After we get back. It's easier to get a marriage annulled during the first fourteen days," he said in a low voice, barely a whisper.

"It's generally not easy to get an annulment."

"It's doable. So if you change your mind after we're back, you can still get out of this."

"But that wouldn't help you at all," I protested.

"I'll deal with the fallout. I just…." He shook his head, as if he couldn't find his words, which was so unlike Hunter. "I'm just afraid that this is going to change things between us, all the pressure, the expectations. You're my best friend, Josie. I don't want to lose you."

"You won't. Who's overthinking things now?" I tried to sound playful again. Yesterday, I'd felt so connected to him. His kisses had felt so real. And last night… he'd probably had a little too much to drink. That was all. I'd been projecting my own feelings onto him.

I spent the rest of the journey watching movies. Midway through the flight, Hunter turned his chair into a bed and slept like a rock. He was used to flying. I, on the other hand, grew restless after only a couple of hours and didn't sleep a wink. When we landed in Dubai, I was already done for, and we had yet another long flight ahead of us.

"If you lie down, you might fall asleep eventually," Hunter suggested.

But lying down made me even more restless. Eventually, the exhaustion won.

I woke up when the stewardess leaned in to say, "The plane is starting the descent. Please put your chairs in an upright position."

I rubbed my eyes, then scrambled into a sitting position, glancing out the window.

"We're over the ocean," I told Hunter, who was still lying down, rubbing his eyes. "The water is dark blue. I suppose it's because it's still deep here. I wonder if it's really as turquoise as it always is in pictures. With all the filters and effects these days, you never know."

Hunter was grinning.

"What?" I asked.

"Your enthusiasm is adorable."

"Why aren't you enthusiastic? You've never been either."

"I am enthusiastic. But clearly, there's normal enthusiasm and Josie-level."

"Don't make me poke you this early in the morning."

"You're welcome to try. I think I know how to win this argument."

He looked at my lips. I blushed, returning my attention to the window. I tried to remember all the activities one could do on the Maldives.

"I can't wait to take scuba diving courses. Do you think our hotel offers them? You bad man. I would've researched if you had told me beforehand."

"The hotel staff will fill us in. Already told them you're eager to try everything."

I turned around to face him. "*We* are going to try everything."

"No, thanks. I'm good at the beach."

"What if I take off with the instructor?"

His eyes flashed, and he leaned in a tad. Just enough that I could feel every exhale on my lips.

"I'll have to sharpen my seduction skills, won't I, *wife*?"

I swallowed, looking away. "What kind of husband are you, leaving your wife to go off on her own?"

"One who thinks she can take care of herself even though she is crazy enough to go underwater with an air tube strapped to her back. Do you know how much can go wrong? And it's all out of your control."

It suddenly clicked in my brain why he was so against it.

"You know what I think?" I asked.

"What?"

"You need to learn how to give up being in control a bit. It'll be good for you."

"No chance."

"I'm going to change your mind."

"You haven't managed that in fifteen years."

I grinned saucily. "No, but... I'm your wife

151

now. I can use so many more tricks, just wait and see."

Chapter Sixteen
Hunter

A car picked us up from the airport, driving alongside the ocean to the hotel. Josie had her nose pressed to the window the entire way.

"I cannot believe it actually is so turquoise. I feel like I'm in a movie."

I'd forgotten how excited Josie could get about anything, how vividly she lived life. Perhaps I'd forgotten because it had been a while since we'd done anything new, whether together or apart. She spent most of her time in that office of hers, which I thought was a damn shame. I'd see what I could do to change that. Having money made a lot of things easier. For example, on weekends, I could have a jet ready to fly us to a new destination when needed. I had three years to give Josie what she hadn't let me do in fifteen years, and I had a good excuse.

"This is so extravagant," she exclaimed when we entered the hotel. Marble and glass surrounded us, decorated with exotic plants as well, giving the impression that we were outside. Plates with fruit and drinks were placed at strategic distances, so the guests would never be without.

"Mr. Caldwell, Ms. Gallagher, welcome to our

hotel." A tall brunette greeted us, holding a tray with four glasses, two with champagne, two with orange juice.

"Can I offer you a drink while you wait to be checked in?"

She led us to a leather couch next to reception. We clinked glasses, sipping our orange juice while the receptionist filled out forms. Josie inspected our surroundings with wide, wonder-filled eyes. Fuck, she was cute. Especially when her lips parted as she realized there were parrots in one of the trees.

She'd applied gloss before we'd descended from the plane, but as far as I was concerned, her lips looked best without any kind of makeup. They were dark pink and full, and so damn tempting. I'd kissed her far more often than necessary during the wedding. I hadn't been able to stop myself. And no matter what I told myself, I couldn't wait to do it again.

When the receptionist excused herself, saying she'd be back after scanning our passports, Josie went to the restroom.

I thumbed some of the brochures in front of me until a blonde approached, placing two glasses of water on the table.

"Thanks."

"I hope you enjoy your stay here. Can I get you anything else?" Her smile was suggestive. It pissed me off. I had a wedding band on.

"I'm good."

"Are you sure?"

"I'll ask my wife when she returns if she wants something else. Look, here she is."

Josie glared at the woman as she sat next to me.

"Josie, do you need anything?"

"No, thank you."

The woman blinked, straightening up.

I chuckled after she left.

"What?" Josie inquired.

"You were cute, going all territorial for a moment. Thanks for saving me."

"What are wives for?" She batted her eyelashes. Was she really jealous or was she just playing her part? Damn it, I *wanted* her to be jealous. I was screwed.

The receptionist returned with our passports a few minutes later. "Your room is ready. I will go upstairs with you, and after you've made yourself comfortable or had a bit of a rest, you can let me know and I'll review all of the resort's activities with you."

I knew before Josie even opened her mouth what she was about to say.

"Can you walk us through all that now?" She'd edged forward on the couch in excitement. "Usually, I love to research and look stuff up online beforehand, but my husband wanted to keep the name of the hotel a surprise."

The brunette looked between us with a knowing smile.

"That's very romantic. I'll go through everything with you right now."

The woman placed a map of the resort in front of us, explaining where each of the twelve restaurants were and what kind of cuisine each served. When she proceeded to explain about the different activities, Josie slid even closer to the edge of the couch. On instinct, I placed an arm around her back to catch her if she slid too much and lost her balance.

When the woman talked about scuba diving lessons, Josie looked sideways at me, smiling.

"Go to town, crazy pants. I know you want to book lessons." I kissed her forehead. What I really wanted was to kiss her lips.

"Should I book them for both of you?" the woman asked. I stiffened. Josie laughed.

"Just for me, for now. My husband is too afraid to try it."

She glanced at me again. *Fuck*. She'd end up convincing me to scuba dive too, I just knew it. I was man enough to admit scuba diving scared the crap out of me, but maybe I'd try it, just to experience it with Josie.

Next, we were led to our room. I'd booked an oceanfront suite for us, which consisted of an enormous bedroom and an even more enormous living room. Despite that, the couch wasn't fit for sleeping. Too short and narrow, and I couldn't ask for an extra bed without raising suspicions. I hadn't booked a suite with two bedrooms because I'd known that if the immigration services got wind of it, it would be a red flag, but I'd hoped the couch would do. Josie was too busy gushing over the view to share my concerns.

I was going to leave the honeymoon with a stiff neck. Maybe I could buy one of those enormous water floaters and sleep on it.

"I'll leave you to change and make yourselves comfortable," the receptionist said.

The moment we were alone, Josie went out on the balcony, peeking over the railing, sticking her ass out a little. My cock twitched. I was so screwed.

"I want to change into my bikini and go straight to the beach," she exclaimed, turning around.

"Sounds good."

Anything was better than being in here with her. I just couldn't stop imagining all the things I'd do to her on that bed, hell, even the balcony.

Only after she changed into her bikini did she seem to notice there was just one bed.

"I thought suites were supposed to have enough sleeping room for a family."

"Only if you book ones with two rooms, but—"

"That would've looked suspicious."

"Yes."

She peeked in the bedroom. "The bed's huge. Won't be a problem. You sleep on one side, right?"

I moved right behind her and whispered in her ear, "But you don't."

She turned around, and her eyes widened.

"I'll manage." Licking her lips, she turned away, walking inside the room.

Could she really be so close to me and not feel anything? Because I sure as hell would know she was in my bed. Especially because I was already picturing her bent over the edge, hands forward as I thrust into her from behind. Or on her back, thighs spread wide as I kissed down her body.

I was losing it. I'd been married to my best friend for a little over twenty-four hours and was already fantasizing about making her come.

We'd both slept a solid eight hours on the last leg of the journey, so we felt fresh. I changed into board shorts, and we headed to the beach. When we reached the sand, Josie bent, touching the sand with her fingers.

"It's so soft. And *so* white." When she glanced at me, her smile was a bit wobbly. "Hunter? This was the best idea you've ever had."

"You're not even going to roast my ass one bit? Progress."

"No, don't mind me when I get like that. I secretly enjoy surprises."

"I'll hold you to that."

She covered her mouth as she realized what she'd said.

"That came out wrong."

"Too late. You can't take it back."

"Sure, I can."

I stepped behind her, wrapping my arms around her waist, lifting her up until her feet were dangling in the air. She half screeched, half laughed, kicking the air a bit but leaning all the way back against me. Her delicious little ass pressed straight against my cock. *Fuck.* This was not the moment to get hard. Not one of my finest ideas.

She laughed when I set her down, and on pure instinct, I whirled her around and kissed her. She tasted like mint and the orange juice we'd drunk at the reception. I could have just given her a quick peck, but I couldn't resist going all in, coaxing her tongue, needing to know if she'd respond again or if she'd only done it yesterday so we would be convincing for the guests. No one was looking closely now. No one would care.

So, when Josie laced her arms around my neck, kissing me back, my entire body felt lighter. Keeping my hands on her waist took all the self-restraint I had. When I placed her back down, she made to move out of my arms, but I didn't let go.

"What are you doing?" I asked.

"Going into the water."

"Not without sunscreen."

"Come on. I'll just put some on afterward."

"Josie, your skin is so white it's almost translucent. Trust me, you're going to need it. The sun here is stronger than you're used to."

She tried to wrestle free, but I kept her close.

"You don't want to spend the rest of the honeymoon hiding indoors because your skin burns. Sunscreen. Now."

She stilled, turning around with a pout. "Fine.

But as punishment, you have to rub sunscreen on me everywhere."

In what world did she think that was a punishment? All right, maybe it was, just not in the way she believed.

I was *very* thorough. I started by rubbing it into her ankles and calves, massaging her legs up to her thighs. I was sitting on a lounge chair and Josie was standing between my open thighs. My head was level with her navel, and then her breasts as I rubbed the cream on her stomach.

How I'd lavish them with attention, suck on those nipples until she squirmed, begging for more, begging for release. I tried to keep my gaze on her belly, but when I moved on to massage the cream on her neck, I couldn't ignore the way her nipples had turned hard, peeking through the fabric.

I was turning her on. Fuck. I glanced up at her, but she only met my gaze for a fraction of a second before turning around.

"And now my back, please." Her voice was husky. Her breaths were more labored.

Don't read anything into it. You just had your hands all over her and weren't being quick about it. Of course, her body reacted.

After I finished, I applied cream on myself, only asking Josie to help with my back, and then we darted into the water.

"This is amazing. How can it be so clear?"

It was one of the most scenic views I'd had the privilege to see, and experiencing it with Josie only made it more special. She half swam, half walked, observing the little multicolored fish swimming around.

"Holy shit, that's a shark?" she shrieked.

"It's a small one. Native to these waters. Completely harmless," I assured her.

"How do you know?"

"Apparently I was more thorough in my research than you were in yours."

"Hmpf. You're sure they're harmless? Even if their teeth are proportionally smaller, they can still do some damage."

I saw an opportunity for teasing right there and then. Or maybe I was just looking for an excuse to touch her again. I placed my hands on her shoulders, pulling her closer.

"How exactly do you imagine you'll get through scuba diving? You're going to get close to large fish. Some might have teeth. Some might even be dangerous."

"Yes, but there will be a pro with me, so I'll be safe."

"I see. So, the sharks aren't the problem here. I am. I'm offended."

She grinned, playfully patting my cheek. "You'll get over it."

"Josie, you don't honestly think I'd risk anything happening to you, do you?"

Her shoulders relaxed. "You wouldn't... normally. But here's the thing. You're more afraid of wildlife than I am. If something really attacked you, I bet you'd save your own sorry ass."

"You calling me a coward?"

"Yes, sir, I am."

Before she could guess my intention, I started tickling her armpits.

She gave an adorable shriek, and I wrestled her to the beach, tumbling with her onto the wet sand. The movement freed her from my other arm, and Josie seized the chance. She gave as good as she got. Her laughter was contagious. Pure happiness, pure relaxation. I wanted to give her more of this. Wanted to give her a reason to laugh like that every day.

I stopped her the only way I knew how—with a kiss. I pinned her wrists above her head, holding them captive with my hands. I'd intended just to surprise her long enough for her to stop tickling me, but as usual, I got completely wrapped up in her.

What I'd do to this woman if she belonged to me. I'd always known that Josie was sexy, but this pushed me to the very edge of my self-control.

I deepened the kiss, trailing my fingers down the side of her body until she moaned against my lips.

Then she tore her mouth away from me. Her cheeks were flushed, her mouth red. She was avoiding my gaze. I'd crossed a line. Fuck. I shouldn't have kissed her like that. Yet, instead of feeling guilty, I wondered just how wet she was for me. I moved over to the side, freeing her, and she immediately scrambled to her feet, heading to the lounge chair. I didn't go after her. I knew enough about Josie to know she needed to be on her own, to digest this. Hell, *I* needed to digest this.

I couldn't go on like this. Kissing her for no reason, claiming more each time. I needed to pull myself together and not screw this up.

I went to the beach bar first, getting a drink for each of us. When I returned, Josie was reading, so I set the tray on the small plastic table between our lounge chairs.

"I brought you coconut water. You've wanted to try this, right?"

Josie lowered her book, grabbing one glass, slurping as if she'd been dying of thirst.

She was still avoiding my gaze. I needed to fix this. From now on, no more kissing and touching if it wasn't absolutely necessary.

She spat out a mouthful. "This is awful."

I laughed, taking the glass from her because the spitting turned into choking.

"That's what you get for trying everything."

She looked at my glass of caipirinha with narrowed eyes. "You knew it tasted like shit."

"I even told you it did. You just said you'd make up your own mind, remember?"

"Ugh… sometimes I think I need saving from myself."

"I agree. Remember that when you book that scuba diving course."

She scrunched her nose adorably before going

back to her book. The title was *7 Habits of Highly Effective People*.

"I've been meaning to get that book," I said, lying back on my own lounge chair. "How is it?"

"Some advice is common sense; some is actually more insightful than I thought."

She gave some examples, and we both came up with ways of integrating them in our routines.

I'd always loved our conversations, the way we built on the other's ideas. It always came easy to me to talk about everything from business to personal issues with Josie, and I wouldn't make the mistake of losing that.

Things between us seemed to go back to normal as the day progressed. We talked about everything from politics to history to discussing some of the local wildlife after Josie bought a book on it from the hotel shop. I also couldn't let the opportunity for teasing pass when she looked at *S* in the animal index.

"Any chance you're researching sharks?" I asked casually. She glared at me. "Admit it, you want to check if they're harmless or not. You don't trust me?"

"You've proven a bit untrustworthy as of late," she said just as casually, flipping another page. Shit. I couldn't argue with that.

I followed through with my resolution only for a few hours. But when Josie emerged from the bedroom dressed for dinner, I knew I didn't have a chance of sticking to my own rules tonight.

She was wearing a light pink dress in a flowy fabric that reached all the way to the floor. From the front, it looked inconspicuous, with a halter neck, no cleavage. But her back was uncovered, and the dress dipped so low that I could almost see her crack.

"Josie." Yes, I knew it had sounded like a growl, but goddamn, I just couldn't do better at the moment. "You look... stunning."

She smoothed her hands down her waist, laughing. "I'm even a bit tan already. You were right about the sunscreen. Even so, my skin itched a bit after the shower. The after-sun lotion helped. Should we go?"

"Yes." Because if I was alone with her for long, I didn't know what I would do.

"Welcome, we have a special table for you tonight," the server informed us when we stepped in the outdoor restaurant. We'd decided on trying out local cuisine tonight. I'd called the concierge to reserve a table, and when the man had asked if I wanted the extra package for honeymooners, I couldn't resist saying yes. The package included a secluded table in a special gazebo, adorned with twinkle lights.

I wanted the best for Josie. Unless I coerced her to come on another trip while we were married, she wouldn't fly here again.

The hostess winked at me, saying, "The best table, as you requested."

So much for this staying a secret.

Josie looked at me with wide eyes once we were alone. "You requested this?"

"Thought you'd like it."

"Thanks," she muttered, returning to studying the menu. "My God, I want to order everything."

"So, do it."

"Ha! I've already had too many empty calories from the cocktails on the beach."

She'd given up on the coconut water after that first sip and ended up drinking caipirinha with me.

"Josie, stop. You're beautiful. If you were any more beautiful, I'd have an even harder time resisting you."

She lowered her menu, looking straight at me.

"What? Don't tell me you didn't notice until today," I said.

She pointed a finger at me. "Stop this."

"What?"

"You know what."

She was calling me out on my flirting. I should take a step back, reevaluate. Instead, I kept pushing.

"You're my wife. If I want to compliment you, I will."

"And you said I'm getting more daring. You're no better."

"What are you going to do about it, *wife*?"

She licked her lips, shaking her head. "You just wait. I'll cook up a revenge plan."

"Here's the thing. I don't think you will."

"Know me so well, do you? What do you

think I want?"

"I think you want me to push and push until you have no choice but to give in."

Josie exhaled sharply before biting her lower lip.

I wanted her to give me a sign that she wanted this too. That she had just as much trouble navigating this as I did.

When she lowered her eyes back to the menu, I had my answer. I'd asked her last night to keep me in check, to be the responsible one out of the two of us, yet I was already changing the rules.

I didn't have a chance to keep pushing right now, because a waitress came to take our order. We started small, with appetizers and sparkling water, but before long, it became a food festival.

We spoke about the wedding and about our families.

"Ryker couldn't believe I was the first one to get married."

She grinned. "If I were a betting woman, I wouldn't have bet on you either."

"Neither would I."

She tilted her head, studying me. "Why not?"

I frowned, taking a sip of water to buy time. I'd never given this much conscious thought.

"I don't know. I think it's just easier. Making that vow, trusting someone, making them happy for their entire life… that's a lot of expectations."

And when expectations weren't met, everything went downhill. My parents had loved each other. I knew that for a fact, because until I was ten, I'd never heard them fight. They were always affectionate with each other.

Yet when Dad's business went downhill, their relationship suffered. I remember the fighting, until they couldn't even stand being in the same room.

"Hunter, that's a lot of pressure to put on yourself. Our happiness shouldn't depend on someone else. Besides, I've known you for a long time. You're a great friend. A great person. Give yourself more credit."

"Usually you give me shit for giving myself too much credit," I teased.

"I'm adaptable."

"I can see that."

"And if you feed me food that is this delicious, I tend to be nicer. Much, much nicer."

"I'll keep that in mind."

We ordered only one dessert, but it was large enough for three people. While we ate, I mulled over her words. They made sense, but it had always been in my nature to make the people I cared about happy.

I was certain that if the person next to me was unhappy, I'd feel not only guilty, but responsible for it.

After we left the restaurant, we strolled through the complex web of narrow paths in the greenery separating the main building from the beach and the restaurant area.

"I love the resort," Josie remarked, stopping

to take a picture of an exotic plant. I wondered if she was slowing us down on purpose and if the prospect of sharing a bed had become daunting since we'd last spoken about it.

When we finally entered the suite, she said, "This day was great."

"Thirteen more to go."

"Can't wait."

Josie took off her shoes, walking barefoot to the bedroom. I followed her. She stood in front of the mirror, fumbling with the clasp of her necklace.

"Let me do that," I said.

"Thanks. It was so much easier to put it on."

I unclasped it in no time but couldn't help myself and let my fingers linger on her soft skin.

"Today has been more fun than I expected. Yesterday too." I didn't know why I'd started talking, but now that I had, I wanted to continue. "I kissed you far more than was strictly necessary."

"Hunter...."

"It's true."

Finally, I looked up, meeting her gaze in the mirror. I let my thumb glide from her shoulder down to her arm, felt her shudder. I flipped her around, bringing her flush against me.

"I don't know how to do this," I admitted. "Be married to you and not want more than friendship."

Her eyes nearly bulged out of her head. I went on.

"I tried, but you can see I'm not very good at

it."

She chuckled. "No, you're not. But I'm not doing much better."

I ran my hand down her exposed back until I reached the fabric, and then even lower, cupping her ass with both hands.

Josie tugged me lower to her the next second, and I kissed her so hard that her knees wobbled, showing her exactly how desperately I wanted her.

I groaned against her mouth. I was already hard. She felt it too, and rocked her hips gently back and forth, demanding more.

ssrीूर

Chapter Seventeen
Hunter

I was hungry for her, and even as I desperately pushed the straps of her dress down, tugging at the fabric until it fell to her waist, and then to her feet, I knew that this hunger wasn't the result of the last few weeks.

It had been there for years, I'd just buried it deep so our friendship wouldn't suffer. I kissed her jaw, tracing a path to her earlobe, biting the shell a little, enjoying the little gasp she gave, the way she pressed herself against me. I tilted her head, moving my lips on the side of her neck. I didn't want to leave one single inch of her skin unexplored. I wanted to touch and kiss her everywhere at the same time. I wanted to watch too, to drink her in. I'd seen her in the bikini today, but this was different. This was just for me.

"Hunter...," she murmured when I twirled my tongue in the nook at the base of her neck. By the way her voice shook on that one word, I knew it was a sweet spot for her. She was already writhing in my arms, and I hadn't even kissed below her shoulders. But I changed that, lowering my mouth over her chest to the silky strapless bra that was so thin I could feel the shape of her nipple under it.

I twirled my tongue over the fabric once before my hands desperately searched for the clasp at the back. I yanked it open, the bra fell to the floor, and I had free access to kiss and tease her until she'd beg me for more.

I led her to the king-size bed, kissing her all the way, until we reached one of the four posts. I ran my hands over her waist and thighs, wanting to memorize every curve and every shape, then I whirled her around, pushing her hair to one side, kissing the back of her neck and lower down her back, following her spine until I reached the hem of her panties.

Her ass cheeks were on full display, round and beckoning to me. I drew my thumbs down the center of each one before licking the same path. Then I wedged a hand between her thighs, inching them further apart. Josie rose on her toes, gripping the bedpost with both hands, as if she already couldn't take what I was giving her. And damn, I planned to give her so much more.

"Fuck," I exclaimed when I touched the part of the fabric covering her pussy with two fingers. It was already wet. My cock strained so painfully against my jeans that I nearly pushed them down and fucked her just like that, against the bedpost.

"You're so beautiful, Josie. So damn sexy. What am I going to do with you?"

I slipped my hand inside her panties.

She gasped. "Whatever you want."

I nearly burst in my pants at her words, at feeling how aroused she was.

"I'll make you beg. And I'll make you come."

I moved two fingers around her tender flesh, teasing the area around her clit. I enjoyed watching her fingers curl tighter around the bedpost, moving her weight from her heels to her toes.

I kissed every inch of her that I could reach, keeping one hand in her panties, bringing my other arm around her middle so I touched her breast, drawing circles around her nipples, mimicking the ones around her clit.

"Hunter, Hunter, Hunter," she chanted. "I'm so close. Please. So close."

She exploded the next second, crying out. Her knees gave in, and I tightened my hold on her waist even as she gripped the bedpost harder. I held her as she rode out the wave of pleasure, laying her head back on my chest, eyes closed. Then I turned her around slowly, drinking in the haze of lust in her eyes before pushing her gently on the bed.

"There are condoms in the amenity kit," I said.

She shook her head. "No need. I'm on the pill."

We hadn't set any boundaries, hadn't talked about whether this would be a one-time thing or not, but I knew that after tonight, things would change between us on a fundamental level.

Josie looked gorgeous, lying on her back, her breasts rising and falling with every breath. I unbuttoned my shirt quickly. Josie moved to undo my belt and the button of my jeans.

When I was completely naked, I leaned to kiss her, climbing in bed on top of her. She opened her thighs, curling her fingers on her lower belly as if she could barely stand not touching herself intimately.

I drew the tip of my erection around her clit, watching her writhe, drinking in her moans, driving her crazy until she moved one hand upward to her breasts and lowered the other one. My vision blurred when she touched my cock.

I drove inside her the next second. She felt so tight, so damn perfect around me. I moved in and out, touching, kissing, biting, memorizing every inch of her body, every sound she made. She pulsed around me, digging her fingers in my biceps.

When her thighs pressed against mine, I knew she was close. I pulled back a bit, wanting to watch her when she climaxed, but I was too far gone. This felt too good, too intimate. I clung to my control only long enough to make sure Josie came first, and then climaxed hard.

It took us both a few minutes to calm down. I kept her close, kissing her neck again, inhaling the scent of vanilla and pepper that I'd associated with my best friend for years. After tonight, I wouldn't be able to smell her perfume and not think about how sensual she was, how responsive. How she'd surrendered her pleasure to me.

**

The next morning, I woke up to an empty bed. I swallowed hard, sitting upright, trying to gather my wits to guess where Josie could be and why she wasn't here.

My heartbeat was erratic as I rose from the bed, and only returned to normal when I heard the water running in the second bathroom.

I debated waiting for her to come out so we could talk... but why postpone the moment?

I grinned as I approached the door, hearing her sing a catchy tune. My Josie was in a great mood. I hadn't known that she sang in the shower, never heard her at the apartment.

I opened the door, grinning from ear to ear at the sight of her. She was dancing under the spray of the water, eyes closed as she rubbed shampoo in her hair, swinging her hips and that perfect little ass from side to side.

I couldn't bring myself to even feel guilty for looking. I merely leaned against the doorframe, crossed my arms over my chest, and watched this fascinating side of my best friend.

Unfortunately, I was so focused on following the movements of her ass that I didn't realize she'd seen me until she yelped, nearly slipping.

"Hunter!"

"Good morning."

"How long have you been standing there?"

"Since the last time you sang the chorus."

"And you didn't think about announcing your

presence?"

"Nope. Had a great view. Got distracted. Can you blame me?"

"I totally can, and I am."

"I'd apologize… but I'm not really sorry."

"I didn't know you were a shameless peeping Tom."

She grinned, and I grinned right back. I stepped closer, then into the shower.

Josie swallowed, lowering her gaze to some place on my chest. I brought my hand under her chin, lifting her head. Then I couldn't help myself and kissed one corner of her mouth, nibbling at the other until I felt her shudder.

"I don't want to forget about last night," I said before realizing this wasn't how I was supposed to go about this. I knew Josie, and she needed time to adjust to changes. Hell, she'd already turned her life upside down to help me. I was supposed to ask her what *she* wanted, be the gentleman, not make any demands.

Josie didn't say anything, but I was still hovering with my mouth over her jawline, feeling her hot, short breaths on my cheek. If she wanted us to forget about it, then I'd respect her wish. The next three years would be excruciating, but I'd respect her wish.

"What do you want exactly?" she asked in a small voice, which was unlike her.

"Why don't you tell me what you want instead?" I wanted to look her straight in the eyes, but one other thing I knew about Josie was that she didn't like eye contact when she was figuring things out. It unnerved her.

"I… I don't know. I mean, last night was incredible. And I don't want to pretend it didn't happen, or that I didn't want it to happen. Because I did. I'm just… afraid this will change our friendship."

I pulled back then, looked her straight in the eyes. "It won't. I promise. You're my best friend."

Something passed through her eyes, quick as a flash. "Are you sure?"

"Yes. Why do you doubt me?"

"Your recent track record about keeping your word is against you." She was smiling now.

"Is that so?"

"Remember what you asked me on the wedding night? And yet here we are, not even forty-eight hours later."

"Your fault entirely for being so damn irresistible."

"You won't even own up to your flaws? You're even worse than I thought."

"I see. No redeemable qualities?"

"If I think about it hard, I could come up with one or two, but you're welcome to prove to me you have more."

"Your wish is my command, wife."

Chapter Eighteen
Josie

"This was amazing. *Amazing*." I felt like jumping up and down on the boat. Scratch that. I *was* jumping up and down. This had been our first scuba dive into the ocean. We'd practiced in one of the pools before, until we got the hang of breathing and managing the equipment.

The scuba instructor smiled, maneuvering the boat back to shore. Hunter sat on the back bench, giving me a lazy smile. He watched me the entire time I took off my scuba diving suit.

My skin warmed up everywhere he looked, as if he had his hands on me… or his mouth.

"You're not saying anything. What did you think?" I asked him later on as we walked to our lounge chairs. I elbowed him lightly. He reacted immediately, wrapping an arm around me, pulling me into him.

"I think that you look fucking irresistible in your bikini."

I rolled my eyes. "I meant what you thought about scuba diving."

"I think I absolutely need a reward for the act of bravery."

He let me go as we reached the lounge chairs, sat on the nearest one. I parked my hands on my hips, tilting my head.

"A reward?"

"Yes."

"And what would that be?"

His smile turned into a wolfish grin. "Beggars can't be choosers."

"So, if I reward you with an ice cream, you'll be happy?"

He pulled me closer. "I didn't say anything about not persuading you to give in to the kind of rewards *I* want." He placed a kiss just under my belly button. My skin broke out in goose bumps the next second.

"Hunter. We're on a beach."

"And I just can't get enough of you."

Somehow, he'd pulled me between his legs again. My outer thighs were touching his inner thighs, but even that small contact was enough to send a sizzle through me. He lazily moved his hand at the small of my back in tiny circles. The man simply seemed incapable of keeping his hands off me. But who was I to judge? I touched him every chance I got after our first night together three days ago. The lines between us were blurring, and I didn't know how to bring that up, or if I should. I was just afraid that I couldn't keep my heart out of this.

"Sooo… what do you think about skydiving? Or a safari?" I asked casually. Hunter stared at me.

"You're doing this on purpose? To torture

me?"

"Maybe." I had no idea what had gotten into me, but I suddenly wanted to experience everything with him. Besides... loosening up wouldn't hurt him. Not everything was controllable, as evidenced by the fact that his visa hadn't been extended, prompting the need for a green card.

I did understand why he felt the need to—or at least I thought I did. When his dad lost the business years ago, it threw his family into a spiral downward. Everything was out of his control. I could understand the drive—the need to ensure you never got in that situation again.

"You're different, somehow," he said.

"What can I say? You're right. As your wife, I keep developing new skills. Nagging, for one. Talking you into trying out silly things for another. What do you say, husband?"

I just wanted him to have fun, be happy.

"Only if you promise not to give me shit for flying your family over for Christmas."

I crossed my arms over my chest, attempting to sound stern.

"That is a conversation we'll circle back to later."

Truth was, I was still melting every time I thought about that, but I didn't want him to get any more dangerous ideas. Meanwhile, I was already thinking about nice things I could do for him. Stuff I hadn't been able to do as a friend. *Holy shit!* A whole new world of options opened up. I could just imagine taking care of him in the evening when we were both home, helping him relax.

"This isn't how it works," I said.

He leaned in closer, playfully wiggling his eyebrows. "No deal, then."

"You're not leaving me much of a choice."

"So we have a deal?"

"Okay."

"You do realize you're letting me get away with a lot more than before, right?"

I shrugged playfully. "What can I say? I'm starting to like being your wife, Mr. Caldwell."

Chapter Nineteen
Hunter

"You're cheating," Josie said. I'd brought my laptop to the beach. We had two days of our honeymoon left, and I just wanted to get a head start on the emails.

"Just checking on a few things to make sure there's nothing urgent."

"I'm not checking anything until I'm in my office. I love being a lawyer, but I apparently love taking a break more. And I have to thank my husband for helping me make that discovery about myself."

I chuckled. I was so proud of her for making it so far. Josie had hustled just as much as I had. Between the two of us, we'd probably covered about every student job there was in this city.

She glanced at my screen. "That project looks sexy. What is it?"

"A school."

"It's a charity project, right?"

I nodded. The company made enough profit that we built one or two buildings for charity a year. This was a public school. The Ballroom Galas also gathered funds for this project.

"Can I ask you something? How come you've gone into real estate? I'm sure you haven't made things easier for yourself."

I hadn't. People still associated the name Caldwell with the huge real estate developer who went bankrupt more than fifteen years ago.

"You know me, I never choose the easier way." I could have left it at that, but something in Josie's expression beckoned me to open up. "I've always liked Dad's work. He put everything he had in it, and I'm not talking about money. It was who he was. He was proud of it, and I spent most of my childhood in his office, watching mock-ups, listening to him explain the ins and out of the business."

Josie kissed my shoulder, skimming her lips up and down my arm. This newfound closeness between us made it so easy to keep talking, even about things I hadn't spoken about before—not because I had anything to hide, but it put me in a mood.

"My dad actually started this school project years ago. It took a while to sort out the legal issues and get all the permits to build, but we got the green light last year."

"Do you need a hand?"

"You want to get involved?"

"Sounds like you need a lawyer for all those permits. I have contacts."

The company had enough lawyers, but I wanted Josie to be part of this. I'd always liked working with my cousins, but the thought of Josie being on it too filled me with a sense of joy unlike anything I'd ever felt.

"I'd love that."

"Just hit me up with whatever you need. Have your people email it to me."

"Yes, ma'am."

I glanced at the screen again, but I couldn't focus. To the hell with it. Everything could wait until I was back from the honeymoon. I shut the laptop, putting it to one side.

"That was awfully quick."

Even though her face was buried in my arm, I felt her lips curl into a sly smile against my skin.

"Someone's demanding my attention."

"Who could that be?" she murmured.

"My wife."

"This wife of yours is a pest, isn't she?"

"Not at all. She's smart, fun, and I can't get enough of her."

She wiggled her ass. I scooped her up, bringing her into my lap.

"Sounds like you like her," she said on a grin.

"Very much. I think it's time I showed her, just so I don't leave room for any doubt."

Her grin widened even more. "Excellent idea."

***

Departure day came all too soon. Josie was in a bad mood while we packed. She slammed her suitcase shut, cursing when the zipper wouldn't budge. I offered to close it for her before she ripped it.

She took a long shower afterward. I surprised her by ordering a slice of her favorite hazelnut cake.

"What's this?" she asked when she returned to the bedroom.

"I ordered it for you. I'm expecting you to spit fire any second now."

She gave me a sheepish smile. "Sorry... I'm usually cranky on the last vacation day."

I tapped my temple. "Learned that today. Stored it right here for future reference. I'll make sure you start your day with cake."

"Fair warning, it might get worse once we're at home."

"I'll keep that in mind."

Her mood improved from the shot of sugar. She snapped a few pictures on the way out of the hotel.

She slept on the first leg of the journey, but when she woke up, she was moody again. Didn't smile, didn't joke.

"You okay, Josie?"

"Yes, just a bit nervous. Managed to forget about the immigration services and everything while we were away, but now I can't help imagining doomsday scenarios."

"Have you thought about the annulment? I can still make it happen."

Say no. Say no.

Just the thought of her saying yes made me

feel as if the rug had been swept from under me and I'd plowed face-first into a wall.

"The annulment," she repeated.

I straightened in my seat, nodding. "Yes. I can ask my lawyers to have everything ready by the time we land."

"Is this what you want?"

No. A million times no.

Since we decided to go through with this, all I've wanted was to keep Josie, and that feeling had intensified after the honeymoon. But I needed to at least attempt to do the right thing.

"This isn't about me. It's about you feeling comfortable. I'll deal with the fallout. I don't want you to feel pressured. Josie, I swear I'll understand if you want to get that annulment. Nothing will change between us."

"I said I'd help. I'm not going back on my word," she snapped.

Instead of feeling relieved that she didn't want an annulment, I was even more unsettled than before, because somehow things were worse between us than before we had this conversation.

She placed headphones over her ears, pulling up a movie on the screen.

When we arrived at the house, there was still tension between us. It wasn't my style to ignore a problem or tiptoe around it, so after dinner, I cornered her in the kitchen. She was making tea for herself. I stood right beside her.

"Josie, what's wrong?"

"Nothing."

"You've been snappy with me ever since we talked about the annulment. If that's what you want, say it. I don't want you to keep doing this just because you gave me your word. That's a bullshit reason to do anything."

Her eyes flashed. "Keeping a promise is bullshit?"

"That's not what I mean. Going through with something difficult just because you gave your word is... necessary sometimes, but not with us. You're mad at me."

"Yes."

"Why?"

"Why do you think?"

"I have no clue, or I wouldn't be asking you."

She was pissed, but so was I. I didn't like guessing games.

"You brought up the annulment as if... as if it was nothing."

She blew out a breath, blinking fast. It occurred to me that she wasn't playing games. She just didn't know how I felt. Probably thought the annulment didn't matter to me either way.

"Look at me." My voice was determined, but she kept staring over my shoulder. "Josie..."

She sucked in a breath when I touched her jaw, tilting her head until we had eye contact.

"It's not nothing. I don't know what I'd do if you said yes, because I need you. I want you."

She sucked in a breath. Her eyes were searching me, uncertain. I wanted to erase any doubt. I cupped her head with both hands, pressing her in that corner, between the counter and the wall.

"Things changed between us, Josie, and I like the way they are. I fucking love it. Being with you, sharing my life with you… it's incredible. You are incredible. I'm the luckiest bastard on earth. I don't know what I did to deserve this, or what this will mean for us… for our friendship, but I don't want to give it up, okay?"

***

Josie

God, the way he was looking at me… as if I was the only woman in the world.

"Okay." I nodded, just in case I'd spoken too low for him to hear. He'd seen right through me, and I felt raw, exposed. When he'd brought up the annulment, I'd felt as if I'd been slapped. I'd been so afraid that I was the only one whose feelings had changed that I didn't even know what to do or say.

But he wanted me. He wanted *us*.

Hunter drew his thumb over my lower lip before claiming my mouth. He hadn't kissed me since we woke up this morning, which was far too long. I gave in to his kiss, responding to his passion with fervor, wanting to give him everything he demanded. When we pulled apart, I was torn. I wanted to kiss him, but I didn't want to break eye contact because that look just about brought me to my knees. So much warmth and affection underneath all the passion. I wanted to indulge in it for as long as he was mine.

He kissed me again, scooping me up in his arms, carrying me to the master bedroom. I touched his arms, the planes of his chest and shoulders, wanting to rid him of all clothes. But where I was hurrying, Hunter slowed us down.

After ridding me of an item of clothing, he covered my skin with kisses. When I was only wearing panties, he took a step back, looking me up and down. All my nerve endings were burning in anticipation, and when he removed my panties too, I jumped right in his arms. He was naked already, his cock wedged between us. We tumbled on the bed, laughing. He pinned my hands at the sides of my head, kissing me so ferociously that I moaned against his mouth.

Life with this man was exhilarating. Being his wife was nothing like I'd imagined, and I meant that in the best possible way. With every kiss, he made me feel alive, adored… *claimed*. With every day we spent together, I discovered new sides to him, despite having known him for fifteen years, and the more I discovered, the deeper I fell into him.

"What are you thinking about?" he murmured, touching my cheek, kissing down my jaw, my neck.

See? He could tell my mind was racing at one hundred miles an hour.

"You."

He smiled against my belly. "I like that answer."

He went even further down, and when he drew his tongue along my opening, pleasure shot through me. He kissed me until I was writhing under him, and then he climbed over me, thrusting inside me.

I gasped, moving my pelvis to accommodate him before digging my heels in the mattress for better leverage. We moved in sync, both of us desperate for release, desperate for each other. Hunter kissed my neck and shoulders while he gripped one ass cheek in his hand, moving me at an angle that allowed him so deep inside me, it spurred the tremors of pleasure. I shuddered, feeling tension gather in my lower body, spreading through me. He brought me closer to the edge with every thrust, every kiss. When he brought his hand between us, touching my clit, I couldn't take the tension anymore.

"Hunter... please."

"I want to feel you come all around me, babe. But not yet."

He pulled out, despite my protests, kissing down my chest again, down my belly, stopping just above my pubic bone. Then he continued the delicious torture by kissing my inner thighs, raining kisses all the way to my ankles. I wanted him so much that I was certain I was going to do something wild if he kept at it. As if knowing what I was thinking, he grinned wolfishly at me, moving further up, closer to me. But instead of entering me, he turned me on my belly. I felt the tip of his nose along my spine, then his mouth.

"Spread your legs," he said in a low, gruff voice. I did as he said, swallowing hard against the pillow. When I felt him slide inside me, I saw stars. It felt even more intense than before. How was this possible?

I climaxed so hard, growing so tight that I felt every delicious inch of him. I moved my hips faster and faster until he came too, grunting out my name, gripping my hips possessively, driving inside me, squeezing every drop of pleasure.

I couldn't think for what felt like hours, could barely breathe. Hunter remained on top of me, caressing the side of my breast and waist, whispering sweet nothings.

When we finally dragged ourselves to the shower, I felt wide awake. The time-zone difference was no joke.

"It's a good thing we have two days to recover from the jetlag," I said as we climbed back into bed.

"Or… you could skip work on Monday."

"Never."

"Want me to take that as a challenge?"

This banter, and even the intimacy felt different than on our honeymoon. I couldn't say why, but I loved it.

I feigned a shudder… but couldn't help smiling. "Oh God no. You have a habit of getting your way when you do that."

He smiled wolfishly before pulling me under him, kissing me so hard that I knew he'd taken it as a challenge   anyway.

Chapter Twenty
Josie

On Monday morning, after dressing hurriedly, I took in my appearance in the bathroom mirror. My lips were swollen from Hunter's wild kissing, my grin was absolutely huge (he was at fault for me being in a hurry in the first place).

I had absolutely no doubt that anyone passing me would know I got loved up good this morning. Then again, I was a newlywed who'd just returned from her honeymoon. This should be expected, right? Swooning and daydreaming were acceptable… I hoped. It would even give the whole thing more credibility, and that was certainly a good thing.

On the way to work, I called my sister. I was dying to speak to Isabelle. I talked her ear off from the second she answered.

"You sound so… radiant," she replied when I finished.

I chuckled. "How can you *sound* radiant?"

"No idea, but you do."

"I miss you so much."

"I miss you too."

"So move to New York."

"You always tempt me with that."

"Well, I always hope to convince you."

"One of these days, you just might."

Holy shit, that was the closest she'd come to saying she'd consider moving. I'd love to dote on my sister, and generally just having her nearby would be amazing.

"I have to go now, but keep me posted on your newlywed bliss."

"Will do."

I started my day by meeting with my assistant and the junior who had handled my workload while I'd been gone.

"So, in a nutshell, we have five contracts waiting for you to sign, and ten others where you still need to double-check certain details we've pointed out on Post-its."

"I'll get to all of those today."

That had gone more smoothly than I'd imagined. Hunter had been right. My entire career wasn't going to collapse just because I'd taken two weeks off. I *did* need saving from my own brain.

I'd have to thank him later. On second thought, maybe I shouldn't. That would only encourage him to continue ambushing me. For some reason that didn't sound like such a bad idea.

My God, was I conflicted or what? Part of my brain was still on the Maldives, relaxing in the sun. It would take me a few days to readjust to the breakneck speed of a law firm.

The day became more stressful by the hour, though. My to-do list was growing by leaps and bounds every time I read a new email, and it didn't help that my brain was working at a slug's pace.

Around lunch, I shot Hunter a text.

Josie: How's your day? My brain is trying to sabotage me. Instead of focusing on statutes, I keep daydreaming about white sand and cocktails and just lying in the sun doing nothing.

Hunter: But not daydreaming about ME? :-)

I laughed, staring at the screen.

Josie: Just a little :)

Hunter: You're jet-lagged, that's why focusing is harder. It'll get better in a few days.

Josie: Hope so, because I'm out of tricks. Already went over my daily dose of caffeine, and I'm still half asleep :-(

Hunter: It'll get better. I promise.

I was determined to make the best out of the day, so I massaged my temples, smelled the small lavender bag I kept on my desk, and attacked my to-do list with renewed focus.

Half an hour later, I was distracted by a delivery guy calling my name. I poked my head out of the office, waving at him.

"That's me."

He'd made so much ruckus that even some of the others had poked their heads out.

"I have a delivery for you, Ms. Gallagher. From Deli's."

My mouth watered. Deli's baked some of the best chocolate cakes in town.

"But I didn't order... I didn't even know you did delivery."

"We don't. But Mr. Caldwell was very convincing."

"Thank you!"

Hunter had sent me sweets? OH MY GOD. Why hadn't I married him before? I took the bag, not even bothering to tone down my excitement. Deliveries at the firm were 95 percent documents. But this was something else, so it accounted for some excitement. Two of my colleagues whistled, and one called out, "Already running for Husband of the Year? Well done."

I was giddy as I retreated to my office. I admired the sweet treat, considering for about three seconds if I should share with my coworkers before settling on *Hell, no*. This was all for me. I dug in and didn't stop until the carton was empty and I'd licked the spoon clean.

I was just about to throw everything away when my phone lit up with an incoming message.

Hunter: Would love to see a picture of you and the cake right now.

He thought I still had cake? Ha! He didn't know me as well as he thought, then.

I took a selfie with the empty carton. I hadn't dabbed at the corners of my mouth yet, so I still had some chocolate there.

I looked like a three-year-old who'd stuffed her face in a hurry so she wouldn't be caught. But the man had requested photographic evidence, and since

I'd practically inhaled the cake, that was the best I could do.

Hunter: You're already done? Hell, woman, I should've sent you more.

Josie: I'll never say no to more cake. Thank you.

Hunter: You said you needed help. What are husbands for but coming to the rescue? :)

I was melting. Yep. Utterly and completely melting.

Josie: Smart man. Had to protect it. (that's why I ate quickly). My entire office got wind of it.

I went out to lunch with Nigel, one of my other colleagues who was on the fast track to become partner.

"So, we didn't have time to chat since you've been back. How was your honeymoon?"

Odd question, since Nigel and I weren't friends. One could say we were in direct competition, even though the firm was big enough that both of us would eventually become partners. They only promoted once a year, though, which meant that one of us would get there first.

"Honestly, it was great. Everything looks just as in pictures: the sand, the water. I could've stayed there for a whole month."

"Ugh, wouldn't want to fall behind on work, though. I only took two days off last year for a wedding and promised myself I wouldn't do it again until I made partner. It's just not worth it."

"Recharging from time to time is good," I said, ignoring the jab. "Besides, it was my honeymoon."

We found an empty table by the window and sat opposite each other.

"So, this moved fast. We didn't know you were seeing someone seriously."

Why was he still asking about personal issues? We usually discussed cases and our bosses.

"It just happened," I said in a monotone voice, in no mood to continue this conversation. I reached for my glass, taking a sip of the icy-cold soda.

"Does Caldwell already have his green card?"

I felt as if someone had dumped all the ice cubes from the glass on top of my head.

"Oh, that? No."

There. I sounded calm, composed. As if the question didn't matter at all. Come to think of it, how did Nigel even know Hunter wasn't a citizen? Then I remembered, there was a plethora of articles available about Hunter, and they often said he was born in England. Regardless, I wished I'd put more effort into recounting a convincing love story.

"I see. Lucky he's married an American, then. Won't have to go through so much paperwork."

Don't panic. Don't panic. I repeated that mantra a few times, drawing on my years of experience as a lawyer. I'd been blindsided by evidence brought in at the last moment more times than I could count. But this was different. This was personal. I considered my next words very carefully. It made no sense to deny this. With a pang of horror, I wondered if the immigration services had started asking around already.

"The two things aren't related." I was proud of how confident I sounded.

"I'm glad to hear that."

I changed the subject to a huge custody battle that had made headlines recently.

I needed to get my bearings before I spoke too much or said the wrong thing. Hunter and I needed a strategy in case more people came up with similar comments.

I could barely concentrate for the rest of the afternoon. I wanted to talk to Hunter but didn't want to put everything into a text, and I didn't want to risk calling him. What if anyone overheard us?

So when Hunter called a few hours later, I barely refrained from telling him everything.

"Hello, husband."

"Hey! When do you think you'll be ready today?"

"Around six. Why?"

"Amelia called. She wants us over for dinner tonight, no excuses."

"Uh-oh. She actually said no excuses?"

"Yes. Also used my middle name when I tried to come up with one."

I laughed. "Ouch. Wouldn't have wanted to be in your place."

"Trust me, *I* didn't want to be in my place."

"Then we'd better show up." I smiled for the first time in hours, spinning in the chair. I hadn't seen Amelia since the wedding two weeks ago, and I already had withdrawals.

"I'll pick you up at six?" he went on.

"Sure." I wanted to tell him about my conversation with Nigel right away, because I was bursting at the seams with worry, but managed to keep silent. I'd tell him everything in a few hours.

At five fifty-five, I practically flew out of the office. I was usually one of those who burned the midnight oil on Mondays, to get ahead of the week, but I could see that pattern changing.

On the way out of the building, Nick caught up with me.

"Josie, you're back. Almost couldn't believe it when they told me you took off two weeks."

"Almost couldn't believe it myself."

Nick and I had dated for six months a few years ago but broke up because both of us prioritized our careers above our relationship. We'd remained friendly, and even though Nick had suggested repeatedly that we could be friends with benefits, I'd never been interested.

Outside the building, I spotted Hunter immediately. He'd come by car, and he'd pulled in the no-parking zone in front of the building. He narrowed his eyes when he noticed Nick.

Guess who knew about Nick's insistent

propositions? Hunter.

"Congratulations, man. Heard you're the lucky one who put a ring on her finger," Nick said, holding out his hand to Hunter, who shook it very briefly, giving him a sardonic smile. The look in his eyes was so intense that for a split second, I thought he'd crush Nick's hand.

"Thanks." Turning to me, he added, "Ready?"

"Sure. See you, Nick."

Hunter opened the door for me, but right when I was about to climb inside, he kissed me. His mouth was hot and urgent on mine, coaxing me to give in to him until I forgot we were not alone. I felt wanted, claimed.

When he pulled back, smiling down at me, I was dazzled. Crap. I'd completely forgotten Nick was still on the sidewalk. I gave him a small smile before climbing in, watching Hunter as he rounded the car to the driver seat.

Over the past few weeks, he hadn't had a chance to wear a suit, and I'd forgotten how hot he looked in one, especially since he was so tan now. The bronze skin contrasted beautifully with his blue eyes and crisp white shirt. The tailored jacket fit him like a glove.

"How was your day?" I asked once he'd climbed in.

"Half my brain was still in the Maldives."

"So was mine." I smiled, but then the corners of my mouth dropped as I remembered the conversation with Nigel. "One of my colleagues is suspicious of our marriage."

"What makes you think that?" he asked calmly, eyes on the road.

"He asked about your green card. I'm wondering if the immigration services been asking around at the office."

"Okay. Okay. If they think it's a sham marriage, they'd tell us."

"Not right away. They'll investigate first."

Hunter pressed his head against the headrest. At a red light, he turned to look at me, touching my cheek.

"Josie, we'll figure it out together, okay? We'll convince everyone this is real, don't worry."

"How will you do that? Kiss the living daylights out of me in front of everyone? Like you did in front of Nick?"

His voice was hard. "He was looking at you as if he still has a claim on you. I had to do something about that."

Will you look at that. Hunter Caldwell was jealous. I felt like a terrible person, but I was secretly enjoying it. Well... apparently not so secretly, because Hunter narrowed his eyes at me.

"You fiend," he said.

"You kiss me shamelessly in front of a coworker, and I'm the fiend?"

"Yes. Because you're enjoying the fact that I'm jealous."

"Drive, Caldwell. The light turned green."

I was grinning as he turned his focus on the

road, feeling ridiculously giddy. *Keep your feet on the ground, Josie.*

This... *thing* was still new, and who knew how long it would last. Hunter had never thought about having a family, he'd said so repeatedly. Would we go back to being friends after the three years were over?

I was slowly beginning to understand that there was no way our friendship would remain the same after all was said and done. I didn't think it was possible to forget all this. At least, not for me.

Chapter Twenty-One
Hunter

Amelia opened the door, looking at both of us with a huge smile.

"There are the newlyweds. Come in and tell us everything about the honeymoon. Is the long flight worth it?"

"It absolutely is," Josie answered. "And if possible, take a scuba diving course. It's so surreal to be underwater, so close to all those forms of life you normally don't see. Even Mr. Grumpy Ass here enjoyed himself."

She grinned proudly. I wanted to kiss her right there, right now, and I wouldn't be quick. She deserved the kind of kiss that made her feel ashamed for calling me that in front of Amelia.

"I don't believe that. You talked Hunter into that?"

"Yes, ma'am, I did. And he even enjoyed himself."

"I never said that," I replied.

Josie narrowed her eyes. "So you went with me on all five trips... why?"

"Just being a good husband, that's all."

She held her hand in front of her mouth,

leaning into Amelia as if she was about to whisper a secret.

"Don't mind him. He had fun. I have photographic evidence."

She smiled brighter, showing her dimples. Fucking hell, that happy smile got to me like nothing else. I made a mental note to immediately plan our next getaway. Nothing too far, but just enough so she could relax. Besides, I had an inkling that once she got the traveling bug, there would be no stopping her. She just didn't know it yet.

Just as I didn't know that I would actually enjoy scuba diving. I had thought I'd panic the minute I submerged under water, but funny thing was, I'd never felt more relaxed. Following the instructor's lead, aware that I couldn't influence anything happening around us was... liberating.

"I'm planning to print some albums. I noticed you have many with various family events. Do you want me to make one for you?"

"I'd love that."

I looked at this strange creature, wondering how she could be this thoughtful, how she'd known exactly what Amelia would want.

I was pissed about her coworker giving her shit. I didn't want her to have to deal with this. She was mine to protect and take care of. She was my wife.

For now.

I had to remind myself that this was temporary. But could it be forever? It scared me how

LAYLA HAGEN

much I wanted the answer to be yes.

"Come on, you two, part of the gang is already here. The rest should arrive soon," Amelia said. "Don't give me any more details until everyone's here, or you'll just have to repeat everything later."

"I don't mind," Josie said, with an enthusiasm that made me think she'd already recounted the details to her family multiple times. It was a powerful feeling, knowing I'd made her happy.

Tess and Skye were already there. I had expected them to pounce on us immediately, demanding details, but they were quiet. In fact, they were looking at Josie and me as if they were suspicious of *us*. Maybe I was simply reading into everything because I was hiding something. Josie didn't seem to share my concerns. She immediately sat between Tess and Skye. Mick gave everyone drinks while Josie described in great detail the room, the water, the beach, the sessions of scuba diving.

"Wait a second," Tess interrupted. "I think I've misheard you. Hunter actually went scuba diving?"

Josie nodded proudly. "He put up a good fight, but I won him over."

Skye clapped, and Tess gave Josie an appreciative whistle. "Proud of you, Josie. I never thought anyone could make him let loose a little."

Ryker and Cole arrived just as Amelia announced that dinner was ready.

We all sat around the table, Josie next to me.

"So, what's this we hear from the immigration services that this might be a sham marriage?" Tess asked.

Every muscle in my body went on lockdown. I felt Josie go rigid.

"Wait until their stomachs are full before roasting their asses," Ryker said.

Cole nodded slowly. "Yes, at least let them eat before you go all gung-ho on them."

I squeezed Josie's hand under the table, gathering my wits.

"What are you saying?" I asked.

"A very unfriendly lady from the immigration services called me. She seemed to be under the impression that you only married because they weren't renewing your visa and you needed a green card," Amelia explained. "I told her of course that she's wrong."

"I too received a call," Tess said. "Sent her running for the hills. I wasn't as calm as Amelia. But just because I was as unfriendly as possible, that won't keep her from investigating. But I am very curious to know the real story."

She narrowed her eyes at me, sitting up straighter in her chair. Fuck. I didn't want to disappoint any of them. The only reason I hadn't been honest with them was because I thought I was protecting them.

Josie blew out a breath. Goddammit. My mind raced, trying to come up with the best solution? Should I deny everything? Just pass it off as natural that a red flag had come onto the immigration services' radar because marriages between American citizens and outsiders were scrutinized?

I glanced at Josie. She was shaking slightly. I couldn't ask her to outright lie. Hell, *I* didn't want to lie to them anymore.

"It's true that my visa wasn't renewed. I was informed very late about it, and I was advised that a marriage with an American citizen was the easiest way around it."

The table fell silent. I felt the weight of their disappointment crush me. I hated the feeling.

"You know what? I'm offended you didn't tell us. Here I was, panicking that you willingly gave up your bachelor status, when in fact there was a simple explanation," Ryker said. Everyone started laughing. The tension was somewhat defused.

"We didn't tell any of you because we didn't want you to have to lie for us in case the immigration services started to ask questions," Josie explained. "Honestly, I hadn't thought it would happen… at least not so quickly."

"We are family. You don't need to pretend with us," Tess said in a clipped tone.

"I'd have an easier time believing this if you weren't still giving me the evil eye," I said.

Tess laughed, and I hung on to the hope that forgiveness was possible in the near future.

"If the immigration services contact any of you, just tell them exactly how things have unfolded since we announced our engagement," I said. "You all know the same version, and it will seem more natural if you recount everything in your own words as opposed to some rehearsed answer."

"Now that's all cleared up, let's change the subject. No need to turn this dinner into an interrogation," Cole suggested. I owed him, big time. Ryker gave Cole a thumbs-up.

"I agree," he said.

"Wait, so no one is interested in juicy details? Just me?" Tess asked.

Skye shook her head. "Tess, we're at dinner."

She was great at calming down Tess's overexcitement and generally being the calming force in a tense situation. She shifted in her chair, focusing on Josie. "When do you have time for a girls' night out?"

Josie's cheeks went pink. She glanced at me with wide, pleading eyes, but I had no clue how to save her from this.

Skye and Tess were looking at her expectantly.

"Umm... I'm not sure. I have a few events in the evenings next week, but I'll check and let you know."

"We could also have lunch together if you're pressed for time," Skye suggested. Right... time for me to step in.

"Skye, Tess, stop pressuring her. She said she'll—"

Tess glared at me. "You, dear Hunter, cannot make any demands. At all. You let us all get our hopes up with the wedding."

Okay. Point taken. I was not yet forgiven.

"I'll let you know," Josie repeated.

"Now that's settled, let's focus on dinner before everything gets cold." Amelia's voice was calm and warm, as usual. I was man enough to admit I'd been avoiding eye contact ever since this conversation started, but now I gathered enough courage to look at her. She didn't seem nearly as annoyed as Tess and Skye. She didn't seem disappointed either. The knot between my shoulder blades loosened a little.

We enjoyed dinner, talking about everything except Josie and me. Every time the conversation veered dangerously close to honeymoon talk, Ryker expertly changed the subject. I was impressed by his skills. Then again, he was a master at avoiding uncomfortable conversations.

After dinner, I pulled Amelia aside in the living room.

"Amelia, I want to apologize. I'm sorry you got dragged into this. I'm also sorry about not telling you from the start. I genuinely thought it was for the best."

"I don't doubt you had great intentions."

"You're not mad."

"My boy…." She gave me a knowing look. Honestly, I preferred her calling me using my middle name too—even if it meant I was in trouble—because at least then I knew where I stood. But that knowing look always felt like a trap.

"I see how you look at her. That's not

someone who's just pretending for the immigration services."

I'd been spot-on. This was why Amelia had been so blasé about everything.

"Amelia...."

"Hunter Jonathan Caldwell." There she went with the middle name. I braced myself. "I might not be your mother, but I know you as well as she does. Whatever is going on between you and Josie, it's good for you. Don't contradict me. And don't ruin this."

"Didn't even cross my mind, ma'am."

She was obviously not done with me, but I was saved by Josie, who hurried toward us.

"Amelia, can I steal Hunter for a minute?"

"Sure."

Josie motioned with her head toward the corner farthest away from where the group was perched on armchairs. I felt Tess's gaze drill into the back of my skull even from the distance.

"Thanks for rescuing me," I said.

Josie folded her hands over her chest, narrowing her eyes. "I'd been watching you for a while."

"And you waited to rescue me... why?"

"Because you didn't deserve it. You didn't rescue *me*."

"From what?"

"Girls' night out. They'll drill me, won't they?"

"They will," I confirmed.

"So why didn't you do something about it?"

"I don't engage in fights I can't win," I said solemnly. Besides, I couldn't deny it… the idea of my cousins questioning Josie was *very* amusing.

"Oh, Hunter. At least tell me Amelia drilled you good."

"She used my middle name."

Josie laughed, throwing her head back. "I feel vindicated."

"You're having a little too much fun with this."

"What are you gonna do about it?"

The urge to kiss her was overwhelming, but I fought it. After coming clean to the family about the immigration services, explaining *this* would just bring another round of questions, and neither of us was ready for that.

"Should I come clean to my parents too?" Josie asked.

"What's your gut feeling on this?"

"I don't think the immigration services will bother with them. They usually conduct their inquiries in the city where the couple lives and works."

"If you want to tell them, go ahead, Josie. Whatever is easier for you."

"I'll think about it."

We returned to the group after that. Tess, Skye, *and* Amelia were looking at us. I could practically see a spark going off in Tess's mind. She patted the empty spot on the couch next to her.

"Josie, let's look through your calendar."

Josie threw me a desperate glance, but before I could come up with anything smart, Ryker gestured for me to join him and Cole. They were still at the dining table.

"So, now that we know you're actually not off the market, let's go out," Ryker said.

"We can even be your wingmen, in case you lost your game in the meantime," Cole added.

Shit. I should have seen this coming.

"Can't do that. Josie and I agreed not to see anyone until I receive my documents. It would raise suspicions."

"How long will that take?" Cole asked.

"Getting my green card? Probably not too long, but we'll stay married for about three years to avoid any red flags."

Ryker looked stricken. "So wait, you're going to have a three-year dry spell? Jesus, I'd rather be deported."

"Wait, you haven't been with a woman since you announced your engagement?" Cole asked.

Karma. This was karma. I'd been amused by the idea of Josie having to face Tess and Skye but looking at the suspicious expressions on Ryker and Cole's face, I was not going to fare much better.

"My priority right now is not to get into trouble with the immigration office. Everything else I can handle." There. That sounded like a smart answer.

I looked around the room, but Josie was still

sitting with Tess and Skye. I felt the need to be connected to her, to touch her.

When I'd told her that today half my brain was still on the Maldives, what I'd meant was that my mind had been on her. After being with her twenty-four hours a day for the past few weeks, it had felt strange to be without her today, as if an integral part of me was missing.

Honestly, I'd never been more grateful that Josie had insisted neither of us see people during these years. I couldn't share Josie. I was starting to wonder how I'd be able to let her go at all.

"Survived?" I asked her as we walked to the car a while later. I undid the top button of my shirt. August in New York was smothering. The humidity made it all worse.

"Yes. You?"

"They weren't as hard on me, but Ryker was already trying to rope me into going out with them. Cole even offered to be my wingman."

Josie stopped in the act of reaching for the car door handle. "What did you tell him?"

I brought a hand to her waist, right over her stomach. She was *so damn* tense.

"No, of course. You and I agreed not to see other people. And that was before I had you, Josie. I'd be crazy to want anyone else. I'm yours."

I felt her muscles go lax. "Okay. Okay. So, now what?"

Even though she had her back to me, I could

feel her smiling. I brought my mouth to her ear, enjoying the way she leaned into me, as if she didn't want to risk missing any word. I trailed my fingers from her shoulder down to her elbow, drinking in her reaction. She sucked in a breath, shimmying against me.

"Now, I'm going to spend the evening proving what a good husband I am, wife."

Chapter Twenty-Two
Hunter

The week after returning from our honeymoon, the immigration services asked me to come in for an interview for my green card. I was relieved they hadn't asked Josie to come in too. Still, I'd be lying if I didn't admit I was nervous as hell when the case worker asked me to come to her office.

"Mr. Caldwell, we've received your green card application, and I'd like to ask you a few questions."

"Sure."

"You've lived in the United States since you were four years old. Why haven't you applied for a green card before?"

"Honestly, I didn't have time and didn't think it was too important. My parents were British citizens, and they'd never had issues with their visa."

She looked down at my file, drawing check marks.

"But yours wasn't renewed."

"Hence why I decided to go directly for the green card."

"And you got married in the meantime."

I stood still, watching her carefully. "I did."

"Thought you'd kill two birds with one stone, eh?"

"Josie and I have been friends for a long time." I was still calm, but I wouldn't be able to keep so for too long.

"A large percentage of sham marriages happen between friends. People rarely trust strangers with something like this."

I could feel myself losing my composure. I had to force myself to keep my voice even.

"This is not a sham marriage."

"That's for us to determine. You have a good track record—a successful business, charity work. But we still have to investigate."

"Any other questions?"

"No."

That unsettled me for some reason. Usually, the less questions the better. But they'd asked me here for an interview, and we'd only covered a few things.

What had been the purpose? Catch me off guard?

By the time I arrived at the office, I was in a worse mood than when I'd gone in for the interview, but there was a small light at the end of the tunnel: Skye and Tess were dropping in at lunch so we could look at their business plan.

To my surprise, when I entered the meeting room, Ryker was there too. On second thought, it made perfect sense. As a Wall Street guru, he knew what investors were looking for. Besides, we all met about once or twice a week for lunch anyway. Before a Ballroom Gala, we sometimes had to discuss details, but mostly it was an opportunity to catch up. Everyone worked in the Manhattan area, so it was easiest to meet for an impromptu lunch than schedule dinners.

Skye and Tess were all smiles, pointing to the take-out bags they'd brought.

"Ladies, this is enough food for ten people."

"We went a bit overboard, but we just couldn't decide. Besides, we know you had your interview today. Thought you might need some comfort food," Skye explained.

"Or just comfort," Tess added. "How did it go?"

I waved my hand. "Not worth talking about."

"But they didn't question Josie, right?" Skye asked.

"No. It was just me."

As I sat down, I became aware that everyone in the room was watching me. I narrowed my eyes.

"Wait a second... your visit isn't just about the business plan, is it?"

Tess groaned, turning to Cole. "You gave us away? We told you we do our best work if he's unprepared."

Cole shook his head energetically. "No, I think he just put two and two together."

"Cole here tells us he worries about you. You can't focus," Skye said.

Tess grinned. "He thinks you're sick. We think you're mooning over Josie."

I blinked. "Mooning? That's a low blow."

Ryker held up a finger. "Um, no. Bringing Mom in would have been a low blow."

"Language aside, it's not all an act, is it?" Skye asked.

"Shit, if I'd known you'd go all gung-ho on him, I wouldn't have asked for your help," Cole said. I looked at him and Ryker. I was completely unprepared to answer my cousins' questions.

"Let's not be hasty," Ryker said.

Tess cocked a brow. "Brother, I'm not sure you'd realize you're in love even if it smacked you at the back of the head."

He grinned. "Love is not my domain, but I can bring in my charm and humor to any situation. I've been told it helps relieve tension," Ryker said.

"Why do you think I asked you over?" Cole teased.

Ryker clutched his heart. "Because my Wall Street expertise will be invaluable for the business plan."

I took advantage of the fact that he mentioned that to switch topics. "That's right. Tess, Skye, I thought you said you wanted us to look over your business plan together."

"Yes, but that doesn't mean we can't multitask," Tess replied.

I narrowed my eyes. "Business plan. Now."

Skye grinned. "Your lack of answer *is* an

answer anyway."

Tess nodded. "We're good with that. For now."

By the time lunch finished, I was in a much better mood. It carried on into the evening. Josie was already at home when I arrived, on the terrace. She was lying on a blanket and had lit candles everywhere.

"What's up with the candles?" I asked.

"I've read this book that says candlelight helps with relaxing. Was just testing it out."

"What's the verdict?"

"So far, so good." She patted the blanket. "Come here. How did it go today?"

I'd only shot her a message after I left the immigration building, because she'd been in meetings all day.

"It was very short… and I just had the feeling that they're baiting me, asking about our marriage."

Josie swallowed, shrugging. "We knew that might happen. Let's not worry unless it escalates. How was the rest of the day?"

"My cousins stopped by for lunch. We looked over Tess and Skye's business plan."

I left out the other *details*. It wasn't just that I hadn't been ready to answer their questions. I wasn't even ready to examine my own feelings.

"Those two are a powerhouse. I'm sure they'll do great. I've always been jealous of your working lunches."

"Join us. I'd love to have you there."

"You forget, I'm a lawyer. I've not only signed off my time to the firm, but also my soul. Lunches are just an excuse for more work. But I'm used to it."

"I can make up for all the stress in the evening." I wiggled my eyebrows suggestively. Laughing, she pushed me on my back on the blanket, propping her chin on my chest.

"How?"

"You tell me."

"You know what? My parents had this tradition where they met on the way home and talked about their day before they arrived. How about we make our own traditions? Catch up on the day just before dinner? We can come out here. Candles optional. I'm still weighing the pros and cons. What do you think?"

My heart started beating faster. I remembered a few traditions from my childhood before things went south. Traditions I hoped to pass on when I had my own family. I'd brushed off those thoughts for years, because some things had seemed out of reach, even for me. Josie was giving me something I'd never had before, never even dreamed of having.

"I think you're a genius. And I'm completely on board with you," I said.

"You're agreeing so fast with me these days, I don't even know what to make of it."

Grinning, I pulled her closer to me. "You'll see, Josie. You'll see."

I wanted more of whatever this was—of

everything Josie could give me.

Chapter Twenty-Three
Josie

"This is heaven. Pure heaven," I whispered.

"You're easy to please."

I opened an eye. "You're joking, right?"

We were in the reading nook I'd arranged in the empty corner between the couch and the window.

In the three weeks since we'd returned from the honeymoon, we'd definitely kept to our tradition, though I had given up on the candles. Way too messy.

We spoke about our day before dinner and either ordered in, or we cooked. About once a week we attended some fancy function where I got to dress up in the elegant dresses I'd bought. On Saturday mornings, we went to a nearby farmer's market.

We hadn't heard from the immigration services. As long as they didn't call me in for an interview as well, I wasn't worrying. But I knew better than to relax. The agency gathered evidence before acting.

"Look at you. You've got hot chocolate and a

book, and you're happy."

"I also have you giving me foot rubs. Don't downplay your role."

"Do you want another hot chocolate?"

"Is the earth round? Yes, please."

He moved my feet away from his lap, standing up. I followed his every movement to the kitchen, drinking in that sexy sway of his ass. He worked out a lot. Aside from his evening runs on the treadmill he'd put in one of the guest rooms, he also went to the building's gym four times a week, where he rigorously trained each group of muscles.

Since I did my yoga routine in the morning, I had no use for the gym, but I did go to the sauna. As a plus, I could spy on this sexy man.

He handed me a cup and resumed the foot rub. Hot damn, how was this man even real? He made me feel like a queen.

"How was your day?" he asked.

"Long and stressful. We're in the home stretch with a case we've been working on for three years, but I swear it's cutthroat now. How was yours?"

"Busy, but in a good way. We need new staff for our Miami branch, and I'm involved in managerial hires. I see about five new candidates a week."

"Live interviews or video conference?"

"I want live interviews. I can read people better in person. First impression is important. For those who make the second round, I'll just do video calls."

He pressed his thumbs on my sole, then expertly massaged my calves. I seriously was in heaven. What could be more perfect than this?

"Anyone giving you trouble at work?" he asked.

"Not more than usual. They do give me the side eye, though, when I brag about a certain someone."

"Who might that be?"

"My husband. I happen to be very proud of him."

He gave me an intense look I couldn't quite decipher. Even as I said it, my heart squeezed. We were growing close in ways I hadn't imagined before. I loved how he always joined me in the nook, bringing me a cup of hot chocolate or tea, or sometimes just worked on his laptop in silence.

I was already getting attached to our life, to the house, and it had only been a month. How could I say goodbye to all this in three years?

"What's wrong?" he asked.

I shrugged, unsure how to put it in words. Did he like this intimacy as much as I did? Or was he sharing because it had become a routine, because we lived together?

"Do you want to look over the to-do list for the school?" I asked, not just to change the subject, but because I genuinely loved the project.

Hunter leaned in, cupping my cheek. "Josie, this is your free time. You've already done a lot."

I hadn't done *that* much, just secured some permits. The great thing about having attended law school in New York was that 90 percent of my fellow classmates were working in the city—some for public institutions.

Knowing that Hunter had gone into real estate partly to keep the connection to his dad, to make him proud, endeared him to me. I was seeing a part of Hunter he hadn't shown me before.

"If I'm thinking about work in my free time, you're doing something wrong, husband." I wiggled my toes, indicating that I was ready for another round of foot rubs.

Hunter pressed three fingers into my arch before skimming his hands up my calves. My skin broke out in goose bumps.

"I'm going to miss this tomorrow evening," I said.

"Why?"

"I have the girls' night out, remember?"

He grimaced. "Wouldn't want to be in your skin."

I poked his waist. "Stop making fun of me. This is all your fault. You could have prevented this."

"If you really believe that, you have too much faith in me and not nearly enough in Tess and Skye."

The next evening, Tess and Skye stopped by the house. We were going to a bar two blocks away. Tess had clasped one of my wide belts around her waist. Skye was trying on some chandelier-style clip-on earrings that looked gorgeous on her. They reminded me of my sister. We'd routinely swapped clothes growing up. I sighed, more aware than ever of the dull ache in my chest. I missed her terribly. But being with Tess and Skye was like having two new sisters.

Hunter was watching us from the doorway of the master bedroom.

"What?" Tess inquired, giving him the side-eye. "I feel that I won't like whatever you want to say."

"Just bring my wife home in one piece."

"Territorial, are you?"

Hunter's eyes flashed. Tess looked between us, and I blushed. Hunter's clothes were everywhere around the room. It wasn't hard to put two and two together. Sure, we could play up the immigration services angle, say that it was best if it appeared that we shared a bedroom because they could always question the cleaning personnel.

"Okay, I say we're done here," Skye exclaimed, admiring her knee-length golden dress in the mirror.

"I ordered an Uber, because no way can we walk two blocks in these heels. It'll be here in two minutes," Tess said. "Let's go. Chop chop."

"You go ahead. I'll be right out. Need to put on some earrings," I said.

Tess and Skye hurried out, past Hunter, who looked at me for a few seconds before taking mercy on me and striding over to help.

"Here, let me do this."

He made quick work of it, but then lingered with his fingers on the shell of my ear before flipping me around and sealing his mouth over mine.

Holy hell, what a kiss. His lips coaxed mine feverishly, until I was so worked up that my pulse was out of control. I was in danger of forgetting that I was supposed to head out. All I wanted to do was stay in with this sinfully sexy man and let him have his way with me.

"Hunter...," I murmured. "I have to go."

"I want to keep you here. I thought you were worried they'll grill you."

"I am, but... I also have an agenda tonight. Skye has been a little morose the few times I talked to her over the phone these past few weeks. I want to get to the bottom of why."

"Skye's in trouble?" He was immediately alert.

"It's just a hunch. Nothing business-related. Just... personal stuff. Anyway, I want to be there for her, just to comfort her... or bury a body if necessary."

"You're amazing."

"I am?"

He nibbled at my lip again, moving his hand upward over my spine.

"I can show you... and I can be very thorough about it, but then you won't make it to the bar at all."

"Then stop touching me, you devious man."

"I can't. Maybe I'll just keep you here. Lock

the door, tie you up."

His eyes flashed. My entire body reacted to his words. Heat simmered on the surface of my skin. I pressed my thighs together.

"You're a bit territorial, husband."

"Fuck yes, I'm very territorial."

"So, I take it that you wouldn't be too happy if I danced with a random sexy stranger tonight?"

"You do that, and I'll throw you over my shoulder and bring you home." His gaze was so determined that I had no doubt he'd do exactly that. "Josie...."

"Kidding. Just checking where you are on the territorial scale."

"And?"

"From one to ten, you're at twenty-five."

He pulled me to him, kissing me again, only letting me go when we heard the front door open.

"Josie, our Uber is here," Tess called.

"I'll be right out."

I walked past Hunter, sending him an air kiss, enjoying that feral glint in his eyes, giving an extra sway to my hips as I moved. I loved getting a rise out of him.

The girls were in an excellent mood, already looking at the bar's menu on their phone in the car.

"If they have a good DJ and quality cocktails, that's all I need," Skye said.

"Don't forget great finger food. That's also a must, or those cocktails will do a number on us," I said.

They exchanged conspiratorial glances, and I instantly knew I'd been right about tonight. They had two purposes. One: have fun. Two: make me spill the beans.

As soon as we arrived at the bar, Skye ordered daiquiris and tacos. The place was relatively full, given that it was a weeknight. I loved the diffuse lighting and low-key music.

"So, anything you want to tell us?" Tess asked.

"What do you mean?" I tried to sound innocent.

Skye whistled. "She's gonna make us work for it."

Tess sat up straighter, winking at me. "I don't mind. Secrets are more satisfying if I have to earn them."

I felt my ears burn hot, and I didn't look Tess in the eyes, afraid she might see right through me. Unfortunately, that just seemed to tip her off.

"You and Hunter looked cozy tonight," Skye said.

Oh, boy. Our daiquiris weren't even here. How was I supposed to survive this?

"We noticed both of your clothes all over the master bedroom," Tess added. "And you both had stuff in the bathroom. Your conditioner and body lotions, his shaving stuff."

"Wow. You noticed all that in the two trips you took to the bathroom?" I asked, just to buy myself some time.

"Don't be silly. I noticed it on my first trip. The second was just so I could confirm they were actually used, not just put there so people could see them."

"Of course."

"Plus, your lips were a bit swollen when you got out of the house. So we're guessing Hunter didn't just give you a pep talk when you were alone."

That was it, I was a goner. I couldn't lie to them anymore. I also didn't want to. Being dishonest was so exhausting.

I hadn't told my family about the arrangement, and I hadn't told Tess and Skye about the rest. I wanted to be one hundred percent honest with someone.

"Wait a second, is she blushing?" Skye said.

"Yes she is. Holy shit, we're onto something. Aren't we?" Tess shimmied in her seat, drumming her fingers on the table just as a waitress placed cocktails in front of us. I looked from Skye to Tess, then took a sip of my daiquiri and nodded.

"You're having sex. I knew it," Tess exclaimed.

I dropped my face in my hands, feeling like a schoolgirl sharing with my girlfriends that the boy I liked had kissed me. I felt my face become even hotter.

"So... what exactly does that mean?" Tess asked.

"We're just... well, it was naive to assume we'd be able to pull this off and that things wouldn't get complicated."

"Define complicated," Tess demanded.

"Honestly, I don't know. I'm trying not to overthink and just... go with the flow. Plus the sex is awesome, and I'm not looking a gift horse in the mouth."

Tess raised a glass. "Hear, hear. Great sex isn't so easy to come by."

Skye clinked her glass to ours too, but her expression was softer. "Do you think things between you two might evolve into more? Just putting it out there, but we think you're a *perfect* fit for him."

My stomach constricted, and I vehemently shook my head. "No, it's just for now. I mean, I think it was naive to think we could just be roommates for three years, and... Hunter is drop-dead gorgeous, so that didn't make things any easier. But the short answer is no."

I couldn't get their hopes up. I couldn't get *my* hopes up either. They nodded, and we proceeded to order a second round of cocktails.

I veered the conversation toward Skye.

"You seemed a bit down when we spoke on the phone."

"That obvious?"

"Yes."

"Can I get a pass tonight?"

"Nope. I did my part. Now, your turn."

Skye pouted. "But I don't want to ruin the mood."

"It's better than to keep it all in," Tess said

wisely. "I already know everything, but... all three of us could send him all the negative karma in the world. The more the merrier."

Skye swallowed, looking down at her glass. "This guy I was seeing from work... he already had a girlfriend. Can you believe that? And I found out when *someone else* at work told me. I've never been more embarrassed. When I confronted him, he said that he'd never told me he was single. I mean... why would I assume that a guy who was hitting on me for months would be single, right?"

"I'm sorry, Skye."

"I don't understand. Why did he bother? And his girlfriend.... It almost makes me want to find her just so I can tell her to cut her losses, and not let that jerk dick her around. But what if she knows and doesn't care? I mean... some people don't mind open relationships. But I do. I just want a guy who wants... just me. Is that so much to ask for? Ugh... he made me feel so worthless."

Tess and I exchanged a glance. Yeah... talking about it definitely didn't help Skye. I knew it helped some—I, for one, liked to talk about breakups to get them out of my system. But Skye had been in such a great mood when the evening had started, and now she looked small and hurt, and I hated it. Tess moved her chair closer to Skye, giving her a heartfelt hug. I loved these girls.

Skye gave us a small smile, leaning into her sister. Tess said nothing, and neither did I. I'd been through enough ugly breakups myself to know that when you felt this raw, nothing anyone said could make you feel better.

This was all my fault. Why had I insisted she talk? It was also my duty to make it better. I brainstormed potential topics that could lift her mood, before the obvious one popped up: me and Hunter.

Skye had been exuberant talking about us, so it was worth a try, even though I knew it meant we'd spend the rest of the evening on the topic. What I wouldn't do for these girls.

Tess must have sensed what I was thinking about, because she focused on me next.

"How do you do it?" Tess asked. "Living with Hunter, having sex with him, and keeping all these boundaries?"

"Yes, do tell," Skye said. She was smiling again, finally. Her eyes were sparkling with enthusiasm.

I'd had three daiquiris, which were two too many for me to be able to play it cool.

"It's hard to keep the lines from blurring. Really hard," I admitted. When I looked up from the glass, they were grinning.

"What?" I demanded.

Tess shrugged, flashing a devilish smile. "This isn't going to help you keep those lines from blurring, but we saw how he is with you."

"We've never seen him like this," Skye confirmed. "Mom thinks the same too, by the way. And I trust her instincts."

"You're so bad for me."

"But what would you do without us?"

I might not have said it out loud, but I couldn't pretend with myself: I was falling for Hunter, and I didn't know how to stop it.

Chapter Twenty-Four
Josie

A few clichés about the lawyer world had proven to be true within my first year.

Ruthless competition? Check.

Long hours? Double check.

The adage that if you don't have a mental breakdown your first three years, it means you're cut out for it? Also true.

I had found ways to cope with my stress, especially since I'd received my own office. Behind the closed door, I could do whatever I wanted, and I took full advantage of that.

Usually that meant kicking off my heels and walking around barefoot. I had various tools to help with the back strain from sitting too long. I was currently sitting on a medicine ball, pressing my feet on a small reflex therapy mat.

September was a busy month for us, and I already needed a time-out. I couldn't believe the honeymoon was already a month and a half ago.

I only had phone conferences for the rest of the day, but no physical appointments. Which was why, when one of my assistants called me, telling me they had someone here to see me, I was perplexed.

I checked my calendar, frowning. "I don't have anything on my schedule."

Drop-ins were highly unusual.

"It's someone from the immigration office."

I gripped the mouse so tightly that I almost couldn't feel my fingers anymore.

"Should I tell her to come in?"

"Of course." I forced my voice to remain calm. I couldn't kid myself that this had anything to do with any of my cases. Immigration officials didn't just come to one's office. But I could pass it off to my superiors as research for one of my cases if anyone got wind of it.

Assistants usually didn't discuss our business.

My legs were shaking a little when I rose from the ball. I immediately rolled it away, drawing my chair closer. I also put on my shoes as I watched the door open.

A woman in her midforties strode in. Her white-blond hair was styled in a strict bun. She wore a suit that made her fit right in here with the rest of us.

"Hello. I'm Josie Gallagher. To what do I owe the pleasure?"

I stepped from behind my desk, extending my hand. She shook it briefly.

"I'm the immigration worker in charge of your husband's file."

Nodding, I pointed her to the chair in front of my desk.

"Please, sit down. Do you want anything to

drink? Water, coffee, tea?"

There. I sounded calm, as if her visit didn't stress me out. I didn't know if I *looked* calm, though. I felt as if I was in front of a judge, about to be sentenced. My entire face felt hot. My mind was racing a mile an hour. I wished I had gone to the bathroom to splash cold water on my face.

The more I tried to calm myself down, the more I panicked. What if I said the wrong thing? What if the agent could read between the lines?

"You know why I'm here?" she asked.

"You said you're working on my husband's case, so I'm assuming it's about that. How can I help?"

I set my elbows on the table, clasping my hands, hoping I was projecting a calm image.

"I won't beat around the bush. You're under the suspicion of having committed marriage fraud."

My stomach bottomed out, but I held my chin high, didn't allow any emotions to show.

"What do you have to say to that?" the officer pushed.

"I'm a lawyer. I work by the credo, innocent until proven guilty. Of course, it's not true."

"The timeline of your marriage is very suspicious."

"And why is that?"

"You went from engaged to married in three weeks."

"My parents met at a wedding, and they were married within the month." It wasn't even a lie.

"Ms. Gallagher, you are aware of the penalties for a sham marriage, right?"

"As I said, I'm a lawyer. You can rest assured I wouldn't do anything against the law."

"I see. And yet your marriage has raised several red flags. Why did you keep your name?"

"You consider *that* a red flag? I'm a lawyer, I have a reputation. People know my name. I didn't want to lose that brand awareness."

"Or you didn't want to have to go through the process of changing it back after Mr. Caldwell received his green card."

"Look, you can twist this however you want. I can just tell you the facts."

"If you were to confess to the sham, I am sure I can work out a lower penalty for you."

I narrowed my eyes. She thought she could turn me *against* Hunter? This woman didn't know who she was dealing with.

"I know you're just trying to do your job, but there's a difference between questioning and intimidation. You cannot intimidate me. Frankly, your insinuations are offensive. So unless you have any more questions about facts, we can wrap this up."

She scoffed, taking out a small notebook from her bag.

"When did you two meet?"

"In high school."

"And you were friends for fifteen years?"

"Yes."

"When did that friendship turn into a romantic entanglement?"

When he kissed me for the first time.

I couldn't say that, of course. Instead, I pasted what I hoped passed as a dreamy expression on my face and repeated the story Hunter and I had concocted. One night about a year ago, after he drove me home from an event we'd both attended, I invited him upstairs and we ended up in bed. After that, we were friends with benefits for some months.

"But both you and Mr. Caldwell were seeing other people at that time."

I bit the inside of my cheek. Who had they been talking to?

"We were not exclusive."

"When did things change?"

"When I told him that I could no longer do this casually. That I wanted more... some sort of commitment. I honestly thought he'd end things. You know men can be fickle when it comes to commitment."

I got no sympathy smile from her.

"Anyway, he surprised me. Said his feelings for me had deepened too."

"Did he propose then?"

"Yes. It was... as I said, completely unexpected. He didn't even have a ring." In a flash of inspiration, I added, "He made this very romantic gesture where he had an employee from Tiffany's bring by a selection at my place so we could choose together." I held up my hand, pointing to my ring finger. "Isn't it gorgeous?"

There. She could check with the store employee and confirm this story.

"How long have you lived together?"

"Two months, I think? He'd been house hunting for a while, but when we decided to take the next step, he involved me in the process too. We had an excellent realtor. Her name is Darla Lopez. She showed us this beautiful house, and I fell in love with it. Hunter bought it right away."

She pursed her lips, jotting down notes.

"*He* bought it? You didn't buy it together?"

"It's in both our names," I said, almost through gritted teeth.

"What is your morning routine?"

"I do thirty minutes of yoga, then hop in the shower. He exercises in the evening, so he sleeps in every morning."

"What kind of aftershave does he use?"

"You're kidding, right? I barely remember the name of my own body lotion."

"What's his favorite food? What is yours?"

"We both like steaks."

The officer threw question after question at me. I also detected some classic witness interrogation traps, such as rephrasing a question several times in the hope that the subject would give different answers.

My experience as a lawyer served me well. I didn't fumble. Still, once she was out of my office and I slumped back in my chair, I discovered that I was shaking slightly. I needed to get a grip on myself, because I had a phone conference in twenty minutes.

I used the break to head to the bathroom and splash some much-needed cold water on my face. That went well, didn't it?

Or was I being overly optimistic?

Shit. I had to let Hunter know—warn him in case he'd be questioned too. I hurried back to my office and sent him a quick message.

Josie: An immigration agent just came into work. I think it went okay.

I wanted to give him more details, but I came up blank. The adrenaline still hadn't left my system and it was making it very hard to focus. *Damn it, Josie. Pull yourself together. You have a conference call with a client.*

I could ask my assistant to postpone it, but I didn't want to give anyone any reason to doubt me. I could pass off the agent's visit as work related. But if I cancelled a meeting right afterward? Someone might put two and two together.

The phone call was scheduled in one of the conference rooms, where we had a professional sound and image system.

I left my office armed with a legal pad and a pen, as well as the client's file, and casually stopped by my assistant's desk.

"Hey. Everything went okay with the officer?"

"Yes. She was here for some research I'm doing. I completely forgot to add her to my calendar."

Eleanor's eyebrows shot up. "That's unlike you."

I smacked my forehead playfully. "Freshly married brain and all that. Don't fall in love. Messes with your memory."

She chuckled, nodding.

"I'm heading to the conference room for the call. It might take longer. You know how these things go. Don't wait for me."

"Sure."

I arranged everything in the conference room, armed with the summary page of the case, listening to the client. But half my brain cells were still rewinding everything I'd told our case worker. Had it been enough? Had it been too much—as if I was trying too hard? Had they questioned Hunter too?

Even though I didn't like checking my phone while I was in a conference, I glanced at the screen, grateful that the client had preferred to do this audio-only.

My phone's battery was dead. Great. Just great. What if Hunter had called or messaged, wanting more details? What if he didn't remember my favorite food or whatever and he wanted to double-check?

"What's that sound?" the client asked sharply. Shit. I was tapping my fingers against the desk. I *needed* to get a grip on myself.

"Better now?" I curled my left hand into a fist, laying it in my lap.

"Yes. So... Josie, do you think we can win

this?"

I was great at my job. I loved helping people, fighting for them. But I didn't like to give them false hope before I'd had a chance to sink my teeth into their case.

"I'm certainly going to do my best. I need to review all the facts, but we're going to put up a good fight."

My mind was still spinning an hour and a half later, when I ended the call. I'd taken copious amounts of notes. I walked straight to the elevator, heading first to my office to drop all the case files and pick my bag.

All the assistants on my floor had already left, but when I descended to the lobby, both receptionists were still there. One of them waved at me.

"Josie, someone's waiting for you."

Was the case worker back? I couldn't deal with her again today.

"I've been fighting with him for half an hour. He insisted on going up to your office. Told him we don't allow anyone in our lawyers' offices alone. He wouldn't take no for an answer."

I had a slight suspicion who *he* was.

"My husband?"

"Yes. He's in the lounge."

"Thanks."

I rounded the reception corner, heading straight to the lounge—an elegant room with leather couches and oil portraits hanging on the wall, tracing the origins of the founders back to the old world.

Why was Hunter here? Had the case worker accosted him too? Had something worse happened?

That pessimistic train of thought came to a screeching halt when I noticed Hunter. He was standing, hands in his pockets, molten eyes trained on me, oozing testosterone.

His tan had faded a little, but his hair still maintained that bronze look, with a few blond waves here and there.

I smiled; I just couldn't do otherwise.

"They didn't let me up to your office," he said.

"We have a policy."

"I'm your husband. If I want to see my wife, I will see my wife."

God, I loved the sound of that. Would this come to a natural end when the three years went by? I wasn't sure how I'd handle it. How could I go back to not having Hunter be such a huge part of my life? How could I be just his friend when I'd had a taste of how he could light me up with a kiss, a touch? When I knew how it felt to lie in bed and laugh with him?

When he walked up to me, cupping the back of my head, slanting his mouth over mine, my worries melted away on the spot. *Oh, Hunter.* Was there anything his hot kisses couldn't just push to the back of my mind?

"Mmm," I murmured when we paused to breathe. "You should be on those danger signs. Like they have for blinding sun… only this would be 'hot guy in a suit.' Warning, don't stare for too long. May cause accidents."

He laughed, and the melodic sound relaxed me as well.

"If that deserves a warning sign, how about this hot guy out of a suit?"

"Are you offering to strip for me?"

"Yeah."

"Not wanting to look a gift horse in the mouth, but what exactly did I do to earn that?"

He traced his thumb on my forehead. "I just want to make this frown disappear from your beautiful face."

My insides felt all warm and fuzzy.

"How can you be so relaxed?" I asked.

"Because I'm sure you did great."

"Has no one from the immigration office contacted you?"

"No."

I relaxed a little.

"So, striptease is on the menu. What else?"

"You'll see."

"Give me hints."

He cupped my jaw, tilting my head up slightly, giving me a quick peck.

"Come on, curious girl. I want to take care of you."

He'd come by car again, and we drove to Brooklyn, getting out in front of a red-brick building. The large neon sign said Climbing Hall.

"Why didn't I know about this place?"

"It only opened a week ago. I knew you'd love to try it out."

He knew me so well. I was ecstatic as they gave me gear, and even more so when Hunter also borrowed some.

"Husband of mine, you're going climbing with me?"

"I'll give it a try."

"You feel awfully brave now after scuba diving, huh?"

He walked right next to me as we headed to the changing rooms. I thought nothing of it until he pinched my ass.

Amusement flickered in his eyes. "You were the one afraid of sharks."

"Any sensible person is afraid of sharks," I countered, but stood a little away from him.

I loved climbing. Reaching for the next milestone, focusing on one move at a time was the best way to shut down the constant mind chatter.

From time to time, I glanced down at Hunter. I wasn't going very fast, but he was still a good way behind me.

"Did you have fun?" I asked after we finished the session.

He waggled his eyebrows. "I had an excellent view."

So that explained why he'd always remained behind me.

"You're unbelievable."

"What's next?" I asked as he led me to the car.

He kissed my hand, opening the door for me. "We're going home, and I'll keep taking care of you."

That sounded like a dream.

He'd ordered all my favorite food, and we arrived at the same time as the delivery guy. We relieved him of the bags, carrying everything to the kitchen.

"Bringing out the big guns?" I murmured.

I intended to put it all on plates, but someone kept distracting me. Hunter kissed the side of my neck, dragging his hands down the sides of my body. How was I supposed to go back to a life where we didn't have all this? He bit my earlobe, pressing my ass against his crotch. Holy hell. He was semihard. He fondled one ass cheek lightly. I gasped, already anticipating his next touch.

"You're so beautiful, Josie. So fucking sexy."

He trailed his fingers from my ass cheeks up my back, resting them over the clasp of my bra before dropping his hand altogether.

"You're mean," I murmured.

"On the contrary. I am on my best behavior."

"But I don't want that."

I turned, flashing him a pout to let him know I was only semi-okay with this. I mean, I wanted dinner, but I wanted Hunter more. Then I decided on another strategy.

"You're right. Dinner is an even better idea

than sexy time."

"Babe, I'm offended."

I peeked at him sideways.

"Offended enough to do something about it?"

He gave me a sly smile, bending to kiss my shoulder.

"You little vixen."

"Learned from the best."

He turned me around, kissing me so deep and hard, gripping my hips so possessively that I couldn't help letting out that moan I'd been holding in.

When we pulled apart, we were both fighting for breath. I smiled, and we both finished putting our dinner on plates.

"By the way, you still owe me a striptease," I informed him as we moved to the living room.

"I'll show you mine if you show me yours."

"You're impossible."

"But you're still into me."

I sighed dramatically. "I totally am. What does that say about me?"

He pulled me close, planting a smooch right on my lips.

"That you're adorable."

Wow. Why was he so attentive? So sweet? Could I keep him? Shit, no, I didn't want to even allow myself to consider that. If I started to think about the day I wouldn't have him every time he charmed me (which was often), I would end up miserable.

Since I was a documentary freak, we settled to watch one about ancient Egypt, sharing tacos and chatting about everything except my meeting with the case worker today.

I sighed. Things were changing fast, weren't they?

"Why are you looking at me like that?"

I shrugged, trying to sound nonchalant. "No reason. Just admiring this sexy man."

He bit my shoulder lightly. "Liar. You have something more on your mind. But I'll make you tell me all about it later."

"Your persuasion skills are pretty impressive," I admitted. When he moved on to kiss my neck, I shuddered, playfully shoving him away.

"Hey. Don't distract me from my pharaohs."

To my surprise, he actually did stop nibbling at my skin.

"You're just giving up?" I asked suspiciously.

"Told you, tonight we'll do whatever you want."

So many things crossed my mind. Where to begin?

"You've got that secretive look on your face again," he said playfully. I grinned.

"I'll let you lure out all my secrets later tonight, mister. Every single one of them."

I wiggled my ass, turning on one side, and almost knocked over the guacamole.

"Shoot. That was close. Did you ever think about getting a leather couch? They're so much easier to clean."

"We can get one if you want to. Or if there's anything else you want to change, just go ahead."

I frowned, placing the bowl of guacamole on the coffee table. "Hunter, you don't have to change anything for me. You'll just have to redecorate again after I move out."

And I'd already gone overboard with the nook. I didn't want to get even more attached to this house than I already was. I had withdrawals already at the mere thought of leaving this behind, and my time with Hunter.

He'd gone quiet. His gaze was lethally calm. Then he gripped both of my ankles, pulling me so close that I almost smacked into him.

"You want another couch, you buy it. You hear me? I told you I want you to feel at home here. I mean it." He almost growled those last few words.

"O-okay," I stammered. My heart was suddenly working in overdrive.

When he slanted his mouth over mine, he kissed me possessively, as if he wanted to mark me. And I wanted nothing more than to let him. I wanted to belong to this man every way there was.

Chapter Twenty-Five
Hunter

The first gala event of the season took place a few evenings later.

"How do I look? Is this okay?" Josie asked, twirling in front of me as we were getting ready. She was wearing the white-and-silver dress we'd bought on that shopping spree. The one that had driven me crazy with lust even back then.

"You're beautiful."

"Your voice sounds a bit growly. Is this too revealing for you, husband?" She twirled again, giving me a view of her exposed back, all that soft skin on display. The dress was long enough that it reached the floor, but the plunging back was just killing me.

"Are you teasing me?"

"Yes, sir, I am."

"You look too fucking beautiful. But... it's... if we go to the event with you wearing that, I'll have to fight off men for you. You're not wearing it."

"Then why the hell did we buy it?"

"Because you look absolutely gorgeous in it."

"See? I have to put it to good use."

"I have an idea. You can wear it just for me. In here."

She narrowed her eyes. "That's a waste of a dress. Right... when I asked your opinion, I just meant if it's appropriate for the caliber of the event. It's the first Ballroom Gala of the season. But I won't change it because you're jealous." She tapped her ring. "This will keep men at bay. Also, you're the host of the event. Everyone will know I'm your wife."

"How? You're not sharing my last name."

She rolled her eyes at me. "If I had a penny every time you said that. Now, come on. Or we'll be late. I'm nervous."

"Don't be."

"This is a huge thing. How did you get the idea?" she asked once we were in the back of a car. We were arranging transport for all the guests.

"Had been reading about Bill Gates, and how he convinced various high earners to donate to causes he'd donated to himself. It's much easier if you have skin in the game. Plus, if you gather everyone in the room, the social pressure to make generous donations is higher."

"You're devious."

"But it works."

"Smart man."

"Besides, it was an opportunity to have a joint project with my cousins. It's a lot of fun."

"I can tell."

I started organizing these the same year the company made the Forbes 500 list. It was a way of giving back, of supporting those who hadn't had my opportunities and my luck.

I'd known what it was to fall from the top. To

have everything and then almost nothing. Those hard years had changed my view of the world.

"Everything okay? You've been quieter than usual," Josie said.

"Just… thinking about my speech."

That wasn't a lie, but it wasn't the whole truth either. My dad's birthday was today, always a day when I could barely keep all my emotions in check. She clasped her fingers with mine. My heart rate sped up. It was a small gesture, but it was as if she knew it would calm me down. As if she felt I needed it. All my cousins were at the venue, at the organizers' table.

"Come on, the raffle will begin right after your speech," Tess said.

Instead of simply inviting one to dance, you had to buy a ticket for the person you wanted to dance with. There was a raffle for every dance—only men bought tickets for the first few rounds, and only ladies for the next ones. All the money went to charity, of course, though this wasn't the main donation, just provided an element of surprise and kept everyone laughing and guessing.

When we were brainstorming ways to keep the balls entertaining and unique, Tess came up with the idea, citing *Gone with The Wind* as inspiration. I had no idea what the movie was about, but Tess talked our ears off, and before we knew it, we'd all agreed to it. It proved to be a success.

"I'm thinking we should also participate in the raffle," Ryker said. As organizers, we'd stayed out of it because we had plenty to do.

Skye laughed, but Cole nodded in appreciation. "I'm with you, brother."

"I'm sure I'd bring in the most tickets," Ryker continued.

Cole cocked a brow. "When I'm competing against you? Ha! No chance."

Josie looked between the two of them. "Well, well. The Flirt vs. the Charmer. I'd pay money just to watch that."

Tess clapped her hands. "We don't have time for brainstorming now. Hunter, your speech. And by the way, your pretty wife could totally join the raffle. Josie, what do you say?"

"For a good cause? Of course."

"No," I said firmly. The whole group turned to look at me. The corners of Josie's mouth twitched. Ryker and Cole shook their heads. Tess and Skye were radiant.

"We need to make the rounds for this ball," I said. "I want to introduce you to everyone as my wife. You won't have much time for dancing."

No one seemed to buy my explanation, not even Josie—the corners of her lips twitched again. I was a territorial bastard. I just didn't want to share her.

"I'm going to the restroom to freshen up before you start introducing me, *husband*."

The second she was out of earshot, my cousins pounced on me.

"So, is it just me, or did he sound jealous?"

Cole asked.

"Not just you," Skye confirmed. She was grinning from ear to ear. If possible, Tess's grin was even bigger.

"Did you tell her how you feel?" Tess asked.

"Not… explicitly," I admitted.

"What are you waiting for?" Skye asked.

"What if it ruins everything? What if she doesn't feel the same?"

Tess tilted her head. "You always take chances, Hunter. You're going to hold back now?"

"What exactly *do* you feel?" Skye went on.

Cole cleared his throat. "Let's not corner him before the speech."

Ryker sighed dramatically. "Yup, let the man focus on his speech. He's a goner for Josie anyway. Even I'm not that clueless."

I didn't get another word in, because the evening's moderator called me into the main room. Showtime.

Getting up on a stage and giving a speech wasn't one of my favorite activities, but over time, I'd learned to view this as an opportunity rather than something to dread. The better my speech, the easier donors would part with their money.

At the end of it, I pulled out a check, reading the sum out loud before handing it over to our treasurer. I always set the bar high, donating six figures. People tended to follow suit.

Josie watched me from right next to the stage for the entire duration of my speech. Tess and Skye were right, of course: I had to tell her, but having the guts to do it was another story.

Josie was the star of the night, and not because she was my wife. Well, partly because of that. Several regulars weren't shy about expressing their surprise that I'd married.

But Josie stole the show with her clever input and her charm. I was proud to be her husband.

"You know, everyone here is a potential client for you," I whispered to her while we danced.

"I'm not here for that tonight. I'm here for you."

She threaded her fingers through my hair, looking at me with happy eyes, as if sensing that I needed all that warmth and sweetness she had to give.

No one had ever cared about what I needed, looked at me as if I was her sole focus, as if nothing else mattered—not the opportunities to strike business contacts or to advance her own career. I almost didn't dare think it, let alone hope it, but... was it possible I was so important to her?

***

When we arrived home, I was restless. I couldn't avoid my own thoughts, sinking into that melancholy I did every year on the anniversary.

"Coming to bed?" Josie asked.

"You go ahead. I want to finalize a few emails."

I was beating around the bush. I doubted I could concentrate on emails. I just didn't think I could lie next to her and not lay every thought bare. I didn't want her to see this weak side of me.

"Hunter, you know you can talk to me about anything, right?"

"Go to sleep, babe. We'll talk tomorrow."

She fidgeted in her spot, frowning before finally turning away.

I simply couldn't sit, or even stand still. Forget emails. I headed to the guest room where I kept the treadmill. I quickly discarded my tux, changing into the running gear I kept there, then hopped on the machine.

Our bedroom was on the other side of the house, so it wouldn't wake up Josie.

I'd intended to only run fast enough to be able to block my thoughts. That usually happened at level ten. It wasn't enough this time. Memories poked around in my brain, the deep sadness twisting in my chest. I kept increasing the speed and the inclination of the slope, until I had to concentrate on the treadmill only, or I risked falling off.

One foot in front of the other. One in front of the other. Faster. Faster. That was it. The effort drowned out the memories, how much I missed him. How much I hoped he looked down and was proud of everything I'd achieved, of restoring the dream he'd worked on for his entire life.

My lungs were protesting. My chest ached

with every breath. The deeper I tried to breathe in, the worse the ache became.

The muscles in my legs started burning. My buttocks were in pain. I glanced at the screen. I'd run for over an hour at this speed? Fuck. I wouldn't be able to walk tomorrow.

I pressed the End Program button, and the speed decreased gradually. The slower I went, the weaker my thighs felt. I didn't think I was able to walk right now either.

I nearly twisted an ankle stepping off the treadmill. My legs almost couldn't sustain my weight. Jesus, what I had been thinking? My throat was as dry as sandpaper. I was completely dehydrated.

A soft whoosh made me look toward the door. Josie was standing there in a white nightgown that barely covered anything, holding a bottle of water.

"Babe… did I make too much noise? I'm sorry."

"No, I just woke up and you weren't next to me, and I went looking for you."

"How long have you been standing here?"

"Forty minutes, give or take. Noticed you didn't have a bottle of water and brought you one." She handed me the one she was holding.

"Thanks."

I guzzled down half the bottle in a few swigs, then tried to gather my thoughts as I put the lid back on.

"I'm worried you'll dehydrate, or that you'll

get sick. You were going so fast... Hunter, what's wrong?" she asked softly.

"I'm fine."

"No, you're not. Don't shut me out."

"I said, I'm fine."

"Right, that's why you ran yourself into the ground. Forgive me for intruding in... whatever this is and worrying about you. Clearly, you have it under control and don't need me."

She spun around, leaving the room. I clasped the bottle so tightly that the plastic gave in.

Jesus, I was an idiot. She'd stood here for forty minutes, ready to hand me water, to listen to me, to just watch me in case I needed something—because she was worried for me. And I shut her out.

Josie deserved better than this, and I needed to find it in myself to give her exactly what she deserved. I just didn't know how. I'd never been one to pour my heart out to anyone, or to voice my inner turmoil.

Ever since I was fifteen, I'd sucked it up and done what had to be done, rarely stopping for any introspection—the exception being Dad's birthday—and never talking about it. It wasn't that I wanted to forget about everything—I didn't. I cherished Dad's memory, and I understood that life sometimes handed you curveballs—I just chose not to linger too much on them.

Taking in a deep breath, I walked after her. She'd gone straight to the bedroom and had closed the door behind her.

She'd *locked* it. What the…? Did she not want me to come in tonight?

I knocked twice. "Josie, I'm sorry. I want to talk."

"Why? To keep telling me you're okay? I don't feel like going around in circles."

"Please open the door."

I waited, holding my breath, only exhaling once I heard footsteps approaching.

She was eyeing me suspiciously when she opened the door. I walked inside, pacing the room before finally sitting at the edge of the bed, resting my forearms on my thighs, staring at the floor.

"I'm sorry for reacting like that. I…. You're right, I'm not fine. I mean, there's nothing wrong… it's just an emotional day. It's Dad's birthday. That's why I start the charity season on this date."

"Oh!"

"So, it's always a tough day for me."

"I'm sorry, Hunter."

She came closer. I snapped my gaze up when she stood right in front of me.

Without thinking, I wrapped my arms around her middle, pressing my forehead against her stomach. The contact calmed me like nothing else.

I'd never felt a calm so deep, so natural, on his anniversary. Josie was everything I needed.

"It's normal to miss him, Hunter," she said softly.

"After so many years?"

"Yes. And missing him doesn't mean you're

not strong. It means that you care about him. I'm sure he's proud of you. I'm proud of you. Not because of everything you've built and achieved, but because you're an amazing man."

I pulled her in my lap, cupping the back of her head, kissing her hard and deep. I was insatiable. I wanted to bury myself in this woman who not only accepted all parts of me but made *me* accept them too.

I didn't want anyone else by my side, ever. I couldn't even imagine it. I wanted Josie in my future with an intensity I'd never wanted anything else.

"Fuck, I want you. I need you, Josie. But I should shower first."

She wrinkled her nose playfully. "Wouldn't hurt. You *are* a bit stinky."

"Am I now?"

She shifted further back on my legs, as if determined to put distance between us. I clasped both her wrists with one hand. She gasped, looking up at me. Hooking an arm around her waist, I flipped us, pinning her against the mattress, blocking her legs by straddling her thighs. Her nightgown hiked up to her waist. She wasn't wearing panties.

I ran my fingers over her bare thighs, watching her skin become flushed and sensitized. Her breath turned ragged when I reached her waist, pushed the nightgown even higher, exposing her breasts. I touched the underside, then the upper part, drinking in the change in her body, the way her nipples turned hard.

She attempted to wiggle out, but she was grinning from ear to ear.

"What are you doing?" she asked.

"Haven't decided yet."

"Can I give you some suggestions?"

"Maybe."

She lifted her head, feathering her lips against mine. I captured her mouth, kissing her until she squirmed underneath me. For the first time in my entire life, I was genuinely, completely happy.

Usually, at least part of my mind focused on the drive to be more, to prove to myself I was capable of making those around me proud. But Josie was proud of me for the man I was, not the one I wanted to become. I was enough for her just the way I was.

The second I relaxed my grip on her hands, she pushed me off her, wiggling out, darting straight toward the bathroom. I chased after her. My grin was just as wide as hers when I caught up with her. I turned on the water. She half laughed, half shrieked when I carried her under the warm spray without removing our clothes.

"You're crazy," she said.

"I know."

After peeling the nightgown off her, I kissed her, pushing her against the tiles, only stopping long enough to get rid of my workout gear.

The water warmed our skin, but covered her scent, her taste. I pulled back, pouring shower gel in my palms.

"What are you doing?" she asked, pouting.

"Cleaning up for my wife."

She grinned, leaning against the tiles. "Now that's what I call a show."

She watched me intently while I soaped up. If I hadn't already been hard, this would have sealed the deal. I'd intended to take her to the bedroom, but I was too hungry for her. The second I turned off the water, I captured her mouth, kissing her until she arched her hips, trapping my cock between us.

"Fuuuuck." I groaned, pulling back a little, lowering a hand between us, sliding a finger in very slowly. She was so damn wet. I kissed her hard, showing her with my tongue and finger the way I planned to fuck her.

Hard, relentless. I wanted to give her everything I had.

"I'll make you come so hard tonight, Josie. With my fingers, my mouth. When I'm inside you."

"Hunter." The last syllable came out in a shaky tone.

When she gripped my shoulders, gyrating her hips against my hand, coming apart, I nearly lost it. I touched her until she rode out the orgasm, then pulled back, barely suppressing a smile when she gasped in protest.

I led us out of the shower, toweling her off first, then myself.

I wanted to prolong tonight as much as possible, to worship this woman the entire night. My entire life.

She climbed on the bed, lying back propped on her elbows, opening her thighs, tempting me. I kissed from her knees up her inner thighs before pushing her on her back completely, moving my mouth on her stomach, watching her, not wanting to break the eye contact, to miss any change in her expression.

I moved my mouth back down, positioning myself between her legs, nipping at her clit before giving her my tongue.

Josie cried out, pushing her hips up against my mouth. I was so hard that it was almost painful. I touched myself, squeezing tight, moving my hand up and down. And Josie was watching me.

"Fuck me. Please, Hunter. Please."

Pulling back, I grinned at her, moving upward, trailing kisses on her stomach, between her breasts, until we were face to face. I kissed her hard, gripping the base of my cock, teasing her clit with the tip, watching her come apart with every touch until her legs shook.

Then I drove inside her and nearly came just from feeling how tight and wet she was. I propped myself on my elbows, watching her, wanting to be connected to Josie in every way possible.

I skimmed my hand up and down the side of her body, feeling her soft skin, teasing her breasts with my thumb, pushing my pelvis against her clit with every thrust until my muscles protested. When she tightened around me even more, I couldn't hold back any longer.

I buried my head in the pillow, cupping her ass with both hands, lifting her up, driving hard inside her, then even harder, until we both went over the edge.

I was so in love with my wife I couldn't even see straight.

Chapter Twenty-Six
Josie

"Now that is how every week should end," I exclaimed, spinning around in my chair. Not that my week was over yet. I still had to send out two emails, and I wanted to read a contract for Monday, to get ahead of the week. I was only taking a short break to call my sister.

"Mine's been good too. I'm looking forward to a weekend all by myself. I'm treating myself to a spa visit."

"I like the sound of it."

"Just me and a good book. What about you?"

"Ah, me and my charming husband. Might sneak in some reading."

"If he can keep his hands off you long enough?"

"Something like that."

"Damn, sister. I'm jealous."

"Catch up again tomorrow? I still need to finalize a few things."

"Sure."

I'd planned my next hour to the last minute. What I didn't plan for? My husband showing up in my doorway twenty minutes later.

"Hunter, what are you doing here?"

"You've overworked yourself the entire week. I'm not letting you do that today."

"You're not *letting* me?"

"No."

"Think I need your permission?"

"Yes, you do, on our anniversary day. I'm taking my wife out to celebrate, and I won't accept anything other than *yes, right away* as an answer."

He was right, it was our two-month wedding anniversary.

My stomach did a somersault, especially when Hunter walked over to me, leaned over the desk, and gave me a kiss. My body hummed when Hunter pulled back, looking at me with warm eyes.

"Ready?"

I pushed him away playfully. "No, I'm not. You just burst into my office. I still had two emails…."

My voice faded at the glint in his eyes.

"Josie, you've been coming home late all week. I've missed you. No way am I letting you overwork yourself on Friday too."

I melted. No one had come to whisk me away from my office before. I mean, I would have probably tossed something at them if they'd tried… but now… all I wanted was to let him whisk me away.

I bit my lip. "One email?"

"I swear I'm going to take you in my arms and carry you out for the entire office to see."

"You're extra broody today."

"Thought you'd need the incentive."

"When is the reservation?"

"An hour."

"But that gives me no time to go home and get my ass out of this suit."

"Josie, if you get your ass out, we're gonna starve."

"I meant to change, you perv."

"And I just gave you an insight into what I plan to do. What can I say? I'm weak for you."

I closed my laptop and smoothed my hands down my skirt. "Okay. Where are we going?"

"The Lightning."

"Oooh… my favorite. Wait, are you trying to bribe me into something again?"

"No, I'm not."

He didn't meet my eye as he said it. What was he up to?

***

Hunter

I'd lied. Sort of. Bribing wasn't what I had in mind, but it hadn't been a coincidence that I'd booked a table at her favorite restaurant.

The second we were out of the building, her body language relaxed.

"You're always so tense when you're inside."

"This building just has bad vibes. Everyone inside is so permanently stressed out."

"You could work from home more often," I suggested.

"Nah, I need people around me."

"I could work from home on the same days. Keep you company. Clothing optional."

She giggled. "Surefire way to make sure I get nothing done."

"You're saying I'm irresistible?"

"You know you are."

I was counting on it. We ordered duck breast and red wine. She sipped from her glass, relaxing in the chair.

It was so easy to make her happy. I wanted to keep her smiling like this. I wanted to be the only one with the right to put that smile there.

"Two months?" she said happily. "Can't believe this. Mom always told me that it took her three weeks of dating Dad to realize he had all the qualities of her ideal man."

"Three weeks, that fast? What qualities should your ideal man have?"

"No clue. Haven't thought about it like that. It's a bit unfair to hold anyone to those expectations."

"Humor me."

"Okay. Let me think." She tapped her finger on her chin, then held it up. "Needs to be a family man. Should be kind and have a sense of humor. Should like kids. Better, actually—should want kids. Artistic ability is a plus, because I have none whatsoever. Being a good dancer would be another plus."

"I'd say I check a few of those criteria."

"You do make me laugh. You give excellent foot rubs. And you bring me hot chocolate when I'm in the reading nook."

"Sounds like I'm a catch." I wasn't the same man from a few months ago. Sharing my home and life with Josie had changed me in fundamental ways—how I saw life, what I wanted out of it. Now I looked forward to building a life with her, having kids.

"I can confirm that." She looked at me funny. "You're acting a little strange tonight."

Fucking hell, I was. My palms were sweaty. I had to know if she could imagine sharing her life with me after this ended, or if all she wanted was to stay friends.

And now I was a coward. Why couldn't I just bring myself to outright ask her? What if she said no? There'd be this barrier between us for the rest of the arrangement. Maybe she'd even want us to go back to being friends right away, so things wouldn't get even more muddled.

I couldn't even stand the thought of that. I kept touching my chest pocket. Right. Better to take the present out right now. I'd planned to wait until dessert, but at the rate I was going, I was clearly just going to give myself away.

"I got you something."

"Ooooh… show me."

I smiled, fueled by her enthusiasm, and

reached for the small jewelry box. She covered her mouth when I brought it out.

"Hunter...."

I opened the lid, and she sighed. It was a tennis bracelet with twelve gemstones.

"I saw this when we went shopping the other day."

I noticed her looking at this very item in the display.

"I know. Asked the vendor to save it for you."

"Hunter... I love it."

"Then let me put it on you."

She sighed again when I closed the clasp, admiring it. In a low whisper, she said, "You didn't have to spend so much for a fake anniversary."

And that twisted a knife right in my gut. If this still felt fake to her... I realized on the spot that I couldn't go on through the next years falling harder for this woman without knowing if there was a chance this felt as real to her as it did to me.

"This isn't fake, baby. Not for me. Things changed during our honeymoon. Even before that. You're the one for me, Josie. I love you, and I want to keep loving you for the rest of our lives."

Josie straightened her back, but kept her head bent, still looking at that bracelet. It felt as if a million years passed before she looked up.

"Hunter... what are you saying? That you want us to stay married after the three years pass?"

"We don't have to stay married. We can

just… take it slow. But I can't imagine letting you go."

"You're already thinking about divorcing me? Well, I won't let you."

My entire body felt lighter as the meaning of her words registered.

"You mean that, Josie?"

She nodded, breathing rapidly. I touched her hand over the table. She was shaking slightly. I pulled my chair closer to the table, cradling her legs with mine.

"Baby, let's get out of here. I want you all to myself." We weren't even halfway through dinner, but I just couldn't wait to be alone with her.

She nodded. I headed straight to the waiter to pay. I didn't even have the patience to wait for him to stop by our table.

The restaurant was only minutes away from home. I wasn't even sure how or when we got there.

I only trusted myself to touch Josie once we were inside. She was still shaking slightly.

"Josie, is everything okay?"

"Yes."

I touched her face with both hands, looking straight at her. "You're shaking."

"It's just… What if it doesn't work out? What if we just mess things up?" Her voice had dropped to a whisper. "I love you." She pressed her lips together, then hid her face in my chest. "Did I just scare you away with my crazy talk? Lie quickly if I did."

"No. I love you, Josie. So much." She pulled

back, enough that I could look straight at her. "And I'll show you, every way I can. I won't pretend that I know how to do this but trust me to figure this out next to you."

She smiled, playing with the collar of my shirt, pulling me closer. "I do."

Chapter Twenty-Seven
Josie

When I woke up the next morning, Hunter wasn't in bed. Where was he? His side of the mattress was cold, but I felt like being lazy for a few more minutes.

And speaking of last night... had it been real?

I hid my face in the pillow, grinning against the fabric. Yes, it had.

Hunter loved me.

I wanted to scream it at the top of my lungs, while also fearing that if I talked about it—or hell, even thought about it, I would lose it, somehow. Like I couldn't possibly be so lucky.

I'd arrived in New York with big dreams—had imagined my life before it had started, but the reality had been different. Difficult. Becoming a lawyer had taken every ounce of will and energy. Dating turned out to be more like an exercise in lowering my hopes and expectations, nothing like the romantic, laid-back dates of my high school days.

But now... holy hell. I had to tamp down my enthusiasm, and this bubbly feeling that my heart was so full, it couldn't fit into my chest. While showering, I pondered how I was going to spoil my man today. I could cook his favorite breakfast. Yeah, I could do that... and as a bonus, I could cook naked. I was sure he'd appreciate it, but I wasn't so sure if I'd get to finish said breakfast... He was known to jump my bones when I wore no clothes. It was like tickling a bear, but I couldn't help myself.

Still, I put on a robe. I'd drop it later, when I found an appropriate moment... for dramatic effect.

Hunter was walking around the living room, holding up his iPhone. I didn't like the frown on his face at all.

"What are you doing?" I asked.

He smiled, but it lacked the usual spark. "Taking some photos."

"I can see that, but why?"

"Just got a call from the case worker. Wants me to send her pictures of the house in the next ten minutes."

The bubbly feeling in my chest vanished instantly.

"Oh God. Okay. Umm... let me just gather some of the clothes lying around, and my makeup... or, I don't know. What should I do?"

"Nothing, I think. It's best if I just send her real snapshots."

"Why the ten-minute timeframe?"

"I suppose it's so I don't have time to fake anything."

"Okay."

I walked slightly behind him, watching his phone. Our privacy was being invaded.

Unfortunately, I knew for a fact that it was legal. I hated it.

And when Hunter said she also requested a picture of me, I felt dirty. After he emailed the case worker, I tried to pretend that this episode hadn't happened at all, and went straight to the kitchen, getting out some eggs and mushrooms.

I tried to remember if this request came at a certain step in the application, tried to guesstimate how long it was until they'd decline or approve his request for a green card.

Hunter stood next to me, cutting oranges.

"Josie, what's wrong?"

I sighed. Of course he'd pick up on it.

"Nothing's wrong. I… just… when you get your green card… will it change things between us?"

I felt his hand slide to my waist, and then he turned me around, practically pinning me against the counter with his hips.

"Nothing will change the fact that I'm head over heels in love with my wife. Look at me."

I brought my gaze up to his. "Okay."

"That's settled."

He moved his hands to my shoulders, pressing his thumbs in the sore spots just above my shoulder blades.

"You're so good at this," I whispered.

"You're tense."

"It's just… I wish this would be over already."

"I know, babe."

I turned around, continuing to chop

mushrooms.

"Let me cook you breakfast," he said.

"Nope. I want to spoil you."

He pinched my butt, nearly making me jump.

"Hunter! Keep your hands where they were before. I didn't say you could stop."

"Your wish is my command."

"That's not your usual MO."

"You're lucky you're so sexy this morning."

"I knew it. You only indulge me when I'm wearing short things."

"You've got me all figured out, wife."

The silly grin from earlier returned. Unexpectedly, he turned me around again before lifting me up on the counter.

"I think you need something more... substantial than a neck massage to relax."

"Another vacation?"

He laughed. "Not what I had in mind, but that works too. I'm really a bad influence."

"*And* you're good at organizing vacations."

"Whatever my lovely wife requests."

"You're being sweet. All prior evidence shows you do this when you want to bribe me into something or butter me up."

"Not at all."

"Hunter... is there something you want to tell me?"

"Is it too early to talk about kids?"

"Ours?"

"No, the neighbors'. Of course, ours."

"What about them?"

"I know that you want two."

Wow. How did he remember? And now that he'd planted the idea in my mind, my imagination ran away with it. All those muscles, the crystal blue eyes. He had some excellent genes to pass on.

I loved kids. Since I'd been a little girl, I'd wanted little girls of my own—braiding their hair, tucking them in at night. But for the first time, this felt more than just a dream. It felt real.

I laced my arms around his neck, shifting closer to the edge of the counter. Closer to him.

"You never said you wanted kids before."

"It wasn't something I consciously thought about. But with you... I want them. Two girls, or boys, I'm not picky. Before... I wasn't sure I could be a good father. I've spent so much of my life just focused on getting to the next step, giving it my best shot, that I didn't know if I was capable of anything more. But you did say I'm a good husband."

I grinned. "And I meant every word. Cross my heart."

"I can also learn to be a good father."

I nodded, too overwhelmed to say anything.

"When do you want to start trying?"

"Hunter, you do remember I said I want to make partner first, right?"

"Yes. But given all statistics, it can take time. Never hurts to start early. I like to go the extra mile."

That grin on his face... damn. I loved that I'd put it there. That I could make him light up like this.

I laughed as he bit the shell of my ear gently. "First, we need to talk about that celebratory vacation. Whisk me away. I don't even want to know where we're going."

He pulled back abruptly. "You're giving me permission to surprise you?"

"Yes."

"Half the fun is you giving me shit about it."

"If you insist, I can always fight you right until we board the plane."

Hunter slid his hands under my ass, lifting me up. I yelped, right before clenching my knees at his sides. He winced. Right. My yoga routine was helping with my flexibility, but not my instincts. I hadn't gotten the hang of wrapping my legs gracefully around him, but I was working on it. For now, I was awkwardly clinging to him like a monkey. Hunter tried to rearrange my arm around his neck. I had a hunch that I was half strangling him.

"Hey, watch the bracelet. A certain someone gave it to me."

I'd slept with it and showered with it and didn't intend to take it off at all. I absolutely loved it.

"And this someone… what exactly do you feel for him?"

"I think he's the best man. And I love him."

His grin softened, turning into a warm smile. Feeling all those hard abs pressing against my belly and his strong arms wrapped around me was doing things to me. My entire body reacted to him. My nipples pebbled, and a familiar ache pulsed between my thighs. I kissed his neck, drawing my tongue in little circles just above his clavicle.

"Forgot about breakfast?" he whispered on a chuckle. Ah, I totally had. All I could think about was indulging in this perfect, gorgeous man.

"I always forget how devious you are."

"Always happy to remind you."

He shifted me a little lower. I gasped when I realized he was hard already. How could he want me so much?

It hadn't sunk in yet. My husband loved me. I was living a life I hadn't even dared dream about. Part of me still didn't dare to hope too much. But God, the way he held me, the way he looked at me. As if I was more precious to him than anything else. How could I not hope?

"Then what are you waiting for, husband?"

Chapter Twenty-Eight
Hunter

Two weeks later, we were lying on the beach in the Bahamas. Josie couldn't take too much time off, so we were here only for an extended weekend—Friday to Monday—but I intended to make every minute count. Josie was lying on her belly while I smeared sunscreen on her back. She insisted on applying it religiously.

"I don't remember you being such a huge fan of sunscreen."

"Now I'm addicted to it. I think it has something to do with the person applying it." She looked at me over her shoulder.

"Glad I'm contributing."

"Always."

I leaned over, biting one ass cheek. She winced, almost falling off the lounge chair. I steadied her, laughing as I straightened.

"Hunter! You can't scare me like that."

"Yes, I can. You're cute, all puzzled."

Shaking her head, she let out a soft hmpf before resuming her position on her belly. She got out a book too, laying it in front of her. I pinched her arm.

"What are you doing?"

"Scoot over, wife. I want to read too."

"Now?"

"Yes. Otherwise, you'll tell me that it's so good I have to read it too. You keep telling me what happens while you read it though. Spoiling everything."

She laughed, throwing her head back. "I do, don't I? I'm a terrible fiction reader. Nonfiction comes so much easier to me. Probably the lawyer in me just needs to dissect everything I read."

She made space for me, but we were a little crammed on the lounge chair. Our sides were touching. Total unexpected perk.

"We're gonna get weird tan lines," she said.

"I don't care."

"I do."

I brought my mouth to her ear, tugging at it. "No one's going to see them but me."

She laughed, leaning into me even more. When it became clear neither of us would do any reading in this awkward position, I sat up, allowing her to be more comfortable. I couldn't believe the beauty of this place: the clear, turquoise water, the green foliage around us. The smell of salt water and rush of waves instantly relaxed me.

"You're reading a lot for someone who's obsessed with trying out everything the resort has to offer."

"Are you saying that you're up for skydiving?" she asked, batting her eyelashes.

Fucking hell. That escalated quickly.

"Absolutely not."

She kept batting her eyelashes. I sensed a trap.

"How about Jet Skiing?" she suggested.

"I can be talked into that."

Josie grinned, shimmying a little on the lounge chair. "Ha! I'm good."

"What do you mean?"

"I knew that if I brought up skydiving, you'd agree to Jet Skiing."

I bit her earlobe again, fondling her ass just so she didn't get even more ideas.

"You're playing with fire, wife."

"I know, but it's so much fun that I can't stop."

I tickled her before she even took her next breath. She shrieked with laughter. I drank up every sound. I enjoyed everything with her: the quiet times and the adventures. Josie made me feel whole in a way I'd never even thought was possible.

***

I was completely tired when I went into the office the following week, but I had to get my act together fast, because I had a mountain of work ahead of me.

Cole also reminded me that the rest of my cousins were dropping by for lunch.

"It's a council this time," he added. More reason to wake up.

Ryker, Tess, and Skye were chatting animatedly when we joined them in the meeting room. We looked over spreadsheets with the funds the Ballroom Galas had gathered so far, brainstorming about potential new activities we could integrate throughout the evening, especially since not everyone wanted to dance. I was in such a good mood that I was willing to entertain even the more... extravagant ideas.

"Someone's happy," Tess remarked. "Second honeymoon went smoothly, by the looks of it."

"It was great. Didn't even want to come back."

"So, now that Josie knows how you feel about her, is she giving the name change more thought?" Skye asked.

"Haven't discussed it."

Tess laughed, drumming her fingers on the desk. "Told you he didn't bring it up. I think he's afraid Josie will stick to her guns."

Skye shrugged.

"My money's still on Hunter convincing her," Ryker said.

"You've talked about this?" I asked, perplexed.

"Just... exchanged opinions," Skye said.

I couldn't help but notice that Cole wasn't his usual self. He was quiet, not joining in on the fun. I didn't want to ask him if anything was wrong in front of my cousins, not wanting to put him on the spot in case he had any kind of troubles.

After everyone left, I asked, "Cole, is anything wrong?"

"I didn't want to bring this up during your first day back, but your case worker was here in the building last Friday, asking questions."

I felt as if someone had just thrown cold water in my face.

"What kind of questions?"

"About you and Josie… your marriage, your life before. The days before you announced the engagement. Things like that."

"What did everyone tell her?"

"I wasn't there to hear what they answered, but I hope she was satisfied."

Fucking hell. What was going on? Had she gone to Josie's office too?

Chapter Twenty-Nine
Josie

After the trip, I came into the office with a big grin. Regular vacations, I'd decided, were definitely going to be a part of my life from now on. I mean, what was better than spending hours relaxing? It didn't hurt that I had a sexy man at my side to fill all those hours with.

I felt reborn and ready to take on the world. I had an appointment with my boss first thing. He'd emailed yesterday evening and asked me to come by his office today.

Hunter and I had made a bet what it would be about. He said it would be about the promotion. While I loved his confidence in me, promotions were not usually awarded this time of the year. I was sure this was about a new case.

My good mood plummeted when I entered his office. I immediately sensed something was wrong. Craig wasn't his usual self. His shoulders were tense, his eyes pinned to the desk instead of me. Shit, what if Hunter *was* right and this was about the promotion after all? Only I wasn't the one getting it?

"Josie, take a seat," he said.

I pushed a strand of hair behind my ear,

taking my notepad and pen out the way I always did during my meetings with Craig, using the familiar routine to calm myself down.

"What is this about?" I finally asked.

"It was brought to my attention that you've had a run-in with the immigration services."

I gripped the pen so tight that my fingers went numb. My mind worked frantically, but I couldn't come up with a good enough solution except to say the truth and work from there.

"Yes."

"I would have appreciated to hear that from you."

"It's a personal matter. It didn't interfere with my work at all."

"It's a legal matter. Personal or not, you should have told me."

I doodled with the pen to keep myself from tapping my foot against the floor.

"I can tell you now that everything will be cleared."

We hadn't heard anything from the case worker after sending the pictures, which was reassuring.

"I'm afraid this isn't so simple."

"What do you mean?"

"I mean that your case worker was here, asking questions. She spoke to me and a few of your colleagues. I can't have that."

Breathe in. Breathe out. Keep calm. Breathe in.

No, no, no. This couldn't happen. I had no

idea how I kept on talking.

"But this is a personal matter."

"That is, I am afraid, of little consequence. Josie, it pains me to do this, but I have to let you go. Word will spread, and I can't allow people to associate these kinds of subterfuge with us. It wouldn't reflect well on me."

"This is not fair."

I kept my gaze fixed on Craig now. I was so angry that I could barely control the tone of my voice.

"The case worker was just asking questions. You can't fire me because of this."

Craig's eyes flashed. "You know I can."

Unfortunately, he was right. Legally, there was nothing stopping him.

"After this, you would have no chance of making partner here anyway."

I stood up. "Really? I have done exemplary work since I started as an intern here. You haven't had one single complaint about me, ever."

"Don't make this even more difficult for yourself. And a word of warning, when anyone calls to ask for references, I will have to be frank about this. I can't afford anyone suing me for withholding information further down the road."

"Your legal obligation is to report on my work."

It dawned on me slowly what this all meant. No one would hire me right away. Craig telling them this would give the impression he thought I was guilty, not just caught up in a bureaucratic process.

"You're young and smart. You'll figure everything out."

I'd worked my whole life only for my entire career to just be taken away from me?

I'd sacrificed so much, dedicated everything to this. I blinked rapidly, because my eyes were burning and I wouldn't give anyone the satisfaction of seeing me cry.

"My decision is final."

"We'll see what HR has to say about it."

"They've already been informed."

"What?"

"As of today, you no longer work for Marks & Partners."

I was stunned. For the first time ever, I had no comeback. Nothing to say in my defense. I felt so utterly defeated that I wasn't sure I would be able to make it out of the building without having a good cry first. What would I tell my parents?

They'd sacrificed so much to help me through law school, and I'd just trampled on all of their hard work.

I went through the motions for the next hour. Down to HR, signing papers. Up again, packing my belongings in the box they gave me. It all took no time at all. No one gave two shits that I was leaving.

I had such difficulties breathing when I walked out of the building, I thought I was going to suffocate. The October chill wrapped around me like an icy blanket. It was raining too.

New York had never looked more depressing to me. But I was going to get through this—I'd always managed to see the positive part. But for the life of me, I couldn't be upbeat now. I hadn't just lost my job. My entire career as a lawyer was in danger. For the first time in years, all I wanted to do was wallow.

Once at home, I read for a few hours, then took the panna cotta Amelia had brought yesterday as a welcome-home treat, filled the Jacuzzi with water and bubbles, slid inside it, and shut out the outside world. I'd break the news to my parents later... and to Hunter.

Now, I simply wanted to focus on the warm water and the delicious sweet treat. What was it about sugar that made any situation a little better?

I knew there was a scientific explanation, but I liked to think that this exquisite panna cotta carried Amelia's warmth and calmness.

The water was almost cold when I heard movement around me.

I took out a headphone, peering at the door. Sure enough, Hunter was propped against it, his eyes dark, his mouth set in a beautiful smile.

"Should've told me you were home already, wife. Would've gladly ditched the last meeting for you."

I placed both earbuds on the floor, and the plate. Hunter's eyes widened when he saw it.

"Holy shit. Was that all the panna cotta? What's wrong, babe?"

"Got fired."

In a matter of seconds, Hunter crouched in front of the tub, until he was at the same eye level.

"Babe, I'm so sorry. What happened?"

"They caught wind of our run-in with the immigration officer."

"Fuck. Cole told me today she's been asking questions at my office."

"She did the same at mine... and, well, long story short, they don't want anyone even remotely connected to a sham marriage suspicion working there."

"That's bullshit. They can't just fire you. I'll have my lawyers talk to their CEO directly."

"No."

"Babe, it's my fault."

"It's not."

"I asked you to—"

"And I said yes. I'm not going to blame you for a decision *I* made. I don't want to go back to a workplace where I'm not welcome. Even if they don't fire me, they'd give me less cases, refuse to promote me. Anything to make me quit eventually."

He swallowed, rocking back and forth. "Okay, then we'll—"

"Hunter... I don't want... I'm not in the mood to brainstorm about solutions."

He sat on the edge of the tub, looking straight into my eyes.

"How can I be useful?"

"You could distract me. I mean, the music

and the panna cotta did a decent job, but they're nowhere as good as you."

A sly smile popped up on his face.

"I see. Well, that's something I can definitely help with. I do need more precise instructions though. How exactly do you want me to distract you?"

"Foot massage?"

"Whole-body massage?"

"Sounds promising."

He slid closer, planting a quick smooch on my lips.

"Whatever the lady wants."

I grinned. "Strip, then."

He stood up, doing a ridiculous twirl (with a delicious ass wiggle) before turning to face me.

"Start with the shirt."

"Yes, ma'am."

He started unbuttoning his shirt with exquisite slowness, torturing me. I watched, enraptured, sighing. I'd never get enough of him. Ever.

"I mean... just look at these muscles. Now, pants off, Caldwell."

"I aim to please."

Once he was completely naked, he jumped in the tub, splashing water everywhere.

"Hey," I protested. "I didn't say you could get in."

"Tough luck, beautiful. Because I'm done watching you. I want to touch you. Kiss you."

He kissed me so deep that I hummed against

his mouth.

"We'll get through this together, I promise."

Chapter Thirty
Josie

For the next few weeks, I tried to gather my faculties, to make an action plan. I didn't tell my parents the real reason I'd been fired, just that it hadn't worked out. They had been so understanding that I felt even more guilty about everything.

I was so grumpy that I could barely stand myself. I wasn't being fair to Hunter, who was so damn patient and sweet, it just added to my guilt.

When he wasn't trying to cheer me up (whole-body massage being his favorite technique), he was offering to get me another job. But that made me feel useless for some reason. That wasn't how I wanted to build my career. A few of my colleagues had come into the firm because a higher-up had twisted my boss's arm, and they were always treated like second-class citizens. Even when they were competent, and even after years of proving themselves, others still whispered behind their back. I didn't want that following my entire career.

"You sure you don't want to come with me?" Hunter asked. He was going to Boston for three days, and had insisted I go with him and relax, since I didn't have any plans, but I didn't want to. All I was

LAYLA HAGEN

doing was relaxing. I wanted to be productive.

"No, I'm good. Besides, you'll be busy all day."

"Yes, but I'd be yours in the evening."

"I'm grouchy all the time, Hunter. I'd just bring you down too."

"You're sure? Grouchy or not, I'd love to have you there."

"I'm sure."

He pressed his lips together but didn't say anything. Damn. Lately I was saying no to everything my man was suggesting. I'd pull myself together by the time he came back.

It was only the day he returned that I remembered why he'd gone to Boston at all: to negotiate a huge deal for his company. It was an important meeting, and I'd just completely forgotten. No wonder he'd wanted me to go with him, help him relax in the evenings.

I was a *terrible* wife. How could I have forgotten? He'd mentioned it only about a million times over the last two weeks, and even in the Bahamas. But I'd been too lost in my head to put two and two together.

I waited by the door, willing to do whatever it took to make it up to him. My man came in looking exhausted. But damn, even tired he worked that suit like no one else.

I wrapped my arms around his neck, rising on my tiptoes and giving him one hell of a smooch. He smiled against my lips.

"What's this for?" he murmured.

"Umm... part of my wicked plan to make up for forgetting about how huge a deal Boston was."

He skimmed his hands down to my waist, pressing me against him. "I like that plan."

"Why didn't you remind me?"

"I didn't want to push you. You have a lot on your plate as it is."

"Yes, but still. How did it go?"

"It was productive. We didn't strike a deal, though. They're tough negotiators, but so am I."

"And don't I know it." I took his hand, drawing him deeper inside the house.

"Where are we going?"

"Somewhere I can put my wicked plan into action."

"The bedroom?"

"Close. The Jacuzzi."

He took me by the waist, walking in tandem. We probably looked ridiculous, trying to walk at the same pace while he was a head higher than me, but I loved the way he held me, as if he wanted as much contact as possible.

"What did you do?"

"I've been looking up jobs online and applied to some."

"That's my Josie, kicking ass. But why won't you let me help?"

"I'm just... I'm not sure."

"Before... all this, the engagement and the marriage, you used to tell me exactly what went through your mind. Now I get the feeling you're filtering things. Why?"

My man was throwing all sorts of difficult questions at me, and I honestly had no answer. He did have a point, though.

"I don't know."

"I don't like that there's a part of you I can't reach anymore. I don't want you to hold back with me."

I pouted. "I'm sorry. I'll try to be more open."

He kissed the side of my neck, feathering his lips up to my ear. "Good. Because I want my wife back in her sunny disposition. You've been down long enough."

Ouch. He was right, but still… *ouch*.

I wanted to be a better wife; at the moment, I just wasn't sure how to go about it.

I didn't sleep well that night, just tossed and turned for hours, thinking about us, about why I was now holding my cards to my chest.

As a friend, I'd talked his ear off about everything (including details he hadn't wanted to know, I was sure of it). As his wife, it was as if I was afraid he might love me less if I laid out all my fears and insecurities.

When we woke up in the morning, we discovered the pipes in the kitchen had broken. As if we didn't already have enough on our plate.

"This is a mess," he said, just as he was about to leave for work.

"I agree. I'll call a plumbing company right

away, but we might have to move into a hotel while they're working."

"Let's do that."

"I'll pack us things for a few days. I can manage everything before we have to go to the function tonight."

"You're amazing. By the way, I'm meeting a lawyer friend today. I can ask him if he has an opening at his firm."

"It's fine. I'm going to send more applications today."

"I can ask a headhunter friend to arrange—"

"Hunter, it's okay. Really."

"I just want to help." He sounded resigned. Damn. I was doing it again… pushing him away. I fiddled with my thumbs, biting the inside of my cheek. I wasn't used to being at odds with him. I'd been irritated for weeks, and I just couldn't seem to be able to get out of that state of mind.

"Have a great day," I said, in an attempt to smooth things over, but he just shook his head.

After he left, I went through my usual routine. I also called a professional firm to deal with the pipes. They arrived within the hour and assessed the damage, informing me that repair work would most likely last four days. The hotel next to the venue where the event tonight took place was fully booked, so I made reservations at a hotel near Hunter's office, packed our bags and moved us there all before lunch.

In the afternoon, I started preparing for the function. I wasn't as excited as usual. I was a social butterfly, always had been, but I dreaded having to consciously keep the conversations from circling to my job... or lack thereof. Since I'd been five, I'd known I wanted to be a lawyer. I'd worked so hard for my career that without it, I felt as if part of my personality had been ripped away.

Hunter arrived at the hotel shortly before we were supposed to leave and came into the room as I put the finishing touches on my hair.

"You look gorgeous," he said.

He stood behind me, glancing in the mirror. My husband was beautiful no matter what he wore, but Hunter in a tuxedo definitely took the cake. I was happy to see him smiling again after the way we'd parted this morning.

"I like getting ready for these functions. Even though it takes me so long. Good thing I have some time on my hands now."

I'd spent two hours dressing up, applying makeup and doing my hair, but now I wanted to leave the hotel even less than a few minutes ago. Biting my lip, I looked at him while he was putting on his tie. When he glanced at his phone, informing me that our driver had arrived, I finally gathered my courage.

"Hunter... would you be terribly upset if I don't come?"

He turned toward me, his eyes brimming with worry. "Are you sick?"

"No, it's just that... I don't feel like making small talk or answering any job-related questions."

"Babe, friends of mine from law firms will be there. I can introduce you—"

"I don't want that," I snapped, then buried my face in my hands. "I'm sorry I'm snapping at you. But I already told you this. It's not how I want to get a job."

"Josie, I don't want to push, but I don't know what to do. You need to help me out here."

His voice was tight, betraying impatience. I looked up, swallowing.

"What do you mean?"

"Every time I come up with solutions, you just shut me down. I want to be there for you, but you just won't let me. I feel like I'm standing outside a glass room, trying to fight my way in. I have to go. If you don't feel like coming with me tonight, I'll just go alone."

"Hunter... wait. We should talk."

He stared. "Now, you want to talk?"

It was clear that he needed it. I had no idea this had been so hard on him. I'd been too lost in my head to pay attention.

"I have to go. The car is here." He just shook his head again, walking with quick steps toward the door. I'd forgotten the car was waiting.

"Hunter... do you want to talk when you get back? Should I stay up?"

"I don't know, Josie. Do what's best for you."

I swallowed hard. Hunter walked out of the room, and then I was all alone with my thoughts.

What had he meant, *Do what's best for you*?

Okay. I needed to get out of the hotel right away and clear my mind. I'd drive myself crazy if I just waited until he returned. These functions usually lasted until well after midnight. But where to go? I didn't want to be by myself, honestly. I debated calling my sister, but she was miles away and couldn't just jump on a plane and come here. I wished she could.

I called Tess instead. She had a cold, so she was sitting out this event.

"Hey... um, are you up for receiving a visit?"

"Holy shit. Don't like your voice."

I barked out a laugh. "Neither do I."

"What happened?"

"I'm not even sure."

"Right. That calls for some major girl time. Don't worry, I've got everything you need."

"I'll uber to your place right away," I said.

"I'll have everything ready."

I loved Tess so much. So much.

I arrived at her apartment half an hour later and walked straight into her open arms. Her nose was a little red from her cold.

"Come on. I'll take care of you, and you can tell me what happened. If you want to. Ugh, that's a glare. So, not going to talk about anything tonight. Just one tiny question."

I laughed. "Tess...."

"Just one. I promise."

"Go ahead."

"You can answer with yes or no, and I won't

pry any further. Will just motivate the rest of the family into action. Does anyone need their ass kicked? Yes or no?"

"Yes. I think *I* need my ass kicked."

Chapter Thirty-One
Hunter

I'd never wanted to leave a function as badly I wanted to bail on this one. I was going through the motions, counting down the minutes until it was acceptable to make up an excuse and leave.

My head wasn't in the game, but luckily, I'd done all the work when I'd invited the guests. Now all I had to do was smile and emcee.

After securing the mic back in its place, I stepped down from the stage, mingling with the crowd.

"Caldwell, where's that pretty wife of yours?" an elderly man asked. Greg was in his late sixties and a little in love with Josie. Weren't they all?

"Wasn't feeling well."

"So what are you doing here, young man? Wouldn't leave that pretty lady alone if I were you."

"I won't be here long."

"I hope to see her at the next one."

I swallowed hard, trying to mask my unease with a smile. So help me God, I hoped so too. I didn't want to be here without her—whispering in my ear incessantly, making me laugh, blushing when I responded with a sinful promise. Fuck, why had I even come here at all?

Sure, gathering funds was important, because that money wasn't going to raise itself on its own. But fixing things with Josie was more important. Truthfully, I'd needed the time out because my temper was about to flare out of control. I was determined never to let that happen, no matter how frustrated I was. My temper and no-bullshit attitude were for the business, not my wife. Even if we were fighting, even if I felt as if she was drifting away and I didn't know how to keep her with me. I needed to go back to Josie. Right away.

Celia was the head organizer, since none of my cousins could make it tonight. I found her next to the bidding box and pulled her to one side.

"Celia, I need to leave early tonight."

"Hunter... at least stay until everyone puts in their bids."

"They won't even notice I'm here. I'm trusting you to hold the fort."

She pressed her lips together but didn't argue. "Anything I can do to help with whatever emergency you have going on?"

"No, I'm the only one who can fix this."

Of course, getting out was damn difficult.

Half a dozen donors stopped to chitchat, asking about a million things I didn't care about. The longer I lingered, the more desperate I grew. I shouldn't have come, no matter how needed I was here. Marriage was about working on things together, and I needed to let Josie know how much I believed that.

Once I finally managed to climb into a cab, I urged the driver to move as fast as possible.

I had that sinking feeling that I'd messed up more than I'd realized, and that I'd already waited too long to head to the hotel.

I expected to find her in the room, but she wasn't there. I froze in the doorway when I saw the bed was empty. Maybe she was at the hotel spa?

I called the reception to ask where that was.

"Mr. Caldwell, the spa facility is closed at this hour."

"Okay. Okay." I ran a hand through my hair, and before I lost my nerve added, "Have you seen my wife tonight?"

"She left a few hours ago."

"Right. Thank you."

My heart was beating so wildly that I could barely hear my voice around the pounding pulsing in my eardrums. Where had she gone? I called Josie the next second, but heard her ringtone coming from the bathroom. Her phone was there next to the sink. I breathed out in relief. If she'd forgotten her phone, it meant she'd just gone out, not that she'd left.

I stayed up late, waiting for her, but eventually fell asleep. When I woke up, the bed was untouched.

Damn, she hadn't returned? I leaned against the TV console, closing my eyes, trying to gather my thoughts, to focus, to not jump to conclusions. The sound of my phone ringing snapped me out of my thoughts.

It was Tess.

"Tess, hi."

"Morning. So, Josie's here. She came last night and we both fell asleep in front of the TV. She's still sleeping. Thought I'd tell you before you panic."

"I was just starting to. I'm coming to your place right away."

Chapter Thirty-Three
Hunter

When the Uber pulled up in front of Tess's building, I practically jumped out of the car and skidded up the stairs. She lived on the first floor.

Holding my breath, I knocked at the door. Josie opened it. She was wearing shorts and a tank top. Her hair was braided on one side.

"Morning," I said.

"Sorry. I came here last night and just fell asleep."

"Tess told me. Here is your phone."

"Thanks."

"I'm sorry about last night, Josie."

"I'm sorry too."

"Let's go to the hotel, and we can talk about everything."

"I was thinking... Tess needs help packing some boxes for their online orders. I could stay here for a few days and help her out."

I looked at her, stunned. "What?"

"We're staying at the hotel, and it's just that... I'm afraid we'll be snappy with each other in close quarters. I'm trying to gather my thoughts."

"What thoughts, exactly?"

"You were right in the things you said… I did freeze you out. I don't even know why I did that, or how to stop it. I'm sorry." She cast her gaze to the floor. My gut clenched. "I'm afraid I'm going to lose you, not just as my husband, but as my best friend too. You think we were better off being just friends?"

What?

I had no idea how I could ever be in the same room with her and not want to kiss the living daylights out of her. Sure, the past few weeks had been a little rough, but nothing we couldn't work out.

"Why can't we be both? That's what we've been doing until now. Just friendship? No fucking way. I love you, Josie."

I couldn't do it. It would be impossible to stop loving this woman the way I did. It was far more than friendship.

She pressed her forehead against the door. "Hunter…."

"What? You just thought I'd step back and say yes, ma'am?"

The corners of her mouth tilted up. "Not really your style, but a girl can hope. If you're worried about the immigration officer, I'll still play my part. We can still go to events together, and—"

"I don't give a fuck about the immigration officer right now. Listen to me, Josie. I love you. And I know you love me too."

I clasped the doorframe, terrified that she might not.

"I do, of course I love you, Hunter. I just… I

think you should give some thought to what I said. And Tess really does need help, or she and Skye will never finish everything. You know how they are, thinking they can do ten things at the same time, and then they overwork themselves."

The way she cared for everyone around her just made me fall more for her. Instead of leaving, I stepped closer, pulling her to me.

"I'll go," I whispered. "Just let me hold you for a bit."

Fuck, how she melted in my arms. I inhaled her sweet scent, and for one full minute let myself believe that my wife was going home with me.

My heart was about to beat out of my chest. I wanted to push, but this wasn't the moment. I loved her too much. I refused to stop fighting, and I wouldn't.

***

I walked out of the building but didn't leave. Every instinct told me to knock on the door again. I couldn't shake the feeling that if I left, this divide between us would grow, but I was afraid that if I pushed, I'd make things worse.

I'd been there for her through highs and lows for so many years, and now I couldn't, and it was killing me. I wanted to make her happy, but for the first time, I was completely at a loss as to how to do that. I sat on a bench for a long time, and would've probably stayed longer, but Mick called.

"Hunter, can you come over later today to give me a hand with the thermostat? It's giving me headaches again."

"Sure, I'll be there in about an hour."

Better to be surrounded by Mick and Amelia, two people I respected and loved, than alone with my own thoughts.

When I arrived at Mick and Amelia's apartment, Ryker was there too, to my surprise.

"Hunter, long time no see," Ryker greeted me.

"Hey! What are you doing here?"

"Mick asked for help with the thermostat."

Which begged the question… why was I there?

"Right. Is it working now?"

Mick nodded. "I think Ryker and I sorted it out. But you can double-check. I have some beers ready after that. We can watch the basketball game."

He pointed to the couch and the enormous TV in front of it. Mick had what he liked to call a man cave in one of the bedrooms. In addition to the TV, he also had a workstation where he tinkered with wood.

I inspected the thermostat for a few minutes before joining Ryker and Mick on the couch. "Everything is looking good."

Footsteps caught my attention. Amelia joined us, smiling. "Boys, thank you for fixing the thermostat."

Something was very wrong. That was the only

reason she'd ever show up here. The man cave was her least favorite place in the apartment. "So dark in here. It stresses me out," she always said.

Ryker frowned. We exchanged glances. He was just as miffed about it as I was.

When Amelia zeroed in on me, it quickly became obvious that *I* was what was wrong.

"Hunter, I've heard some worrying news."

"How?"

"Tess brought me up to date."

"Right." Of course she had. I glanced to Mick, who was focusing on the TV as if he didn't want to miss one second of the commercials.

"I take it you didn't really need my help?"

Amelia was the one who answered. "Well, no, Ryker was already here. But then Tess said you'd been sitting on a bench in front of her building for a while, so clearly, *you* needed *our* help."

"Knew the thermostat was the easiest way to get you here," Mick said.

I chuckled, because it was true. Whenever Mick called to ask for my help with anything, I always pitched in.

Ryker nodded. "Listen to whatever Mom has to say. She always knows best."

Amelia looked at her youngest through narrowed eyes. "So, if I know best, why do you never listen when I tell you to stop acting like you don't ever want to bring a girl home?"

Ryker shook his head. "Walked into that one on my own. No one to blame but myself."

"You'll figure it out, Hunter," Amelia said gently. "Just give yourself time. Give Josie some time. You can come here after work for dinner if you don't want to go home."

"Wait a second, whenever you think I need advice, you talk my ear off, but all Hunter gets is *you'll figure it out*? I feel like a second-class citizen right now."

"Don't be so dramatic. You two are different." Winking, Amelia patted his shoulder. "I need to tailor my advice accordingly."

The game began shortly afterward, and we all watched in silence.

But I wasn't really watching. I was… figuring things out.

I couldn't believe I'd left for the event that evening. I should have stayed home and been her anchor, the way she'd been mine that night when she'd found me on the treadmill. She'd just been there for me. How could I have left? How could I have thought that was what she needed? We challenged each other because we both had fiery personalities. We were bound to clash from time to time. I loved that fiery, funny woman. She added so much to my life. I'd learned to enjoy life every day, not just the big achievements. Learned to try out new things and let go.

I hung on to this thought, feeling like I'd made a major breakthrough. By the time the game was over, I was feeling one step closer to victory.

Chapter Thirty-Two
Josie

The best part about spending time with Tess? She was so bubbly and full of energy that it was catchy. And we had *so much* work to do. How she'd thought she'd finish everything by herself was beyond me.

On Sunday, we had our very first semi healthy meal—chicken salad with chips and guacamole on the side.

"You still haven't said one word about Hunter. Oh, okay. You're still glaring when I bring him up. More chips?"

"I'll never say no to that."

"I'm thinking, we need to shake things up a bit," Tess said once we'd finished our salads, placing her hands on her hips and scrunching her face up in concentration.

"Uh-oh. Should I be afraid?"

"What? Not at all. When have my plans ever been dangerous?"

"Umm… when haven't they been dangerous?"

"Girls' night out?"

I shook my head. "Your cold is still not one

hundred percent over."

Tess continued undeterred. "Girls' night in?"

I laughed. "I forgot you never give up."

"Ha! Nothing is impossible if I'm making it my mission, and I totally am."

I smiled, despite myself. Tess did her nickname justice. She *was* a damn hurricane. And camping here, in her apartment, I felt bad.

"Tess, have you ever just... felt lost? Like you're not sure what's best?"

"You're talking about your career?"

"No, about Hunter. I love him. So much. I'm just afraid that I'm mucking things up with him. Being his friend was always so easy... I'm not used to things being strained between us."

"Is there something more that you're afraid of?"

I swallowed, deciding to own up to all my fears. Tess would give it to me straight.

"I'm afraid that maybe we got carried away, what with the marriage and living together, but that we're first and foremost friends... I mean, if he hadn't needed my help, we would have stayed just friends forever."

"Ha! No, you wouldn't have. You two always had this *spark* I loved. And of course, you're going to have growing pains. Honestly, I think that's true of any marriage or relationship. Everything happened so fast between the two of you, though. I can understand that you're afraid. Just take your time. And as for your question... Josie, I'm human. Of course, I've had my moments of doubt and uncertainty. After Dad left, Mom was depressed for months. She tried to hide it, but it didn't work. And for a while, we just let her do it, thinking it would pass. I mean, we were kids, didn't know any better. But then after a while, we realized we had to help. Every time we saw her disappear into herself, instead of leaving her alone, we'd take her out and about and just be silly."

"How could you do it?"

Tess gave me a sad smile. "Don't tell anyone, but... I actually hoped my dad would come back. Hoped right until we found out he married that woman. Cole and Ryker were super sweet when they found out. They hugged me and said they'd never leave us. And then we took Mom for ice cream. But enough about that. Let's focus on you. I just had an idea. How about some girly activities? Facials, painting our nails? Just messing around? Take your pick. And because your need is greater than mine, I'm also willing to donate my bathtub."

I grinned at Tess. I just loved her.

Later that evening, I did something I'd never *voluntarily* done before: went for a run.

After twenty minutes, I stopped. Since I wasn't a regular runner, I couldn't go on for too long, but I was feeling reborn. This felt amazing. I couldn't believe I'd been firmly in the *I'm not a runner* camp for so long.

In the months I'd lived with Hunter, I'd given his treadmill a few tries, and gave up because I was bored stiff. But I could get used to running outside. Tess lived near a park , and breathing in fresh air, being surrounded by greenery gave me a much-needed boost of energy. More than that, my mind was clearer during the run.

I loved feeling productive again. It also felt good to finally have a plan, and it didn't include begging anyone for a job. From now on, I was going to bust my ass for myself. I planned to open my own place. My experience practically spoke for itself, and I was confident that I could convince two other colleagues to join me.

My specialty was corporate law, and theirs were family and estate law, so we could cover a broad spectrum between us.

Why didn't I feel good? I missed Hunter like crazy. I hadn't seen him at all since he'd showed up on Tess's doorstep two days ago, and I had Hunter withdrawals.

I grinned when a message from Hunter popped up on my phone. Was he thinking about me as often as I was thinking about him?

Hunter: I need a friend's advice. Can I call you?

Josie: Sure.

He called the next second. I leaned against a lamppost, just smiling at the phone like a lunatic for a few seconds before answering.

"Hello, beautiful."

"Hey. How can I help?"

"What?"

"You said you need a friend's help."

"That was a ruse. I just wanted to make sure you'd answer."

I laughed, cradling my phone with both hands. "I wouldn't ignore your calls."

"Didn't want to take any chances."

"Forgot how devious you can be. So... you have me where you want me. What now?"

"If I had you where I wanted you, you'd be home right now, in our bed, underneath me. We'd be naked. You'd be calling out my name. But we're not there. Yet."

I was glad I was leaning against that lamppost, because my knees had weakened a little. My entire body reacted to his sinful voice, to that vivid image he'd painted.

"Hunter—"

"No, no, no. Don't finish that sentence. Sounds like you want to reprimand me, and you haven't even heard what I want to say."

"Okay, let's hear it."

"I want us to talk every day for one hour."

"One hour?"

"It's not negotiable."

"So what are you going to do if I say no?"

"I'll come by Tess's house and throw stones at your window until you open it and talk to me."

"You're taking devious to a whole new level." I laughed; I couldn't help it. "Tess and I were just talking about you before the run."

He didn't answer, which made me slightly suspicious.

"Oh my God... Tess told you about our conversation, didn't she?"

"Yeah. She said she had a vital piece of information I had to know. Her words. So now I have a simple mission."

"Do tell."

"No, not how this works."

"But it requires talking one hour every day?"

"Yes."

"I see. And does that devious plan of yours begin right now?"

"If you have a free hour, then yes, ma'am."

"My schedule happens to be free."

I walked right back to the park, sitting on one of the many benches, toeing off my sneakers and bringing my knees to my chest.

"So... what do you want to talk about?" I asked.

"Whatever you want. Tell me about your day."

"I've just finished a run."

"You're running?" Disbelief colored his voice.

"Yep. Turns out that all the benefits you laid out are true. I just didn't like doing it indoors. I should listen to you more often."

"I completely agree."

I laughed. "Shouldn't have said that. Have a hunch you'll use it against me."

"You have no idea."

Oh, my. What exactly did he have in mind?

"I've made a plan. Want to hear it?"

"I'm all ears."

"I'll open up my own practice. It's a bit risky, since I won't have a big name to back me up anymore, but I don't want to bust my ass for anyone else anymore. What... what do you think?"

I was on the edge of the bench now, holding my breath. His opinion was important to me.

"I think that's the best thing you can do. You're an excellent lawyer and have enough cases under your belt."

"Exactly."

"I'm proud of you, Josie."

"Thanks."

"How was your day?" I asked.

"The usual. Except I keep thinking about a certain someone. I think my colleagues are starting to notice."

"That can't be good."

"I disagree. I'd rather be with her on a beach, lying on lounge chairs, letting her talk me into scuba diving or some other god-awful activity."

I was melting. Honestly, I was. I vividly remembered that day, how much fun we'd had. How much we'd bickered.

"You keep giving me shit for that, but you liked it."

"Maybe. If I say yes, will it earn me points?"

I grinned. "Maybe."

I now had a suspicion about where he was

going with this.

***

Every day, he called at the same time, five o'clock. At four thirty, the butterflies in my stomach started spreading their wings. At four forty-five, my palms were sweating, my pulse sped up. Starting with four fifty-seven, I just couldn't take my eyes off the screen of my phone.

"Hello, beautiful."

That greeting was just what my lovesick heart needed. We spoke about our day, and then invariably one of us would bring up a memory.

"I got the call from the workers yesterday. All the pipe work is finished," he said.

"So you're at the house now?"

"No. I don't want to go there without you."

"Hunter... that's silly. It's your house."

"It's our house. I miss making you hot chocolate, bringing it to you in that nook."

"I miss the nook," I said.

"The nook? Not me, the nook?"

"You too," I admitted. I'd missed him since the second he left. I missed him so much, it felt as if I'd left a part of myself at the house. I had no idea what else to say. As if knowing I needed to change topics, he asked about my plans for the practice.

We spoke for longer than an hour, right until I heard a light knock at the front door.

"Wait, there's someone at the door."

"I know."

I stopped walking. "Is... are you here?"

"No, but it sounds as if you wish I were."

"How do you know there's someone at the door?"

"Open up and you'll see."

Hunter had sent dinner for Tess and me. She wasn't home yet, though. It wasn't just any dinner, but sushi from my favorite restaurant.

I ate at the kitchen counter, straight from the take-out box.

"It's delicious. No wonder it's my favorite— hang on, are you trying to bribe me?"

"What makes you say that?"

"You do have a history of feeding me my favorite food when you try to talk me into something."

"Okay, I confess. I do, and I'm not even sorry about it."

"You're not just devious. You're downright shameless."

"I've been advised to use my strengths... which include shameless tactics."

"Who advised you?"

"Common friends."

"Sounds like something Amelia would say."

"Right on the first try."

"I need to attend a function tomorrow evening. Come with me."

"You think you're going to have problems with the immigration office if you're not seen with me?"

"I don't care about the immigration office. I want you there as my wife. Sorry—I misspoke. As a friend."

I chuckled, even as my chest filled with so much joy, I felt like doing a happy dance. I was going to *see* him.

"You misspoke? Really? That's your excuse?"

"I've been advised not to pressure you... to give you your time."

"And this is you following that advice?"

"I'm halfway there. But I think me not showing up at Tess's place, throwing you over my shoulder, and taking you back home counts for something."

"It definitely does."

"I'm an impatient man."

"And don't I know that?"

"I just want us to spend time together, Josie. As friends, whatever makes you comfortable. I'll be wearing a tux, by the way."

"More bribing. Wow. You're taking this to a whole new level."

"You haven't answered me yet."

His voice was playful, but I detected worry behind all that. Apprehension. This was our decisive moment. And God, I wanted this so much. I wasn't giving up on us as a couple. Yes, we were best friends, but wasn't that the very best thing that could happen to a husband and wife?

Oh my god! That had been his exact plan with

the phone calls. I smiled, shaking my head. He knew me *so* well.

"I'll be there. And I'll be wearing something pretty."

The function tomorrow was about celebrating the opening of the school that Hunter's company had built. It wasn't a Ballroom Gala. It was a party in his honor at a restaurant.

"Then you'll forgive me if I flirt with you, *friend*?"

"Hunter...."

"No, don't answer that. My fault for asking anyway. I'll pick you up at six."

"Can't wait."

I was grinning by the time we said goodbye, hugging the phone to my chest.

The next morning, I woke up early with far too much energy. Running didn't help shed it. On the contrary, I had more energy. Probably adrenaline.

If I thought I'd been nervous anticipating his calls, boy, that was nothing compared to how I felt now. I had Hunter on my mind. Lodged in my heart. Under my skin. To kill time, I started preparations for the night right after lunch, beginning with a trip to a nearby beauty store.

Half an hour later, I learned a valuable lesson: do not go to a beauty store when you're on pins and needles.

You might end up emptying your bank account buying beauty products.

I came home with no less than four products for my hair and three for body care. The vendor had patiently explained how and when to use each, but I forgot all about it by the time I brought everything into Tess's bathroom.

Holy hell. How was I going to make it through tonight if I was already such a nervous mess?

Come on, Josie. You're a lawyer. You can still recite two hundred laws you learned six years ago. You will not be defeated by a freaking hair care program.

I figured it out eventually. The oil needed to be applied one hour before washing my hair. Conditioner and the second oil came before the mask.

The body care collection was easier to figure out. The first step was dry brushing. I was particularly looking forward to that. I'd seen so many ads and celebrity endorsements swearing by the benefits of dry brushing: smoother skin, better circulation, and my favorite—improved appearance of cellulite. I wondered if it was true, or just another fad. No time like the present to test it. After rubbing oil on my scalp, I brushed my thighs and bum with a lot of dedication before jumping in the shower and finishing the hair program.

I was so proud of myself for doing all this. So proud. Until I stepped out of the shower and felt my thighs and buttocks itch. I glanced in the mirror. *What the actual hell?*

I had scratched myself all over the back of my thighs and my ass. I applied the hydrating oil I'd bought with one hand, googling "is it normal to scratch yourself during dry brushing" with the other.

Of course, it wasn't. It took a special talent. That was why I never bothered. I was clumsy. But I persisted with my efforts, curling my lashes with an eye-curler before applying mascara. Deciding on my outfit took ten minutes. I was ready and dressed by five-fifty. Talk about being punctual. I was—

The doorbell rang, and just like that, everything returned with a vengeance: the butterflies, the sweaty palms. More than ever, I wasn't sure how I'd make it through tonight. But in order to start it, I had to open that door.

He was wearing a tux. Hot damn. That was my kryptonite. How was I supposed to not say yes to anything he demanded? And judging by that smoldering look, he planned to demand a lot. He was also wearing a shirt that required cuff links. Hmm... really? He knew I loved cuff links. If I didn't know better, I'd say he was out to seduce me. Who was I kidding? He totally was. And I wasn't sure I could resist him.

My heart, which had already felt twice its size, just seemed to keep growing.

He didn't say anything at first, just slowly raked his gaze over me. My body reacted as if he'd trailed kisses everywhere. I could barely withstand the simmering heat.

"Fuck, you're beautiful."

I chuckled, twirling around, pretending to be showing off. Instead, I was steeling myself, hoping his gaze wouldn't smolder as much when I faced him.

Nope. No such luck. If anything, he'd turned the heat up. We both laughed. His hand shook slightly. Was he as overcome with emotion as I was?

I stole a glance at him, focusing on the pure joy in his eyes, but then my gaze landed on his lips. They looked so kissable. So, so kissable.

He drew in a sharp breath. Damn. He'd seen me looking. I carefully avoided his eyes, focusing instead on his outstretched hand.

The second our fingers touched, my skin sizzled. He didn't miss it. I was too caught off guard to be able to hide it. And just like that, the air around us thickened with tension. He flashed me a sinful smile that turned downright smug when he caught me looking at his cuff links.

Yeah, he was definitely wearing them on purpose. He drew his thumb slowly up and down my hand.

"Ready?" When I didn't reply right away, he leaned in slightly. He was so close. *So, so* close. His cheek was nearly touching mine. I could feel the warmth of his skin, the five o'clock shadow on his face. He moved his hand from the top of my hand up my arm, finally resting it on my waist. I sucked in a breath, completely overwhelmed by his masculine charm. When the corner of his mouth touched mine, heat speared through me. I needed more of his touch, of him.

I couldn't help but lean in, searching more of

his warmth. He grinned.

"Careful, friend. You might fool me into thinking you want more than my friendship if you keep at this."

I'd asked for this, hadn't I?

"Stop looking at me like that," I said.

"How?"

"Like you want to undress me."

"You look gorgeous. You can't fault me."

"I totally can. And I am."

Chapter Thirty-Three
Josie

On the way to the venue, I tried to steel myself against his charm, because I wanted to have a long and honest conversation with him before succumbing to said charm... but it was pointless. The man deserved a medal for his tenacity. Every smile, every touch set me on edge. By the time we arrived, I was already a basket case.

The room was large, but nothing like the ballroom where the galas took place. There were several round tables spread throughout it and an open bar in the corner. Waiters served drinks at the tables, but guests could also get their own.

We mingled with the other guests, exchanging pleasantries and making small talk before sitting at our table. It was a grand event to celebrate the opening of a public institution, but I supposed it was to be expected because it had been built entirely through private donations.

The room fell silent when the host went to the front of the room with a microphone in his hand.

"Ladies and gentlemen, thank you so much for joining us here. It's a great night. After a year and a half of hard work, we're finally at the finish line.

This wouldn't have been possible without the help and contribution of a lot of people, so brace yourselves while I thank everyone. Christina and Alex, thank you for taking on the immense task of organizing everything. You kept us all on schedule, and that was no easy feat."

Christina and Alex, who sat opposite us, laughed as everyone clapped. The host went on to thank so many people that I was reminded of Oscar speeches.

"And last but not least, a huge thank-you to the man of the hour: Hunter Caldwell. It goes without saying that without your contribution, this wouldn't be possible at all. We have a surprise for you. We had a hell of a time keeping this from you, giving how involved you've been, but we did it. We decided on a last-minute name change for the school. It'll be named after you and your father. After all, he was a pillar for us back in the day."

I felt Hunter stiffen next to me. I touched my hand to his under the table, interlacing our fingers, squeezing them lightly. He didn't react at first, but then he squeezed them back.

He nodded at the host, but only managed a tight smile. When the host stepped down from the stage, the chatter began again. Since the servers had cleared the plates, the guests started mingling again. We rose from the table with the others. Those closest to us wanted a word with Hunter.

He was still tense. I laced my arm with his. "I'm staying right here with you."

Some of the tension left his body. He glanced at me, giving me a smile just as strained as he'd given the host.

The situation did not improve over the next half hour.

Holy hell! Everyone wanted to congratulate him, talk about his dad. I mean, obviously, the naming of the building was a cause for celebration. Hunter had worked hard to clean up his father's reputation, and this was proof he'd succeeded in making people remember the good parts too, not just the sad ones.

But I knew my husband better than anyone else. He didn't like to talk about these things. It made him melancholic and broody.

I had to get him out of here before broody turned into moody and the evening's vibe changed from celebratory to melancholic.

When he started to tug at his bowtie, as if it was strangling him, I knew I had to do something.

"Christina, sorry to interrupt you, but I need to talk to my husband alone for a few minutes."

"Of course."

I steered us toward the exit of the room, walking quickly enough to make it clear we were heading somewhere with a purpose, not just mingling. It worked. No one stopped us.

Out on the foyer, I noticed a window looking into a small courtyard. I led us through the door next to it.

"What's wrong?" Hunter asked the second we

were outside.

"Nothing. You just looked like you wanted to get out of there."

He laughed, and finally, finally, the tension seeped from his shoulders.

"You messed this up." I reached to his tie, rearranging it. "Here, let me fix it for you. Better?"

"Yes. This was a pleasant surprise. I'm *happy* about it. I don't know why I'm so worked up. I'm an idiot."

"No, you're not. Everyone has their own way of dealing with things. You internalize them."

"That's just a more polite way of saying I'm an idiot."

"Not at all. You're broody. I happen to find it sexy."

He gave me a wide, beautiful smile. I breathed out in relief. It was the first heartfelt smile since the speech.

"You do?"

"Yes."

"What else do you find sexy about me?"

I attempted to take my hands away from his tie, but he clasped my wrists, keeping them in place. I splayed my fingers on the sides of his neck instead.

"Your flirty side, your swoon-worthy side. Although that one is just irresistible."

"And yet, you've been resisting me just fine."

His tone was playful, but his gaze was determined. He placed his palms over the backs of my hands, pressing them against his neck, stepping forward until we were but an inch apart.

"Thank you for being at my side tonight, Josie. I needed you. How did you know?"

I always wanted to be at his side. I wanted to be there for him no matter what he needed. Not as his best friend, but as his wife.

"Because I love you. And I've been afraid, and silly. I've been a lawyer for so long and have always wanted to be one, so it felt as if some part of me was just ripped away. I got lost in my head, and then when I realized how unhappy you were, it just... made me doubt that I could be more than your best friend, that I could make you happy as your wife."

I'd realized that he was trying to fix things for me because it was in his nature to make those he cared about happy.

"Don't be afraid, okay? I love taking care of you, making you happy. I admit, I don't always know how to go about it, but I'm learning. I'll be a happy man to keep learning all my life. I love you, Josie. I always will. Don't doubt that. We're both stubborn and passionate about what we believe in. We're bound to clash. But that doesn't mean we don't belong together, or that we can't be happy together. That's what makes us work. We challenge, push each other. I can't promise you that we won't clash, but I do promise you that I will love you for the rest of our lives, Josie."

"I love you, husband."

He kissed me, hard and unapologetically. I

went on my toes, deepening the kiss. I'd never need anything more than this. How did I think we didn't belong together? I'd been a fool.

He moved his hands down to my waist, and then to my ass, pressing me against him. He wanted me, and I was too caught up in his charm to resist him.

Except... we were in public.

"Someone can walk in on us. Or, you know... see us through that window."

"I can't stop kissing you."

"Then you better take me home and have your wicked way with me."

He looked me straight in the eyes, touching my face, resting his thumb on my jaw.

"Our home?" he asked.

"Yes. Let's go home."

"Whatever you want. I aim to make my wife happy." His smile gave way to a grin.

I grinned right back. "So you don't want the same?"

"Right now, I can't think past how much I need you."

"Lucky I don't lose my head so easily... even with all your sexy charm."

His grin turned wolfish. "Is that a challenge?"

"Not really, but feel free to take it as one and prove me wrong."

"It'll be my pleasure, wife."

I was so wrapped up in Hunter on the way home that I didn't register anything during the car ride other than *him*. We sat in the back. He had an arm around my waist, holding me so close to him that I could straddle him if I wanted. That would give the driver a show. I sat next to him, kissing his cheek, his jaw, inhaling the delicious scent of his cologne.

We climbed out of the car the second it came to a stop, hurrying toward the building.

After unlocking the door, he scooped me up in his arms. I giggled, bracing my palms on his shoulders.

"What are you doing?"

"Getting you past the threshold. I want this to be a fresh start for us, Josie," he murmured. My heart seemed to grow in size tenfold. I drew the tip of my nose up and down his neck, resting it in the crook, just as I'd done on our wedding night, only then, I'd been afraid of my own feelings. Now, I wasn't afraid anymore.

He carried me to the master bedroom, setting me down near the bed, caressing my face, my shoulders, as if he couldn't stop touching me. He kissed my mouth ferociously before descending to my neck. His fingers shook slightly as he lowered my zipper. Every kiss felt like a promise; every touch somehow deepened our bond. My skin sizzled everywhere he trailed his mouth, everywhere his fingers marked me. I shivered when my dress fell to the floor. I was standing in front of him wearing nothing but tiny panties. The dress had had sewn-in cups, so I had no bra on.

He drew in a sharp breath, touching the valley between my breasts before lowering his hand, drawing small circles around my navel.

"I love you, babe," he whispered, watching me with so much warmth and happiness that I almost teared up. Hooking his thumbs into the sides of my panties, he drew them down my legs. He kissed his way back up, placing my right leg over his shoulder, teasing my inner thigh. I gasped at the first stroke of his tongue over my center. My knees gave in a little, but he held my hips in place, sustaining me, keeping me right where he wanted while he slowly tortured me with his mouth.

"Ohhhhh…."

Pleasure pulsed through me, lighting me up, driving me closer and closer to the edge, until every muscle was tight with tension.

"Hunter… please, I need…."

"I know what you need," he whispered against my tender flesh. Pleasure shot through me, and I almost buckled. "And I'll make you come so hard, babe."

He didn't relent—not the iron grip on my thighs, nor the lashes of his tongue.

I came apart at the seams, holding on to his shoulders, crying out his name. And yet, he wasn't done with me. He was going to give me no reprieve… and I was completely on board with that. I gave him a wicked smile as I removed his shirt, taking my sweet time feeling up those gorgeous muscles, kissing down his chest as I reached for the zipper of his pants. I intended to return the slow torture, to take my time until I drove him crazy, but when I went on my tiptoes, kissing just under his Adam's apple, he let out a low and delicious sound— somewhere between a hum and a growl—and I completely forgot about my plan. I wanted him *right now*. He planted small kisses on my shoulders as I pushed his pants down.

"You should walk around commando," I murmured.

Hunter chuckled. "What?"

I smiled sheepishly. "Umm... didn't mean to say that out loud. Would just make all this more convenient."

He smirked, pushing down his boxers at lightning speed while I admired... the view.

"Or you can do that," I conceded.

"So impatient, huh?"

He pulled me closer, strumming his fingers upward on my rib cage, touching my neck, resting his thumbs on the corners of my mouth. And that look in his eyes... heavens, I wanted him to look at me like that every day. As if I was the most precious thing in the world.

We tumbled on the mattress, laughing, and then Hunter rolled us over until I was on top. His cock was trapped between us, and I slid up and down his length without taking him in, just drinking in his reactions, even as the ache inside me grew and deepened.

"Fuck, Josie."

He gripped my hips, lowering me onto him in one swift move, filling me up completely until I cried out his name. I attempted to move, but he didn't relent his grip on me. He was in charge again.

"I just want to stay like this, connected to you. To feel that you're mine. That you'll always be mine," he said.

"I promise I will."

He lifted his head from the pillow, and I met him halfway, swiping my tongue over his lips before kissing him. He started moving beneath me with slow, undulating motions that simply made me fall apart. With every thrust, he gave me more pleasure, demanded my surrender. My orgasm built so damn slowly. He never broke eye contact, never looked away, and I couldn't either. Didn't want to. He let go of one of my hips only to bring his hand between us, pressing his thumb against my clit, gently at first, and then without mercy.

Everything was magnified: the sensation of having him inside me, filling me up... The sound of our bodies pushing against each other with more urgency. My entire body was on edge. This was too intense. So much pleasure. Too much. My inner muscles clenched.

"Look at me," he rasped. He trapped my gaze with his. I'd never felt so adored and loved.

Feeling him widen inside me while his thumb circled my clit sent me over the edge. I came apart so hard that my vision faded for a few seconds. All I could do was ride the wave of pleasure, feel him come apart just as hard. When he loosened his grip on my hips, I lost my balance, toppling over him.

"I've got you," he whispered, laughing. I laughed too, even as I hid my face in his neck.

I tried to slide off him, but he hooked an arm firmly over my back, trapping me.

"Stay here. I want to feel you close."

I smiled against his neck. "My husband's a tyrant."

"Damn right I am."

I wiggled my ass, even though I had no intention of sliding out of his arms, just to rile him up. And I succeeded. The next second, he flipped us over, and he was on top, resting his forearms near my shoulders, propping his knees next to my thighs. He wasn't crushing me, but I couldn't get away either. In other words, I had him just where I wanted him. Pressing every single delicious muscle against me.

"There. Now you can't try to get away."

"Who said I was trying?" I asked, unable to mask the mischief in my voice.

He feathered the tip of his nose up and down my neck, laughing. "I see. So, you were just messing around with me?"

"No, but I love it when you think you have to lay on the charm to convince me to do things your way."

He pulled back a notch, looking me straight in the eyes.

"I've got something for you," he said in a low, raw voice, reaching for the nightstand. He opened the drawer. My heartbeats became lightning-quick when I realized he was taking out a small jewelry box. Sliding off me, he sat at the edge of the bed, holding the box for me, opening the lid. My sapphire engagement ring!

"I've had this for a while. I wanted to give it to you on our one-year anniversary, but didn't want to risk them selling out, so I bought it…. Anyway, I don't want to wait anymore."

He took my hand, caressing my ring finger, the diamond engagement ring.

My eyes were misty, my throat completely closed up with emotion.

"I love you, Josie. When I slid this ring on your finger, we both thought it would be just for a while. I don't know what went through your mind, but I was already doubting that I could avoid falling for you."

His voice faltered on the last words. I clasped his fingers, letting him know that I was right there with him.

"When I slide this ring on your finger, I want you to have the certainty that I will love you for the rest of our lives."

I barely had enough patience for him to slide that ring on before wrapping my arms around his neck, practically straddling him. "Thank you. It's beautiful. But you didn't have to get me a new ring."

"I wanted to. And you love it."

I grinned but didn't argue. What could I say? He knew me well. I drew him close, peppering his cheeks and neck with kisses. I just couldn't get enough of him. But he *wasn't* touching me with the usual enthusiasm... which could only mean one thing.

"Is there anything else you want to tell me?" I asked.

He blinked, clearly taken aback. It gave me immense pleasure that I knew him just as well.

"As it happens, there is one thing... how would you feel about becoming Ms. Josie Caldwell?"

I threw my head back, laughing, before straightening up, attempting to sound serious as I spoke, pointing to my ring.

"Was this a bribe?"

"No. As I said, I've had it for a while. But I thought that asking you right now might increase the chances of you saying yes."

"Using your devious strengths again?"

"Guilty." Bringing his mouth to my ear, he whispered, "But if I really wanted to use devious tactics, I'd be doing this...." He drew his mouth down my neck, pushing my thighs further apart with his leg. I gasped, rolling my hips into him before playfully pushing him away.

I debated whether to make him sweat a bit, but even though I loved keeping him on his toes, I loved seeing that big, happy smile even more. When he'd first suggested it months ago, I hadn't seen the point. Why change it only to revert back to my maiden name further down the road? But things were different now. And I couldn't wait to be Mrs. Caldwell.

"Fine, you opportunistic man. I'll change my name." And there it was, that huge, heartfelt smile. I loved it so much. "I love you, Hunter."

I held him tight to me again. I'd just decided I wouldn't let go tonight when a phone started ringing.

"That's my phone," I said, attempting to wiggle out of his arms, but he held on tight.

"How about you don't answer it?"

I grinned. "No can do. That's Tess's ringtone. She made me promise to tell her every single detail as soon as the evening was over. If I don't answer, she might come banging at the front door."

He flashed a grin. "Wouldn't put it past her."

"I will need you to let me go to answer the phone."

He fondled my right ass cheek. I narrowed my eyes but couldn't help shimmying a little.

"Or, I'll tell her I couldn't make it to the phone because you've been fondling me. Pretty sure that won't earn you any cousin of the year award."

He pinched my other ass cheek too. "By the looks of it, it might just earn me husband of the year, won't it?"

That damn shimmy gave me away. But he couldn't blame me for liking his hands on me, could he?

"Don't get ahead of yourself."

"I like my odds."

To my astonishment, he did take his hands off me, practically freeing me. Letting an opportunity for naked time slide by was very unlike him.

I became even more suspicious when a smirk that was a little too self-indulgent appeared on his handsome face.

"What's that?"

"What?" He promptly schooled his expression, but he wasn't fooling me.

"That... smirk."

"Can't wait to hear what Tess has to say when you tell her about the name change. She was so convinced you'd never agree."

"Wait a second. When did you talk about this?"

"When we returned from the Bahamas. She was at my office. One thing led to another...."

I shook my head, at a loss for what to say... but then an idea popped into my mind.

"In that case, I might tell her that I'm still *considering* it."

He grinned. "Changed my mind. Won't let you answer after all."

"Is that so?"

"Yes."

I could give just as good as I got. Well, almost as good. Hunter was still a master at this, but I had plenty of time to learn. I attempted to wiggle out from under him. Rookie mistake. The next second, he clasped my wrists in one hand, pinning them above my head.

"See? Not going anywhere. Got you just where I want you," he teased.

"So, what are you going to do with me?" I giggled as he drew the tip of his nose on my exposed underarm. Not what I was expecting.

"Tickle me at your own risk, husband."

Chapter Thirty-Four

Hunter
One month later

"What do you mean, it's a surprise? I want to know where you're taking me," Josie said.

"Always impatient, Mrs. Caldwell."

She rolled her eyes, grinning. "Are you ever going to call me by my first name again?"

"Sure, just not anytime soon."

She'd been Josie Caldwell for one week and two days, since we'd finalized the paperwork. And yes, I might have called her Mrs. Caldwell ever since. It just rolls off the tongue so easily.

"Are we going to celebrate that you've received your green card?"

"Maybe."

Our case worker contacted us as soon as Josie forwarded the request for the name change, demanding an explanation.

Josie told her that since she was setting up her own firm anyway, she could just as well do it as Josie Caldwell. I received the approval for my green card two weeks later.

"Insufferable man." She sighed, crossing her

arms over her chest. Then she squirmed in her seat, sitting up straighter as I stopped the car at a red light.

"We're going to your office?"

We were on the Upper West side, in the area of my office.

I winked at her. "Close."

Instead of taking the road to my building, I turned right onto a side street. Watching Josie try to piece things together was one of my favorite things to do. I loved keeping her on edge, surprising her.

I parked the car in front of a red brick building, announcing, "This is us."

We climbed out of the car, and I took Josie's hand, leading her inside.

"What's this about?" she asked when I unlocked the door, opening it.

"You've been office hunting for a while. Thought you might like this one."

"I've searched for spaces in this area. This didn't come up, or I would have put it on the list."

"It's not on the market."

"So how do you know about it?"

"Pulled a string or two."

"For me?"

"I'd do anything for my wife."

She glanced at me over her shoulder, and that affection in her eyes just slayed me. I didn't think there would be a day it wouldn't.

"Thank you."

She sighed as she stepped inside. I remained a few steps behind her, wanting to give her time to soak it all up.

"Wow," she murmured.

The space was perfect for a law office, in a building that was elegant but not snobbish.

It boasted high ceilings and large windows that let in plenty of natural light. It had three separate offices and even a small meeting room with an adjacent nook that served as a small kitchen.

I knew she could already see herself here—specifically, in the middle office.

"This is big enough that I can put a recliner armchair in one corner. I can take powernaps when I'm exhausted, or just sit more comfortably when I have a lot to read. And the kitchen is perfect for coffee breaks."

She grinned, turning around slowly, taking in the room before heading to the window. I walked up behind her, pushing her hair to one side, kissing the back of her neck.

"I can join you. My office is not far."

"Midday foot rubs and hot chocolate?"

She shivered, goose bumps appearing on her arms. I ran my palms over the sensitive skin, nibbling at her ear. I loved the effect I had on her. "Maybe a sexcapade."

She elbowed me lightly. "I'll have colleagues."

"Who'll go out to lunch, have meetings."

"I'm taking it. How much is the deposit?"

"I already took care of that."

She turned around, blinking.

"Plus the first month of rent. I have a

perfectly good explanation."

A smile tugged at the corners of her lips. "Let's hear it."

"I passed by here on my way to lunch a few days ago, saw them carrying out furniture. They were about to put it on the market, and I went inside to check it out. I thought you might like it, and I didn't want you to risk missing out on it."

"I don't think you could be any sweeter."

I winced. "How about romantic?"

"Why, Mr. Caldwell, am I offending your manly sensibilities by calling you sweet?"

I winced again. She giggled.

"Fine. I promise not to use that word again. About the deposit and the rent—I'll pay you back."

"No, you won't. Let me do this for you. You've given me so much, Josie." I placed my hands on her waist, keeping her close. "You're the love of my life, Josie Caldwell. You've been my best friend for so long, and now you're my partner, my better half. I'll be here for you, cheering for you every step of the way. Loving you, taking care of you. You've changed so much in my life. You've showed me what it feels like to be loved...." Drawing in a deep breath, I touched my forehead to hers, needing the connection.

I kissed the corner of her mouth, then her lower lip and the bow of the upper one before capturing her mouth, kissing her long and deep, entwining our tongues. I moved one hand to cup her cheek, tilting her head at the perfect angle so I could explore her.

I kissed her until we were both panting, needing more. When it came to Josie, I'd always need more. I smiled against her lips when I realized that so did she.

She pressed her hips against me, pulling at my collar with one hand, digging the fingers of the other in my arm, as if she was a few seconds away from taking off my shirt.

I skimmed my hands up her waist, touching the underside of her breasts with my thumbs. She moaned against my mouth, pressing her thighs together. I nearly pushed her against a wall. I *did* hike her skirt up her legs, desperate for skin-on-skin contact. I ran my hand up her inner thigh, until my thumb grazed the hem of her panties. Josie fisted my shirt. How could I be so crazy for her?

I dropped my hand, pulling my head back a notch. The contour of her mouth was red, her lips slightly puffy. I'd marked her as mine with that kiss.

"Let's go home, wife. I want you so much that I can't even see straight, but I won't have you here. Too chilly, too uncomfortable."

She laughed, running her fingers through my hair. "Sorry... I know I promised, but that was the perfect word for you. Sweet."

Epilogue

Christmas
Josie

"We really went all out," my sister commented. I grinned, looking around the room at the decorations. My family had arrived two days ago, and today everyone was at our house to celebrate Christmas Eve in style. My sister and I had gone shopping for food and... *additional* decorations yesterday, and today, we'd set them up together with Tess and Skye. I'd felt like a kid again, lost in that catchy enthusiasm for all things Christmas.

"You mean overboard, right?"

I'd always loved Christmas, had longed to have a room tall enough for an enormous tree... and a fireplace... and our living room was just perfect for the occasion. I'd intended to only use a decent amount of decorations... and I'd completely failed, of course. One thing led to another, and now there wasn't just a huge Christmas tree—I'd also bought stockings for every single guest, hung them on the mantelpiece, and stuffed them with presents. Strings of lights were hanging from the ceiling, along with mistletoe branches.

"Maybe just a bit," my sister conceded with a grin just as the front door opened and Hunter came in. He'd been out to buy a few last-minute presents. His eyes bulged the second he entered the living room.

"Babe, are we filming a Christmas commercial I don't know about?"

That earned him a pinch right on that delicious ass, but no teasing, because my sister and Tess and Skye were looking at us.

"It's family tradition to… go overboard," I explained, because well, it truly was.

"And we've promptly decided to declare it a Winchester tradition too. I mean, where's the fun in *decent* decorations?" Tess asked.

"We went to pick up the tree with Dad every year. Made a big deal of it. Why not carry on the tradition?" I suggested.

Hunter's expression softened inexplicably. He glanced around the room, a small smile playing on his lips.

"Any other traditions you want to pass on?" he asked.

"I'll make a list."

He drew me closer, planting a kiss on my temple, whispering, "Do that. And then… we can start working on those kids. We have to pass those traditions on to someone."

Usually, I teased him when he brought up kids, but right now, I couldn't do anything but melt in his arms, soak in all that happiness he was radiating. I had an interminable list of traditions and planned to spoil him with every single one.

"Bought all the presents on the list?" I asked.

"Wouldn't dare show my face without them." He pointed with his thumb over his shoulder at the mountain of bags in the foyer.

"Smart husband."

I made to walk past him to start stuffing the last of the presents in the stockings, but he caught my arm. "Doesn't even earn me one kiss?"

"We've got company," I whispered. As of late, we couldn't keep our kisses PG-rated. I couldn't imagine why.

But the heat and determination in Hunter's gaze told me that he'd claim that kiss one way or the other. Hmm... we could manage one small, PG-rated kiss, right?

I rose on my tiptoes, intending to give him a quick peck, but before I knew it, I had my arms around his neck and his hands gripped my waist in a deliciously possessive way. I felt every finger pressing against my flesh as he kissed me harder, deeper.

"Anyone feel like a third wheel?" Tess's voice resounded through the room. "Anyone? No? Just me?"

We pulled apart, chuckling. Skye was watching us, tapping a finger against her chin. "Right. We need to split you two up, or we're never going to be ready in time."

To my surprise, Hunter nodded. That was

unlike him... missing any opportunity to be around me, sneak in a kiss, a sinful touch.

My mouth formed an O. "Are you just trying to get out of the way so we don't put you to work?"

"Possibly. But I have a good reason. I'm supposed to pick up your parents from the hotel. Your mom wants to buy something on the way here. Can't start messing up traditions already, can we?"

Ah, of course. Mom hadn't had a chance to bake her famous apple tart, so she'd ordered one at my favorite bakery—a small shop in Brooklyn that sold homemade goodies.

"Definitely not."

He winked before leaving. I sighed as I headed to the girls. They still had three strings of twinkling lights to hang. I caught myself singing along to Christmas carols as I contemplated the best place to hang them (I didn't have that many options, really, considering we'd already covered most of the living room with lights).

Tess and Skye were exchanging conspiratorial glances.

"What?" I asked.

"You're humming... and Hunter has never been in such a good mood at Christmas. I mean, he's never been the Grinch or anything, but usually he was melancholic..."

I could relate. I couldn't explain why, but the past few Christmases had been a melancholic affair for me too.

"I think he's just excited at the prospect of...

what was the phrase? Having someone to pass the traditions on to?" Skye asked.

"You heard that?"

"Every word. Very creative way of saying he wants to get down and dirty with you." Tess grinned. I felt the tips of my ears turn hot.

Two hours later, the entire gang arrived. Hunter with my parents, Amelia and Mick with Ryker and Cole. I loved having a full house, and by the looks of it, so did Hunter. In fact, I was pretty sure he was conspiring with Dad right now. Not just whispering. Conspiring. How I knew? They looked more than a little guilty. Plus, from time to time, one of them glanced over his shoulder.

I snuck up on them. They stopped talking abruptly upon seeing me.

I batted my eyelashes, looking from one to the other. Surely one of them had to give in to my charms, right?

"What are my two favorite men in the world plotting?"

"Nothing," Dad said a little too quickly.

"You think I'm buying that?"

Hunter cupped my cheek, feathering his thumb just under my lower lip.

"Planning the next get-together."

"Already?" My voice was a little uneven, overcome by sudden emotion. This man. What did he have in mind? Fly them over for every holiday?

Oh, God. I had a hunch that was *exactly* what

he planned. I had to make a concerted effort to keep my hands at my side and not jump right in his arms.

"You've got a great man here," Dad said.

"I do, don't I?"

I left them to their secrets and made the rounds, smiling from ear to ear. I'd had no idea it was actually possible to be this blissful, and just... content.

I found Ryker and Amelia inspecting the stockings hanging from the mantelpiece.

"Got to say, these look lovely. Any chance we'll have an extra stocking next year?" Amelia asked.

I beamed. Here she went again.

"We're working on that," Hunter said, appearing next to me seemingly out of thin air.

I half turned to him, narrowing my eyes. "I think what you meant to say was, we're still negotiating."

I was working hard on establishing my law practice. So far, so good. I'd managed to lure my colleagues into it, and we were taking on as many cases as possible. Some of my clients had left the old firm, insisting that they wanted to work with me, and they didn't care about my run-in with the immigration services.

It would take a while to create a steady income stream, and the fact that I didn't have a paycheck deposited in my account every single month sometimes kept me up at night, but I had full confidence I'd figure everything out. And even when

I didn't have confidence, my sexy man made sure to build it for me, one hot chocolate and one foot rub at a time.

A naughty twinkle appeared in his eyes. What *else* did he have in store for me? Clearing my throat, I looked around for a change of subject… and found a scapegoat instead. Poor Ryker.

"Maybe we *will* have an extra stocking." I patted Ryker's cheek. "You'd make a handsome groom."

Amelia grinned. "You really would."

"It'll take a lot to tame the flirt. But I'm sure the right woman will be up for the task," I teased.

Ryker looked as if he'd swallowed his tongue as Amelia, Hunter, and I burst out laughing. Our amusement attracted attention. Tess joined our group, studying us.

"What's everyone gossiping about?" she asked.

"Nothing," Ryker said quickly, which, of course, made his sister even more curious. I felt a little guilty, since I was the one who'd gotten him in hot water.

"How about we open the presents?" I suggested.

"Before dinner?" Amelia asked.

"I've already caught some of the family trying to peek into the stockings. *All* the stockings," I emphasized.

Tess's cheeks turned pink. "It's your fault for not putting a name tag on each."

"I did that on purpose, so no one would peek. Clearly, I underestimated you."

She grinned, rubbing her palms. "So, which one's mine?"

As the group gathered around the fireplace, I indicated which one belonged to whom. I *loved* giving presents, watching everyone's expression light up once they opened their stocking.

I knew what was in each stocking except mine, of course. Hunter had done that one, and I couldn't wait to see what he had in store for me.

I nearly broke a nail in my enthusiasm to open it. The two of us sat next to the tree, inspecting the gifts. I'd gotten him a set of cuff links—a little something to remind him of me when he was at work. He'd gotten us *plane tickets*. We were going to the Maldives again, where we'd fallen in love. He didn't know how to do things any other way except on a grand scale.

He grinned when I looked up at him, then held his palms up in defense. We were leaving at the end of February.

"You said things move slowly in the industry around then," he said.

I threw my head back, laughing. He'd asked me that out of the blue one evening while we were relaxing in the Jacuzzi. I should have known it wasn't just a random question.

"Sneaky husband. What will I do with you? Thank you for the tickets. I can't wait to go. I'm going to book a scuba diving instructor as soon as I get a chance."

"For me too."

I felt my eyes widen. "Wow. You want to come again? Wasn't expecting it."

"Can't let the instructor steal you, can I?"

"Really? That old excuse again? Why not just admit you liked it?"

"Might give you ideas."

"You mean more than I already have?"

He smiled devilishly, pulling me just behind the tree and out of sight, giving me a kiss that was definitely not PG-rated.

Once he let go, I sighed, snuggling up to him, just breathing him in for a few moments, right until, Ryker said loudly, "We know you're there, FYI."

Grinning like Cheshire cats, we stepped out from behind the tree. Everyone besides Ryker was minding their own business, enjoying the presents.

"I think we did great with the gifts," I whispered to Hunter.

"That's because my wife's a genius." He pulled me in a half hug, kissing my temple, which was innocent enough... except for that hand on my back that kept traveling south. I pushed him away playfully, shaking my head.

He always said I was the one with *ideas*, but he could top me when he put his mind to it. He grinned at me, lifting a brow. I loved our first Christmas as husband and wife, and I couldn't wait for the rest.

***

The end
***

Other Books by Layla Hagen

The Bennett Family Series

Book 1: Your Irresistible Love
Book 2: Your Captivating Love
Book 3: Your Forever Love
Book 4: Your Inescapable Love
Book 5: Your Tempting Love
Book 6: Your Alluring Love
Book 7: Your Fierce Love
Book 8: Your One True Love
Book 9: Your Endless Love

The Connor Family Series

Book 1: Anything For You
Book 2: Wild With You
Book 3: Meant For You
Book 4: Only With You
Book 5: Fighting For You
Book 6: Always With You

The Lost Series

Book 1: Lost in Us
Book 2: Found in Us
Book 3: Caught in Us

Standalone

Withering Hope

Printed in Poland
by Amazon Fulfillment
Poland Sp. z o.o., Wrocław

81508844R00214